MY COSPLAY ESCAPE

A ROM-COM

AMY TRENT

My Cosplay Escape

DEDICATION

To Mr. Trent
Happy Anniversary

AUTHOR'S NOTE

This is fiction. All of it—the characters, dialogue, events—all fiction. If this resembles reality in any way, it is a coincidence. The end. Okay, moving on to cosplay. My favorite, and probably your favorite, superheroes and heroines are largely trademarked brands, and I respect intellectual property rights. So to write a rom-com including everything I love about cosplay, I had to get creative with my approach. (Really creative. There are so. many. superheroes out there.) Hope it works for you!

CHAPTER ONE

"You can't work here."

Before I can tell Brent I have no intention of working at his stupid orthodontist office, he wrinkles his nose and grimaces. "Did you run here from Mom's house?"

I shove my hands into the front pocket of my sweat-stained hoodie. Sure, we could both use a good wash and rinse, but then I'd have missed my training run this morning. And I had to do laundry. "No. I ran here from Mount Soledad by way of the beach, then bay—"

"That explains the smell." Brent rises from behind his computer, and I hardly recognize my big brother. He has a surfer's tan now to match his blond hair, which is weird because last time I checked he hates the beach. Everyone says Brent is the spitting image of Dad, but that's just because he's tall. "You do know that bathing before a job interview is standard practice?"

"I don't want to work here." Staring into mouth after mouth of crooked teeth is not my jam. Plus, Brent and Jen take type A to weird places. If I push a pen out of place, someone in bubblegum-pink scrubs will come running with a ruler to fix it. Judging by the lingering antiseptic smell, an entire bottle of rubbing alcohol would disappear in the cleanup effort. I know Brent tries to make his practice feel surfer-chill—they heavily analyzed and researched optimum office aesthetics, ask me how I know—but it's still an orthodontist office. People are still in scrubs. People still call him Dr. Brent and his wife Dr. Jen. I can't handle it.

"Should have thought about that sooner, Sarah." Brent shoves a still-warm stack of papers into my hands. He plays the role of exasperated-older-brother-with-the-perfect-life-once-again-inconvenienced-by-screw-up-little-sister with gusto this morning.

"What's this?" I ask.

Brent swigs some of his bulletproof coffee. "A two-week lifeline."

I flip through a temp contract, pay agreement, and HR policy. "I'm not working here. I only came by because Mom insisted you needed to see me this morning."

Brent pinches the bridge of his nose. The glint of his platinum wedding band winks at me. Wedding bands are such a-holes. "Mom also insisted that Jen and I hire you. 'Where else will she find a job with benefits?'"

That stings a little, knowing that my only family in the world thinks I'm unemployable. Also stings since the job I'm interviewing for at the gym has no benefits. No point in telling Brent any of this. It'd just give him more ammo against me. I drop the packet of hiring papers on Brent's desk. "You need to square your shoulders the next time you quote Mom. Maybe put a hand on your hip. Her power stance, you know?"

"Sign the papers, Sarah."

"Why don't I just tell Mom Dr. Ken and Dr. Barbie wouldn't hire me?"

"You'd do that to Jen? You'd pit her against Mom?" He folds his arms across his chest, wrinkling his white lab coat. "She's been nothing but kind to you."

I roll my eyes and check my phone. Twenty more minutes until I am due at the gym.

Brent continues on in that same tone he uses to scold his patients who don't wear their retainers. Stuff about responsibility and brushing after every meal. Flossing, too, probably. And then he lands the final sucker punch. "Come on, Sarah. You've had a mother-in-law," he says.

I deadpan a laugh, but it doesn't help. I need another run. I need to scream and break something, anything, maybe one of the many stupid surfboards hanging on the walls. But breaking stuff, throwing a bunch of stupid papers back in my brother's face, and running as hard and as fast as I can until my body is too weak to hold in the anger wouldn't be very adult. And that's what I am now. An adult. A responsible, mature adult who is not going to let her past torture her anymore.

Maybe I could do some sprints after my follow-up interview at the gym is over.

Oh, who am I kidding? My eyes are too full of liquid rage to focus on anything but that stack of papers on my brother's lacquered desk. I push them away with a single finger. "You specify the type of lip gloss your employees can wear?"

There's a tap at the door, and Brent rises. "Weren't you supposed to be a business major? Any edge in a competitive industry should be exploited."

I scoff. "How is lip gloss an edge?"

A spunky-looking redhead in pink scrubs stands in the doorway and chuckles. "Why don't you show up with blue hair and black lipstick and find out?" She holds out a pair of purple surgical gloves to Brent. "We're ready for you at station three, Dr. Brent."

"Thanks, Gwen." Brent nods at me with long-suffering professionalism. "Gwen, this is my sister, Sarah. She's going to be covering the front desk next week while Viv is out."

"No, I'm not," I say.

Gwen flashes me a quick smile. "I was kidding about the blue hair and lipstick, of course, Dr. Brent. Shall I show Miss Sarah out?" She hands Brent his gloves and waves him out the door.

"So you're Brent's kid sister," Gwen says.

"Yeah. That's me." I smile briefly but avoid eye contact. If I don't look anyone in the eye, I can avoid knowing if they know about the divorce and sob story. I can bypass the pity and sad-puppy eyes and almost feel like a real-life, twenty-two-year-old grown-up.

She leans in and whispers conspiratorially, "I think you should totally show up with blue hair and black lipstick. Create some excitement for all of us."

"I'm not working here." For the millionth time. I follow her out of Brent and Jen's office.

"Viv." Gwen drums her acrylic nails on the counter and smiles at the brunette behind the reception desk. "I'm gonna show Sarah out and grab my coffee."

Gwen pulls me along with her to the coffee shop on the corner of Felspar and Cass. "So what's the deal?" she says as we get in line. "You keep checking your phone."

"I have a second interview at Fit Gym 24 in fifteen minutes."

"The one down the street?"

I nod but stay quiet as she buys her coffee along with a scone and a pack of pickles. She offers to buy me a coffee, but I politely decline. Caffeine and I have never gotten along. Anyway, I'm not sure why I'm even here with her. I guess it's better than awkwardly loitering in front of the gym?

We find a seat outside on the patio, and while you can't hear the beach from here, you can see bits of the ocean through the cars and buildings, lines of soft blue that push through the clutter of the streetscape.

Ten minutes now until my interview. I should just leave.

"So what do you want?" Gwen says around a mouthful of blueberry scone. "Do you want this job at the gym?"

I want a time machine. I want to erase that one stupid night sophomore year of college and get the life I was supposed to have. But I'll settle for a free gym membership. I'm definitely not taking a job with Brent and Jen. That would be settling. The forever kind of settling. Just the thought of it turns my stomach.

"I don't know," I finally say. "It beats working for my brother."

Gwen narrows an eye at me. "What did you want to do when you were staring daggers at Dr. Brent?"

She saw that? "That's a two-way mirror in his office?"

"Ew. Gosh, no." Gwen laughs. "It's tinted glass. A two-way mirror would just be creepy." She laughs again.

And somehow her laugh makes everything okay. I stare out across the street and focus on the blue water hedged by clouds of gray. I smell the dark green jasmine blooming behind us as I inhale deeply, obnoxiously. "My brother brought up a sensitive subject."

"Your divorce?"

So Gwen did know. Oh, who was I kidding? Everyone knew. For all of San Diego's size, Pacific Beach itself is a small town. "Yeah. While I was 'staring daggers' at my brother, I really wanted to be running sprints. Maybe see if I could get a faster mile down than this morning."

"I hear that."

"You're a runner?" I don't know why my tone is so hopeful. Goldfish, I sound pathetic.

"Ew." Gwen shudders. "No, but I can understand being madder than hell over a breakup."

I sit up straighter. "I don't miss my ex—"

"Girl, I know. That doesn't mean you couldn't go ten rounds with a punching bag and still want to scream yourself to sleep." Gwen eats a pickle slice from her snack pack. "You want one? They're spicy."

I'm about to shake my head but take one instead. "Thanks."

Gwen smiles. And while her smile is blindingly white and very straight, I notice her teeth on the bottom are all kinds of crooked. "You and I are gonna be friends," she says. "Now, then, what's the plan? For the interview."

My tongue burns from the pickle. "I need to land this job and start ASAP, or else I'll be forced into working for my brother and sister-in-law, where I will single-handedly drive their practice into the ground."

"You would not," Gwen says, taking another bite of her scone.

"Nope, but that's the fear. 'Sarah screws up everything she touches.'" I smile. I know it's a joke. I know some things weren't my fault. I know that I started the whole fudging mess, though.

Gwen licks a crumb from her finger. "How old are you?"

"Twenty-two." I should be done with my undergraduate degree by now, not trying to figure out how to restart it.

Gwen nods. "And school?"

I shake my head. "I didn't finish college." My lower lip starts to quiver. Maybe I could do lunges after my sprints. Oh goldfish, my eyes brim with tears for the second time this morning.

"Those pickles are spicy, huh?" Gwen scoots the bag toward me. "Have another."

I all but sob around a mouthful of pickle. "I'm such a loser."

"Honey, please. When I was twenty-two, I had a bad set of highlights, a perpetual hangover, and not much else."

"How old are you?"

Gwen looks up pointedly.

"Sorry," I say, and I catch my lip on my next bite of pickle. "You don't have to answer. It's just... you look my age."

Gwen visibly brightens. "I'm twenty-eight, baby. What I meant was, are you going back to school anytime soon? Do you need to be up-front about needing to work around your classes?"

"Yeah... Um, Tony mentioned that classes wouldn't be a problem so long as I could work weekends." How much going back to school will cost, on top of my already-in-default student loans, is a problem. A big, nasty, messy problem.

"Okay." Gwen thoughtfully munches a pickle. I hazard a glance up at her, and she is seriously stunning. Like, Greek goddess meets Disney princess meets prom queen. Gwen is exactly the type of girl I'd never have spoken to in high school because my fragile ego and bitchy streak couldn't handle ever being compared to her. Goldfish,

I'm glad I'm not back in high school. "We'll make sure to get it in writing all the same." Gwen's emerald-encased phone buzzes. "We've got to move."

I follow as Gwen marches down a block and stops traffic as she weaves down a side alley. She seems to glow, which is saying something, because the marine layer is still firmly in place this morning. I pull the strings of my hoodie and sigh. Some women just have it. I never quite puzzled out what *it* was until now. In Gwen's case, *it* is a pair of ridiculously pretty blue eyes, an enviable hourglass frame, a confident smile, and piles of auburn hair that I bet outshine new pennies when the sun's out. Next to her, I am a flat-chested, scrawny, dishwater blonde that could be mistaken for a twelve-year-old boy.

"Do you always wear sweatshirts?" Gwen asks.

"So long as June Gloom is a thing. Everyone expects San Diego to be paradise in the summer. No one remembers that it's usually foggy, cloudy, and cold until the end of July."

"Fair point." Gwen stops short in front of a pair of glass doors. "Take it off."

"What?" Oh. No. Did Gwen mistake my sad, pathetic desperation for a friend to be sad, pathetic desperation for... more than a friend? I mean, yeah, I was just staring at her and thinking about how gorgeous she is, but it was in an envious, mentor-me-and-my-sad-frizzy-hair-and-combination-skin way.

"You can't interview in a sweaty hoodie."

Before I can say anything, Gwen has my sweatshirt up and off and shoves me through the sliding glass doors of Fit Gym 24.

"Hey, Sarah," Tony, the jacked dude behind the check-in desk, calls. He perks up, and a flash of a smile surfaces when Gwen walks in behind me.

Before he has a chance to launch into his membership pitch, Gwen leans against the desk and smiles. Sometime between the sweatshirt and now, she managed to pull out her ponytail, and her red hair hangs in long, loose tendrils around her shoulders. I blink, and for a minute, I imagine bright green tendrils wrapped through it, with tight stippling giving way to gorgeous color shadow. I give myself a little shake. Today is not going to be the day I crack.

"I'm Tony Morales, club manager." He holds out his hand to Gwen, and now he can't hide his smile. What is it about men and redheads?

"You're hiring my friend and giving her a signing bonus," Gwen says, flashing her very white teeth.

"Excuse me?" Tony and I both say. Well, actually, I say, "Dude, what the holy fudge?" Okay. Maybe I didn't say *fudge*, but I will next time. Too many of my mom's church friends come to this gym. Like I said, PB is a small town.

Gwen doesn't take her eyes from Tony. "Sarah, tell this man what you were telling me about your running and sprints."

I mumble about my distance running, but honestly, I could have been shouting about my insomnia, swearing habits, or long-standing superhero fetishes. Wouldn't matter. Tony is completely enraptured by Gwen.

If I'm being cruel, I'd say Tony is one of those guys who needs to lay off the supplements, because he is approaching an abnormal BMI, but really, he looks like a Captain Patriotic Man double. Maybe a little browner. Maybe a little stockier. But yeah, a dead ringer for Roy Stevenson after the testosterone injections.

I need to get a handle on my cruel streak.

"See?" Gwen says, pulling away from the counter. "She has the brains and a body that will get people into your club. Let's talk scheduling. Let's talk numbers. And make this fast. I need to get back to work."

By the time Gwen finishes shaking Tony's hand, I have a job and a small signing bonus with some clause in my contract that prioritizes scheduling around my classes when/if I ever go back to school, Gwen has a free three-month membership, and poor Tony has the most unbelievable, palpable case of instantaneous crush I've ever seen.

"We'll put you on the front desk and Kids Club. Can you start this weekend?" I know he is talking to me, but he's totally focused on

Gwen, and his eyes are electric. They'd take up an entire panel in a comic book—a glossy, overly detailed, close-up splash page with Gwen reflected in his pupils. Maybe even with those visible shock lines radiating from him with vague/not-so-vague hearts floating in the periphery.

"How did you do that?" I murmur as Gwen and I head back to Brent and Jen's tooth palace. They hate it when I call it that.

Gwen pushes open the building door. A gust of conditioned air catches her hair. My sweat-dried fringe remains plastered to my face.

"How do I thank you?" I ask as we climb the stairs to Brent and Jen's corner suite.

"Oh, please. You didn't need me. But here." She hands me her phone. "Text me funny stories about work, and we'll call it even."

As I put in my number, Gwen pulls her hair into a tight ponytail. "What do you think of your new boss?" she asks. "What's his name?"

I hand back the phone. "Tony?"

"Yeah, Tony. What'd you think?"

"He seems..."

Gwen's eyes narrow. "Too muscly?"

"Maybe?"

"But nice?"

"Could be." I nod. "Maybe layered underneath a heavy façade of 'I can't be bothered to give two Shirley Temples.'"

Gwen looks at me sideways.

My cheeks burn. "The drinks, I mean. Not *Rebecca of Sunnybrook Farm*." Although that was one of the movies Mom had on frequent rotation while I was growing up.

Gwen's smile flickers before she pushes open the office door. "Only one way to find out. I saw him first. We'll find someone else for you. K?"

Time to quote Hamlet. *O, my prophetic soul.* Etcetera, etcetera. Except it's not my soul. It's Gwen's soul. And I'm not about to bare my soul to my new friend. "K," I mumble.

CHAPTER TWO

If my life were a Jane Austen novel, I'd say Gwen and I became "fast" friends. I'd splay a hand across my collarbone, bat my eyes, and totally seal my fate as an idiot, like Lydia Bennet. Which is hardly fair, because I've always thought of myself as a Lizzie. Except everyone thinks of herself as a Lizzie (thank you, Mr. Darcy). So, I am an Elinor. Elinor Dashwood would totally have been a distance runner, too, had Lululemon and Asics been around. She would have pounded out her frustrations on all those miles of gravel walks and muddy country road.

But my life is not Austen. So I'll just say that in the month since I've met Gwen, we've become friends. She comes to see me after work at the gym most days. And while I'm not stupid and know that she's coming mostly for Tony, I don't mind. It's been too long since I've had a friend, particularly a friend who includes me on any of her guy stuff. Even though I want nothing to do with men for the next two score years, I still like hearing about them. Prince Charming is still a nice idea, even if I don't believe in him anymore.

Gwen holds on to the counter of the Kids Club desk for a deep quad stretch. "But you do believe in soulmates?"

"I do." I reach for the stray crayons from under the kids' table. "But I'm the type of person who's going to find hers when she's sixty-five, and he's forty-three. Not much point looking now. He's still running around in diapers."

"He'd be in here." Gwen gags and shudders, surveying my Kids Club kingdom of broken crayons and foam-covered plastic. "You can't be serious."

"Of course not! But I'd not be serious with any guy I'd meet right now. So what's the point?"

Gwen's smile turns all sultry and suggestive. She arches a brow, and I toss a foam block at her. She swats the block into the bin. My eyes add blurgits to her actions. "Say you did meet Mr. Right right now?"

"I'd be Shirley Temples out of luck. Because I'm not doing anything even close to dating for the next forty-three years." It's one of my rules. I tug the corner of the tumbling mat straight. "How are things going between you and Captain Patriotic Man?"

Gwen's eyes twinkle. "Slowly. New topic. How is life? I know you live here now."

It's not far from the truth. The perk to my employment is a free membership. When I'm not working, I train. Not for any one event or purpose, but because pounding on a treadmill or strapping myself to a rowing machine feels better than being stuck at home in my mom's office/spare bedroom. Especially now that San Diego schools are out for the summer. The gym is always open. And I've come at two a.m. some nights and cried myself silly while rowing in the empty gym, CNN flashing silently above me.

"I'm very popular since I don't mind working nights or picking up other people's shifts on weekends." I look up and stifle a laugh. Tony must have found his courage. "He's coming over."

Gwen laughs again, and fudge, but it sounds genuine. I've never learned how to do that. Not that I want to learn now. "No flirting" is also one of my rules.

"What's so funny?" Tony asks.

"Sarah was telling me she sells more memberships when she works the front desk than any other employee." Gwen winks at me while Tony is busy admiring how her pistachio-colored tank hugs her torso.

I turn red. "I do not."

"I wouldn't be surprised." Tony arches an eyebrow—just for Gwen, no doubt. "She does know half our members by name."

I don't know what to do with this conversation. I've become a weird subject for Tony and Gwen to get their flirt on. "I think my mom got everyone at the school and her prayer group to join just so she could keep an eye on me." I forbade—well, implored—her not to get one herself.

Gwen pulls her arm back in a classic bicep stretch. "You should give her a raise, Tony."

"Is that so?" He's nearly pinned Gwen against the Kids Club check-in desk.

Not this again. No way am I going to field a phone call from an irate parent asking what exactly goes on in the Kids Club after she drops her angel off and runs away without saying boo. "Hey, Tony." I catch Gwen's gaze and wiggle my eyebrows while Tony is hypnotized by the sight of Gwen grabbing her elbows for a deltoid stretch. "Gwen was asking about the TRX straps. I'm supposed to stay put in the Kids Club. Do you have time to show her—"

"Yeah!" Tony says enthusiastically before correcting himself. "Yeah. This way, Gwen." Tony holds open the Kids Club door and beams at Gwen, who turns to wrinkle her nose and roll her eyes at me. Still, she goes willingly. Tony, of course, is beside himself.

Two hours later, Gwen finds me. "Sarah, what are you doing next Saturday?"

I'm about to answer that I will be working when she stops me.

"Doesn't matter. You're going to Comic-Con with me!"

Bright light and Ben-Day dots flash in my eyes. "What?" My heart starts to race, and I swear my hands are shaking.

A little pigtailed toddler pulls on my leggings. I scoop her up. "What's going on, girlfriend?"

She pulls a fistful of my hair and screams with delight.

"Okay. Let's put on *PJ Masks*. You wanna help?" I hand the TV remote over to the toddler, who runs away, screaming joyously. I, too, feel like screaming, but not from joy. Suppressed inner geek maybe.

"We're dressing up too," Gwen says. "I'm going to be a mermaid. You can be one too."

I hear the *flip, flip, flip* of pages, and my world starts to segment into panels and speech bubbles.

"What?" I check in another member, actually a mama with a four-year-old and a crawler.

"I don't like you!" the four-year-old hisses.

"I have candy if you change your mind," I tell him.

His scrunched-up nose unwrinkles as I press a Starburst into his hand. "One now and one when your mom comes back. If you're good."

He runs away, and I rescue Gwen from the chubby crawler, who is using her legs to try to pull himself up. "It's been a crazy day." I'm trying to change the subject. I'm trying to stop this train before it derails. Rule number one: No comics. Not again. Not ever.

Gwen is not having it. "So, Comic-Con! We're going as mermaids."

Sounds are starting to illustrate themselves into onomatopoeia. *Thunk!* go the blocks. *Crash!* go the toy cars. I clutch my stomach, feeling like I am about to faint as my heart hammers into small, yet readable words near my chest. *Thump. Thump. Thump.* "No. We're not."

"Okay, not mermaids. But I have to be somebody with red hair." Gwen pulls out her phone, no doubt to scan Pinterest for redheaded heroes.

I shake the crazy off before it unravels into something weirder. This is real life, and I'm not about to let my demons out of their cage.

I'm not revisiting the past. I'm not doing this. "I can't go to Comic-Con."

Gwen isn't listening. She's smiling at her phone. "Who else has red hair?"

"MJ," I say without thinking.

Gwen snorts. "He didn't have red hair. White glove, yes—"

"No, Maybell June, the girl from Cicada-bro," I say. Images of blue and red spandex, red wigs, and random characters flash through my mind like snippets of a highlight reel. Is the music in the gym too loud today? Or is that just more memories of that fudging awful night sophomore year? I try breathing long and deep, but the smell of rubber tumbling mats and Diaper Genies makes me cough.

Gwen twirls a strand of her hair around her finger. "Yeah, I'd rather be a mermaid. My abs are pretty good. I should get a tan. I bet if we peeled away all your layers, we'd find you wouldn't need one." She mumbles something about rock-hard abs, and I blush. No amount of working out can undo what my abs have been through. Not that I don't try.

I want to lie down. Instead, I plank on the floor of the crawlers' corner. "Not happening."

Gwen rolls her eyes. "Yeah, whatever. K. I'm buying tickets."

A crawler has found me and attempts to use my back as a table. "You can't just buy tickets for Comic-Con. You have to register first."

"Fine, I'll register."

My arms shake. "They sell out the day they go live. In March. And they're not tickets. They're badges." I assumed she had tickets when she asked me to go. Though that was clearly a stupid assumption.

Gwen pauses and looks up slowly from her phone. "Holy jeepers, Nightbat. Sarah's a closet nerd."

My face is crimson, but I can blame it on the strain of planking with a teething baby trying to climb on top of me. "Am not. Can you give me a hand?"

Gwen hops on the counter instead. She thoughtfully narrows her eyes at me, the hint of a smirk haunting her face. "Name five super-heroes who have red hair."

My exercise buddy has pulled himself into a stand and is slapping my back with howls of laughter. The words come even as I try to stuff them back in. "Admiral Autumn is one of my favorites—"

"Clock is ticking."

Fine! "Fascination, Dr. Jillian Slate, Batty Nightgirl, Cardinal Flame, Poison Hemlock, Ruby Carmine, Viscountess Incarnadine." The crazy is out of the cage. And it's not going back in. I collapse out of my plank with a groan. "There is an unrealistically high representation of redheaded heroines in comics because the colorists needed to punch up their palettes."

"Total nerd," Gwen says with wide eyes and a grin. She laughs in disbelief, and that's good. I need to be reminded that my love of comics is laughable. "How have we been friends all summer, and you kept this from me? We're going to Comic-Con."

My stomach is spasming from my plank. "I don't have a badge," I pant.

"Do you have a costume?"

Holy Shirley Temples, Nightbat! You don't ask the addict if she kept some of her stash for the memories.

I hop to my feet and check to make sure all the Kids Club kiddies are still breathing and still reasonably entertained. "No." I sink to the floor to clean up a pile of blocks.

Gwen leans back against the counter and inspects her nails. "You gotta stop turning bright pink when you lie."

A little hand tugs on the hem of my polo. "I went poop!" Evan, a frequent Kids Club flyer, says.

I try not to inhale. Working the Kids Club might permanently damage my ability to smell. "Okay, honey. I'll call your mama." I join Gwen at the counter and quickly scroll through the list of sign-ins. "Janet Stephens to the Kids Club, please. Janet Stephens to the Kids Club, please."

"Why do you even want to go to Comic-Con?" I ask Gwen.

"Tony mentioned it. He said he was going this Saturday and asked if I was going to be there." She shrugs, but in my comic book brain, her eyes start to shimmer. Faint pink heart bubbles may burst and pop around us. Oh my gosh. Who would have thought comics withdrawal would manifest like this?

Gwen pulls me back to the present with a squeal. "Then he started tittering about how we could meet up outside if I didn't have a pass. So I told him I was already going with some friends."

"Please tell me you didn't name me."

"No. First rule of keeping a guy interested is to be vague, silly. I thought everyone knew that." She flips her hair.

I reflexively tug my tight stub of a ponytail tighter. Holy insecurities, Nightbat. "And I thought everyone knows Comic-Con sells out within seconds."

A sweaty Janet Stephens shows up and whisks her poopy cherub to the bathroom.

"Oh, please." Gwen twirls a strand of her hair between her fingers. "There has to be some nerd forum where we post our pictures and say Poison Hemlock and Fem Fantastic want to be your date to Comic-Con, and then the internet breaks with all the desperate, lonely nerds who want to go to nerd prom with the pretty girls."

I try to smile as I greet another parent, this one a dad, who has no qualms checking out Gwen's butt. It's the exact kind of behavior that warrants a pithy line, but I've got nothing.

"Hey?" Gwen asks when we are alone—well, as alone as two women can be in a room full of children. "What's up?"

My lip wobbles. "I met Daniel—my ex—the last time I cosplayed."

Gwen forms her lips into a perfect O, but says nothing.

"And after what happened..." I stoop to pick up a crumpled coloring page. "I swore off comics."

"More of your rules, huh?"

"No more comics—rule number one. No more cosplay—rule number two." I rub the back of my neck and wince as my eyes dart to the bright LEDs in the ceiling. Comics and cosplay are gateway drugs. One taste, and I'm a goner who has trashed her life worse than a trash panda in the compost bin. "I didn't trust myself, so I sold off all my costumes before I moved back home..." I trail off, blushing so intensely I must look catastrophically sunburned. Once again, my eyes are focused on the toes of my Asics.

Gwen gently bumps my shoulder with her own. "Hey. I know you have at least one costume left. Add not looking up at the ceiling and then down at your shoes to your list of non-options the next time you have to lie."

"I never finished my Catstrike costume. You can't sell incomplete costumes." And while I did manage to scrape a few bucks together for my collection, not finishing this costume had been such an easy excuse to keep one cosplay skeleton packed away in the suitcases under my mom's guest bed.

Gwen stretches her quads. "A memento from your badass cosplay days?"

"I've never so much as run my finger over the zipper of that bag." My voice is a weird mix of forlorn and loathing.

She straightens. "Let me take you to Comic-Con, and you can wear it just once. It will be your farewell tour."

"It's sold out."

"Challenge accepted. Now come on. Perk up. We're going to have fun, and I'll personally make sure you do not end up leaving Comic-Con married or—"

"Pregnant," I blurt out. I drop my face into my hands and sink to the floor. Face-palm GIFs have nothing on me right now. "I left my last cosplay misadventure pregnant."

Gwen slides down beside me.

"It was really stupid. I was really stupid," I say into my hands. I wince, as I know a barrage of questions are about to tumble out of Gwen's mouth.

"Hey." She pulls my head onto her shoulder, solidifying that she is the big sister I never had. "It's okay."

It's not okay. Nothing I do can ever make it okay. "I know." I tug the twisted seam of my leggings straight. "But I really do not want to talk about this at work." Or ever.

Gwen nods. "Okay, but if you ever do—"

I know. "Please don't say anything to Brent or—"

"Hon, I'm your friend. If I had known, I wouldn't have even brought up Comic-Con. Or mermaids."

Oh, Shirley Temples. That's how it starts. The walking-on-eggshells self-editing that leads to canceled friendships. Things are already getting weird, and I cannot lose my only friend standing over this. "I want to go," I blurt out.

Gwen blinks. A shower of foam blocks rains down on us, accompanied by a stampede of little feet and giggles.

"Oh, no!" I cry in my exaggerated Kids Club staffer voice, the kind that makes grown adults cringe. "I'm going to get you."

More giggles and shrieks.

"You sure?" Gwen asks. She's scrutinizing my every twitch now.

But I am sure. I'd do anything to keep my new friend. Even break my rules one last time. "Just promise not to leave me alone with any shady guys. Or sperm-bank reps."

Gwen laughs. She puts an arm around me and gives me an encouraging squeeze. "It'll be fun. There are only so many chances a woman has to parade around in spandex looking ridiculous and sexy for a crowd."

"I think you just described the nature of a gym." I perk up into my promotional pitch voice. "And we are open twenty-four hours a day, every day of the year."

Gwen laughs.

"You have noticed how the moment you walk through those glass doors, everyone gives you the elevator eyes?" I groan. "It's like you sign some imaginary waiver that you're okay with everyone checking you out."

"Come on, you do it too," she says.

I grin. "I work here. I'm supposed to keep an eye on things."

Gwen rises to her feet and pulls me up with her. "So I'll meet you at the convention center?"

I press my palm to my forehead. A run and twenty minutes in the sauna would be nice right about now. "Finding the badges this late will cost a fortune and will be, you know, slightly illegal."

Gwen puts up her hand and makes shushing sounds. "My crazy idea, my treat. Yes or no, Saire?"

I open and close my mouth. It's my last chance to say no. I'm supposed to say no. I have rules in place for a reason. I know how I can get carried away with cosplay and/or guys. I'm supposed to be an adult. Comics are for teenagers and boring, middle-aged white guys. They were part of my past, but are not part of my future. The same future that consists of insomnia runs, babysitting kids at a gym, and late-night cross-training, all while doing my best to vanish from functional corners of society. My shoulders hunch and my spine rounds just thinking of it...

But one last hit of cosplay wouldn't change my future. I'm living in my mom's office/spare bedroom, for fudge's sake. It's Comic-Con, after all. You can't really say you're from San Diego if you've never been to Comic-Con.

"You wouldn't tell anyone it's me?" The times I've had to tell people how I met Daniel... It's mortifying. A complete joke. "I mean, if my mom found out, I don't think I'd be let out of the house ever again."

"You can come in costume, and you'll just be another crazy in the crowd."

I try to groan, but it comes out a nervous laugh. "And you wouldn't ditch me?" The real heart of the matter. I cannot let my friendship with Gwen unravel.

Gwen crosses her heart. "Friends don't let friends cosplay alone."

"Thanks, Gwen." I inhale, not realizing I was holding my breath. "Sure. I mean, yes. I will meet you there."

CHAPTER THREE

My mom is a religious zealot. Okay, maybe not a zealot, but she is definitely a church lady. I think it's what happens when your spouse tragically dies during the evening commute, and you are left to raise two kids on your own. Help has to come from somewhere. May as well be church. And if going to church once a week is good for the soul, finding a way to be there nearly every weekday is even better, right?

Growing up, I thought church was just what everyone did. I thought everyone's mom took issue with skirts above the knee and sleeveless dresses. I thought everyone's mom insisted on "clean language" and put her foot down when it came to entertainment in her home that "crossed the line." Not that the line was clearly defined. We watched *The Sound of Music* a lot back in the day.

Brent got more slack. He's a boy. He needed boyish things. He needed an outlet. He needed role models. Sure, he could go see the new Cicada-bro movie with his friends. Meanwhile, I needed to go change because my shirt was too tight. Meanwhile, I started to read more comics than Brent or his friends ever read combined. Meanwhile, I started putting all the home-economics skills I learned at church to good use amassing my cosplay collection. What Jesus and sewing have in common still escapes me, but I will forever be grateful to Sister Grace Eldrich for teaching me how to staystitch nylon on pleather. At least, I thought I would be forever grateful. Right now, I'm not so sure.

All I can think about is how my life would end if my mom decides she doesn't need to go to church this Saturday morning for the Book of Revelation study group and instead comes home to find her daughter clad head to toe in the tightest, shiny, black vinyl catsuit imaginable. Besides the fact that Mom doesn't approve of sexy costumes or masks, there's also the issue that she doesn't know the half of what I got up to in my sophomore year. I mean, she knows I got married. She doesn't know that Daniel got me pregnant before he even knew my name.

"You do remember my name?" I asked that awkward afternoon six weeks later when I told Daniel about the dollar-store-pee-on-a-stick positive.

"Yeah. You're..." He snapped his fingers, trying to remember. The fact that I had to explain I was Cicada Nymph (*you mean the Cicada-bro chick?*) should have been a dead giveaway that Daniel was a class-A douchebag.

Anyway. Mom doesn't know Daniel is a douche. She doesn't know I miscarried at twenty-four weeks. She knows only that we divorced and that I didn't take her advice and try marriage counseling with the pastor first. Kinda hard to go to marriage counseling when you're stuck in Michigan and your husband is thousands of miles away hiking the Pacific Crest Trail and "finding himself."

A text from Gwen makes my thigh buzz, pulling me back from my memory lane funk. Gwen: There's a cosplay contest!

I tug at my cowl. The chin strap bites into my neck just the same. I try to tap out a response with my clawed fingers. Yes, it is cumbersome, but it also feels more natural than it has any right to.

Me: No. Way.

Gwen: Come on, Saire. Don't bail on me now.

Me: "Angels and ministers of grace defend us!"

Yeah, I like quoting Hamlet.

Sitting in the back of my Lyft is a reality check of the most humiliating order. The driver, Tim, keeps glancing at me in the rearview mirror. His eyes nearly pop out of his head, his smile is so wide. I'm a grown woman parading around in a skanky, homemade costume that screams, "Desperate for attention." This is why I quit cosplaying. And yeah, there was the sex on the bathroom counter with Cicadabro, who turned out to be the world's biggest douchebag. One shotgun wedding, quickly followed by a divorce—yeah, it's a bio for the ages.

Gwen: The villain groups always win.

Gwen sends a GIF of a pouting puppy. I scoff and roll my eyes, and I swear that somewhere I've just become a meme.

"Everything okay back there?" Tim asks.

I stare down at my vinyl-clad thighs. The enormous shiny black boots are heavy and sweaty on my legs. They push my knees up to an unnatural angle in the back seat. "Can you turn up the AC?"

Tim pretends to busy himself adjusting vents and whatnot. Clearly, it's not every day you drive Catstrike, AJ Comics' sexiest villain and Nightbat's naughty crush, across town. Thank merciful heavens I am wearing a mask.

I'm not really the praying type, but I find myself begging the cosmos that Tim's sedan breaks down, pops a tire, or crashes, but our drive downtown to the convention center is uneventful and unimpeded.

We arrive, and Tim swivels in his seat. "I'm happy to drive you around the block again. Or, you know... anywhere." He adds the last bit too quietly, furiously blushing.

I take back everything I thought about wishing his car would break down and bolt out of his back seat. Not easy to do in platform boots.

The San Diego sunshine glints on my black vinyl corset, and I can smell the ocean all around me. It's a morning that promises plain, wholesome California fun, and I am a dark-'90s freak fantasy. People are staring. I run a hand across my stomach, but it is no use. I can't hide anything now. I feel like I'm going to be sick.

There is a roller coaster, an old, rickety wooden one, at Belmont Park that has just a lap bar to keep you from flying out. And as you climb up to the top of the big drop—*click, click, click*—you think, *Fudge. What have I done?*

Then comes the feeling of absolute panic, the one that urges you to start screaming for the emergency exit. You'd rather take the long, creaky service steps down than go through with the rest of the ride. Panic turns to dread. They stopped making wooden coasters for a reason, right? You think, *Just let me die.*

You'd pull the e-brake if you could. But you can't. You're strapped in. Can't go over. Can't go under. Must go through.

I used to feel this way about my long runs. I'd panic the day before. The panic would turn to dread as the sun set. Once, I tried putting it off for a day, but that only fed the panic beast. The only real solution was to just do it.

So you do. Not because you want to. But because that's how you make it stop.

I feel that way now. But then there is something else as I edge closer to the convention doors. You don't buy a ticket for the roller coaster because you take a perverse pleasure in suffering. You do it because it is fun. All of it—the nerves, the excitement, the rush. You live for it.

The causeway is littered with cosplayers and conventiongoers. We're all shuffling toward the main entrance. I tug on my mask—not easy to do with my claws. My phone pings with another text.

Gwen: Stop fidgeting.

"Seriously," a familiar voice says. "You look amazing. I don't even recognize you."

Gwen stands beside me in fishnets, green bustier leotard, and hair that is longer, thicker, and redder than I thought possible. She's got some intense green makeup going on around her eyes, but no mask.

I give my friend a hug and swear I hear a dozen phones snap a picture. "How'd you know it was me?"

Gwen swipes on a layer of nude lip gloss. "I didn't until you got my text."

"Epic costumes, ladies," a dude with a press badge swinging from his neck says. "Where'd you find them?"

Gwen drops the tube of gloss back down the front of her bustier. Good goldfish, what else is she hiding in there? "Mine's from this Etsy shop, but Saire is a purist. She made her own."

The dude whistles low and long, and his eyes linger on my hips as he asks for a picture. Gwen strikes a pose.

"Thanks, Dr. Hemmel," he says.

"Who?" Gwen asks, practically dislocating my arm as she pulls me in step beside her.

"Dr. Penelope Rose Hemmel. Poison Hemlock's alter ego," I clarify.

Gwen flips her long red hair over her shoulder. "Whatever. We are badass villains. We're entering the cosplay contest. And we are going to win."

More people are stopping to pull out their phones.

"Why does winning matter?" I ask, swaying uncomfortably in my boots.

"Because, Sarah, it is fun."

A phone flashes, and I cringe. "Fine. I'll do it if you promise not to say my name all day."

"Deal. Now quickly, Catstrike. To the nerd cave."

A weird ASMR buzz starts at the back of my scalp as we enter the convention center. Equal parts anticipation and adrenaline. I usually get tingly before my mile sprints. But Comic-Con is different. Today is different. I can feel every single pair of eyes on my black vinyl. "Goldfish," I whimper. I miss my hoodie. I miss the layers of fabric between my waist and the eyes of so many others. I take big, gulping breaths.

Comic-Con is massive, and the scale of it hits you first in your ears. It is loud. The roar of humanity deafens. I swear, and not of the Shirley Temple variety, but no one hears me. It's that loud.

Gwen laughs and tugs me into step beside her. "This is amazing. Look at all the nerds!" She has to shout for me to hear her.

"You're one of them now," I yell back.

"Don't be silly. This is just camouflage," she says, gesturing to her green leotard.

I scoff, and my ankle wobbles in my boot.

Gwen takes my arm, smiles, and waves at an entire group of digital SLR-wearing fanatics. One even carries a separate flash. Gwen pulls me into a pose beside her. "Wearing leopard print doesn't make you a leopard."

My vinyl catsuit makes an odd crinkling sound as I walk that I'm sure only I can hear. It was little sensory details like this that got me into cosplay. What does it feel like to smile when wearing a Cicada Nymph face mask? Tight, and it totally squashes your nose flat. Can you really dance with a broadsword down the back of your blue dress? Not comfortably. "There are other places to people-watch," I shout.

We shuffle past a group of cosplayers. I have to duck to avoid someone's wings. Queen Cockatoo, I think. The level of extra in these costumes is inspiring. Or it would be if this wasn't my cosplay farewell.

"Like where?" Gwen's green fishnets glow in the San Diego sunshine that streams through the walls of windows.

"The beach. The zoo."

"I've been to the beach. I've been to the zoo. This is more fun." Gwen pulls out her badge and waves it in front of security. "Besides. You needed an excuse to wear your catsuit."

"Not really." In fact, I was determined never to wear it ever. I pull out my badge for the security check. They're being really tight this year, checking badges on every floor and hall. "That ship sailed off to China, where it teaches English to all the adorable and Instagram-worthy schoolchildren before it wanders into the mountains, where it will hopefully die of exposure, never to return." But instead, Daniel's Instagram posts just keep coming. And always with captions about how hard, but so very important, it is to take time to find your true self, even if it takes you to the other side of the world. You know, in case months spent hiking the PCT wasn't enough.

Gwen lets out an exasperated moan. "Where is the AC, people? I don't want to sweat off my glitter."

Gwen is right. The convention center feels like a greenhouse. We wander the halls until we are in the middle of one of the vending galas, and then it's worse than ladies' night at... Well, the theoretical ladies' nights I envision in my head when I'm too tired to brood or work out.

"Me-ow!"

I turn with clawed hands up and a hiss to a smattering of applause.

"Easy, boys." Gwen sashays into the fray, and if I don't follow, I'll probably never see her again.

"Hemlock! Poison Hemlock, can I get a picture?" a group of Space Monk-dressed boys asks.

Gwen tosses her hair behind her shoulder, and for a moment, I imagine the word *flip* faintly penciled in around her as emanata radiate off the Space Monks. "How about the two of us?" She drapes herself around the two cutest monks.

"Crowd in, boys." My voice has become a rough, velvety purr. I arch my back as a Space Monk rests his hand just above my waist.

We make our way to the main ballroom with the most impressive displays and vendors. "Those Space Monks were definitely not of the pious, entropy-fearing order," I hiss.

Gwen's eyes light up at the nearest vendor booth. "Ponies! I need all of them!" She stuffs merch into a conveniently-placed shopping basket. "Why didn't we dress up as ponies? OMG. There's a pink one? With red hair?" Gwen is ecstatic. "Next year, we're coming as ponies." Gwen shoves her way, merch first, into the crowd of shoppers.

"How did you score badges for this year?" I trace my name on my badge with one clawed finger before sliding it back in my thigh pocket with my phone.

Gwen smiles and wrinkles her nose. "The internet is a magical place. Particularly when you have a Venmo account ready and waiting."

"I'm sure your picture didn't hurt either," I say, and goldfish, I'm using my Catstrike voice again.

We edge our way to the front of the queue.

"Do you want a commemorative shopping bag?" the cashier asks, gesturing to the display of reusable totes plastered with images of ponies.

"Honey, of course I do!"

The cashier struggles to fit all of Gwen's purchases into the bag.

Gwen checks her phone before dropping it down the front of her bustier. "Now what am I supposed to do with all these goodies? I'm not carrying them around all day."

A Dragon Wolf cosplayer slides up his helmet. "There's a coat check on the first floor."

Gwen winks at Dragon Wolf. "Care to show us?"

He grins before a Fascination cosplayer tugs him away.

"I'm not walking back to the front." I point to my boots. "I can't." I haven't worn heels in years.

"I promised not to leave you alone." Gwen looks dismayed. She hefts the bag of bulging pony paraphernalia onto her shoulder.

"I'll be fine." I shoo her toward the escalators.

"I'll be right back. Don't wander too far."

Not a problem. It is physically impossible to wander far in these boots.

I make it exactly two steps before Cicada-bro and MJ ask for a photo. I make it another couple of feet before a group of preppy wizards stops me for pictures. After that, I am inundated with a group that is either Dr. Leto or Sherlock Holmes. It's hard to tell, what with the overpowering smell of bodies needing to shower. Holy sweaty socks, Nightbat. I will sign that petition floating around the forums for public showers at all Comic-Con International conventions when this is over. I hope the smell doesn't linger on me.

Selfie sticks are banned at Comic-Con, but somehow props like faux spears, axes, and any kind of wizarding staff are fair play? Maybe I should have brought my whip after all.

After my fourth photo op with yet another Nightbat, I have to sit down. My boots send spikes of pain up my ankles and lay waste to my spine. I may never run again. I'll have to take up swimming, or worse—surfing like Brent. Hours bobbing up and down in the seaweed. Not even breaking a sweat.

"How about a picture, sweetheart?" A jerk grabs my wrist.

I nearly lose my balance as I wrench my hand free. "I'm fine, thanks," I snarl.

"Come on," he moans. "Don't be like that."

He reaches for my waist this time, but I grab my phone and snap a picture of his sorry mug. The flash makes him blink.

"I said no. Now back off. I'm out of your league, and I'm this close to sharing your picture with security."

"Sorry," the idiot slurs, skulking away.

He earned a major eye roll, and again, I hear phones click. People really need to work on their cosplay etiquette.

Calls of approval and questions about the costume follow me as I search for someplace to just chill until Gwen returns. Past Sarah would have been cooler with the attention, maybe even flattered. Oh, who am I kidding? Past Sarah would be enamored of the idea that behind every cowl could be an equally passionate, attractive, kindred überfan searching for a soulmate to validate the importance of comics (for both their artistry and storytelling) and argue over who was the best Nightbat, all while making heart eyes at each other. Now, I can't stop thinking about facial recognition software that may flag me in my mom's Facebook feed or if my platform boots are going to permanently throw off my running. I am all too aware of the crazies who come out to cosplay to indulge in any of my cosplay comic book fantasies.

"Need an escape?"

I turn around, bracing myself for another photo request. Instead, I'm blindsided by a wide smile belonging to a guy in a white T-shirt. I literally sigh out loud, because after posing for a billion Snapchats with a bunch of other cosplayers, a plain old tee is the breath of normal I need.

The guy is probably mid-twenties, in jeans that are as Normal Guy as the shirt. He's taller than me, but only by about an inch or so, with me in the RuPaul heels. And he is delicious, but not in the overt, Ralph-Winston-sans-red-cape, good-looks way. He has that I-do-yoga-and-am-completely-comfortable-in-my-own-skin type of vibe, but judging by the veins that wrap around his wrists and the muscles I can count in his forearms, he does more than yoga. And that confidence sans costume in this place makes me curious. Interested.

Like a breaking wave that sweeps up the shore, I feel it. The cosplay is taking control. My head cocks. Suddenly, my boots don't feel so painful. Fudge brownies, are his eyes blue?

"What've you got?" I purr. Cosplay all of a sudden feels a lot more fun.

Burst lines, the gorgeous ones that need both ink and a colorist, radiate from his smile. He proffers a box to me. "Open it."

I take the box carefully, because of my cosplay claws. It is covered in the type of switches and buttons that would have fit in on an old-school Starship Cruiser set. "Why?" I ask.

He laughs, and that ASMR buzz comes creeping back up my spine. "Most people ask how."

I shift languidly in my boots. "I'm not most people."

"Clearly." His grin turns cheeky for a fleeting moment. His chest swells with a deep inhale. "It's an escape box. You open it. You get a prize."

I look past him to see a couple in Mask Master T-shirts and a father-and-son pair, each with a similar box. I lean a shoulder against the obliging pillar. My feet ache. I pass the box back to Handsome T-shirt Guy. "Show me."

"Too intimidating?" His eyes flash and lips press together. Oooh, this one makes me want to play. Those forearms, that smile. So much confidence without even a whiff of cynicism. "We have a junior version, if you want to wait for that one."

I stand up straighter and saunter closer. I run my gloved, clawed hand gently down his cheek and chest before pulling away. He doesn't flinch. "I don't want to scratch your toy." My voice has slid into that rough, throaty purr. I sit on top of his table of merch and lean back confidently. "What are the prizes?"

He slides a stack of flyers out of my way. "Have to play to find out."

The father and son hand back the open puzzle box to White Tee Guy.

"Good fun," the dad says in a German accent.

I wink at White Tee before turning to the pair. "What'd you win?" I ask.

The dad squints at the paper in his hand. "Buy one, get one coupon to Superhero Escapes. May we have a picture?"

White Tee jumps to his feet to take it. I smile with my lips pressed together, my eyes not leaving this guy. I don't know why—I mean, maybe I do, he's easy on the eyes—but there's something else. My mind stumbles through half-remembered passages of Jane Eyre, memories of my grandma and grandpa playing pinochle, until I land on the memory of my mom sighing over Captain von Trapp all those Sundays from so long ago.

Maybe there was another reason why my mom insisted we watch *The Sound of Music* so much.

"Thanks for playing, guys. Make sure to check out the Sable Siren raffle inside the Halifax Sisters Studios tent."

I arch an eyebrow. "Coupons?"

"Some have actual tickets. Others have key chains, pins, even a few T-shirts." His eyes travel up and down my figure, and I almost kick my feet up and lie down on his table, purring. "Is your suit custom? The fit is..." He trails off.

I put a hand on my hip. "The fit is...?"

His eyes snap up to mine. "It's all really well done. I mean, I can tell you took inspiration from *Nightbat Returns*, but you made it your own." He tosses the escape box back to me. "Go on. Give it a try. If you're really worried about scratching it, you can take off your gloves."

I smirk and shift my weight. All my vinyl crinkles and crunches. I hope this guy is standing close enough to hear. "Why stop with gloves?"

He tugs at the neck of his tee and adjusts the lanyard of his vendor's badge. "Your shoes do look really uncomfortable." He catches my eye with a playful smile that almost distracts me from the slight blush on his cheeks.

No way. White Tee is a gentleman.

I look down at the box in my hands and swing my feet. Why not have some fun? I roll onto my back and toss the box up in the air and catch it. "This panel with the flashing flat buttons, it's a sliding-block puzzle." I slide the buttons that flash around. "There's got to be a clue somewhere about the order." I twist the box, pulling and pushing and looking for instructions. There are two spring-release buttons. I push them together, and a drawer pops open that contains a pair of flimsy red and blue 3-D glasses.

I roll onto my stomach and smirk up at this guy before I position the 3-D glasses around the cowl of my costume. He scoffs, a cute involuntary release of both laughter and disbelief, before running a hand through his hair.

I love cosplay. I've missed cosplay. Never in a billion years would I do anything even remotely like this in real life. But here I am, living my dream and shamelessly flirting with a handsome stranger with no reservations.

White Tee works his vendor space. I've amassed a bit of attention, if I do say so myself. Guess the extra hours of hand-stitching last night were a good idea. Not that White Tee is slowed down by any of this. I track him as I fiddle with the puzzle. He gives a couple of hints to the Mask Master fans without coming across as douchey. He chats with a Chupacabra cosplay troupe. He smiles easily. Laughs sincerely. Clearly, he's done this before. The thought makes me curious but also irritated. What other cosplayers has he ensnared with his wholesome T-shirt and charming smirk of a smile?

Back to business. With the 3-D glasses on, I see a picture is visible in the sliding-block puzzle. A single panel of a vintage Redemption Ring, AJ Comics' band of most successful superheroes.

"Do you do other cosplay?" White Tee asks as I shift the squares around.

"Hey, Catstrike!"

I look up before taking off the 3-D glasses and recoil at a phone just inches away from my nose.

"Dude." White Tee is more startled than me, but laughs off the fan with the phone good-naturedly. "You scared me. A little more warning, okay?"

I shift the last square in place, revealing another spring-load button. This one releases the top lid, revealing a keypad.

"What you working on there, Sai—

I look up at Gwen pointedly. "Sabine," I say.

"Who's Sabine?" she says, nodding and winking to an impressive Cyborg Queen and Admiral Starship Cruiser gender-bend.

"I am."

"I thought you were Catstrike."

White Tee laughs. Gwen perks up. "I like your shirt," she tells him.

Every hetero woman alive would like his shirt. It pulls across his chest and hugs his torso in all the right ways.

He shrugs. "My Nightbat suit was in the wash."

Gwen giggles, and I have to tamp down my bitchy streak. I'm no longer the prettiest girl at the booth. I don't have a connection with this guy. I am a crazy in cosplay who has been embarrassing myself by lounging all over his table. My ego came out to play, but it has to go home now. Bye.

I straighten to a stand and hand the box to Gwen. "Your turn."

Gwen frowns at the box I dropped in her hands.

"We need a four-digit code," I explain.

"When did Magnificent Man first fly?"

"1936. Nightbat was 1939," I say.

Gwen punches in the codes. But no luck. "Maybe today's date?" She tries it, but again nothing.

"Need a hint?" White Tee asks without leaning in, without checking out Gwen's butt or boobs.

I punch in one last number. 1959.

The lid swings open.

"We won a free T-shirt," Gwen squeals and seizes the coupon.

I toss the box back to White Tee. I should do something. I should have a snappy parting phrase or a wink and smirk at the ready for a goodbye. My mouth parts. My eyes search him and land one last time on his impossibly normal shirt, before Gwen drags me into the very crowded HS Studio tent.

"What made you guess 1959?" Gwen pauses to flash a peace sign next to a girl who just turned around for a selfie.

"The year the Redemption Ring first came out." I nod toward the visual vomit of Redemption Ring promotions surrounding us.

"You knew that? #NerdAlert." Gwen rummages through the racks of T-shirts. I'd like to say that Gwen is oblivious to all the attention she garners in the shop, but she isn't. She catches someone's eye and winks. Clearly, Gwen is the life of the party. And I get this weird pang of déjà vu mixed with something like regret. That used to be me when I cosplayed.

I slowly slide back a couple of empty hangers on the rack. They make a terrible screech. "You know he probably had the free tees under his table out there."

"But I like this one."

She's found a vintage Conundrum shirt, chartreuse and covered in little black question marks and exclamation points. "I'm sure it's okay."

It isn't, but after five minutes and a tense moment while the cashier checks Gwen's badge, Gwen and the vintage tee, along with a bag of free swag and a complimentary soda, emerge victorious.

"I don't know how you do it," I say.

"Magnificent Man, eleven o'clock." Gwen flings her hair over her shoulder, purses her lips, and retrieves her phone. "May we?" she asks in her most sultry supervillain voice. Unfortunately, Magnificent Man is too wholesome to do more than beam at the phone.

"So what does a supervillain do at Comic-Con? Besides shop," Gwen asks, sipping on her Diet Coke.

My neck aches from twisting, but trying to catch a last glance of White Tee is worth it. He was an eye oasis. A yummy, much-needed break from the crazy all around. But he's gone. And I can't pretend anymore that there was a spark of connection. "And walking around posing for pictures with strangers? Wait in line for panels. Collect autographs. Ogle rare and expensive comics. I hear the nachos in Hall H are edible."

Gwen gags.

"You want to check out the food trucks?" I ask.

"OMG, yes!"

We stop off at the coat check one more time for Gwen to add to her dragon's hoard and head off toward B Street.

"How are you walking so fast?" My boots send spikes of pain up my ankles and destroy my spine. For reals. I'll be an invertebrate by the end of the day. All I want to do is sit down.

"There's a sweet spot when it comes to heels. I could walk all day in these." Gwen stops in front of the first open table we find and pushes me into a chair. "You want kimchi?"

"Yes, and I wouldn't say no to sushi." I scramble to fish out my debit card.

Gwen snorts. "Hon, please. It's on me."

After lunch, and an unfortunate run-in with a *Union-Tribune* photographer, who I desperately hope will not publish my picture in Sunday's paper, it's time to meet up with Tony.

"You swear you won't tell him it's me?" I ask Gwen.

"Cross my heart." She lets out an ear-piercing squeal when she sees him.

Gwen launches herself into Tony's arms. She must know what she's talking about with the heels, because she's running, not just walking, when Tony catches her. He's obviously a little overwhelmed by Gwen's splendor. And obviously tickled. "Tony—I mean, Night-bat, this is my friend. Catstrike." Gwen is beaming.

"Hey," Tony says. Thank every single last goldfish, he doesn't start rasping in a fake Nightbat voice. "Good to meet you. Thanks for bringing Gwen."

"Don't mention it," I mutter.

"So what have you girls been up to so far?"

"Shopping, sushi, making new friends. Speaking of which..." Gwen strains onto her tiptoes and waves frantically.

I cycle through recognition, embarrassment, and shock as the white-tee guy approaches. I frantically look for somewhere, anywhere to hide. Fudge it, I'm going to dive into the crowd and run.

Gwen instinctively grabs my arm. "Hey," she says. "We were just talking about you."

White Tee pauses like there could not be more flattering words before breaking into a friendly smile. "I'm glad you waved me down. I didn't get a chance to introduce myself earlier. I'm Adam. Adam West McKinney."

Shirley Temples. He looks even better than I remembered.

"You want a picture, honey?" Gwen asks Adam. She's touched up her makeup and looks incredible. I'm sure Adam would beg for her number if she weren't hanging on Tony.

"Would you take one of me and Catstrike?" Adam hands his

phone over to Gwen, who fumbles for a moment before she gets us in focus.

Adam stands by my side, but unlike half the other guys at this convention, he refrains from draping an arm around my shoulders.

"You going to come back tomorrow?" he asks.

I turn from the unblinking eye of his phone to him. I lean in close. Because he is yummy and because I like that he comes to these in his own skin with nothing to hide. "Wouldn't you like to know?"

He thanks Gwen and swipes through the pictures on his phone. "You photograph well."

I step away from his side. Part of me, the stupid part who forgot how I became married then divorced, wished I could have stayed there a little longer. "Is that surprising?"

"A lot of cosplay looks amazing in person but doesn't translate in photos." He slides his phone into his pocket. "Do you do other cosplay?"

This guy has me fighting my cosplay urges hard. "I did. Not anymore. Nice to meet you, Adam." I roll my shoulders back. "Come on, Hemlock," I say. "Let's check out Hall H and plan our cosplay victory."

"Well, clearly, we should just make out onstage. Right, Tony?"

I blanch. Nightbat Tony stops moving.

Gwen laughs and sidles away from Tony to slip an arm through mine. "Don't worry. You're not my type." She turns and gives Tony a wink. "But seriously, if we work the sexual-tension angle, I think we'd have a shot." Gwen's voice drops. "What did the hottie in the tight white T-shirt want?"

I stumble in my heels and bump into a Tournament of Crowns, no, a Robotman Tournament of Crowns cosplayer. He scowls at me until he sees Gwen.

I imagine the sound effects *grind* and *grate* hanging descriptively near Nightbat Tony's clenched jaw as Gwen and I flank this impressive cosplayer who's utilized both carbon fiber armor and genuine fur in his costume. "Feel free to bump into me at any time, ladies," he says.

We wander through the tables of artists. We pose for more pictures. I nerd out at the AJ Comics exhibition. They have Jane Lee originals, from *Numb*, no less. I ogle. I lose my Shirley Temples.

"If you're into Jane Lee, she's supposedly going to be on a panel later," Tony says.

I whimper. "Are you serious?" All my Comic-Con dreams are coming true. Cosplay is awesome. Trying on a sexy, confident, badass character and escaping for those fleeting moments is awesome. Jane Lee's panel is awesome. Even the contest, being up onstage and knowing that it doesn't matter for a second that I live with my mom, is awesome.

We don't win. Two girls dressed as Robin Hood and the Sheriff of Nottingham do. Ironically, they made out onstage.

Gwen and Tony are stuck in a huge line at coat check as I stare at my phone and hail a Lyft. Comic-Con is over and so is my turn at being the sexy, badass villain.

Tall stripes of white and blue flood my peripheral vision. "Congratulations."

It's Adam. He's pulled a blue button-down over his white T-shirt. Maybe his eyes are gray. "We didn't win," I say. We didn't even place. I'm not a sore loser. I'm just sore from the heels and the corset that compressed my rib cage all day. My mood has nothing to do with this being the end of Comic-Con and the end of my cosplaying.

"You were a crowd favorite." He pulls out his phone and shows me his IG feed. "#Catstrike. That's you. That's you again. You and Poison Hemlock. Oh, and you again. Let's search #Comic-Con. You're the third hit. How about #cosplay?" He holds out his phone, and my face is studded all over his feed.

"What do you want, Adam?"

The hall is deafening, and he leans in closer. "I have a proposition."

You've gotta be kidding. I guess Adam isn't a gentleman after all. I fold my arms across my chest, my claws sticking out menacingly. They've snagged on all my stuff today, but right now, I'm glad I'm still wearing them.

"Have you been to an escape room?" Adam asks.

Gwen props an arm on my shoulder. "She hasn't, but she's a poor example. Keep pitching. This is fun." I think Gwen found a drink somewhere before the contest. She's been even more outgoing than I thought possible.

"Name two things Millennials and Gen Z have in common," he says. "They're bored, and they love superheroes. I provide them entertainment via my superhero-themed escape rooms."

"Adult entertainment?"

"No. No!" Adam tugs on the collar of his shirt. "Hear me out. Every single Millennial in this room has a superhero fantasy."

"Ew."

"Let me finish."

"Yeah, Saire—Sabine. Let the man finish." Gwen sways a little.

"They have a superhero fantasy. And Gen Z is the same. They want to be Nightbat for a night. Ralph Winston with the Magnificent Man suit ready to go. Robotman. Catstrike. Huh? They want this." He gestures to the throng of conventiongoers all around us. "They want access to this. That's it. No one is being a jackass in here. No one is asking to sleep with you—"

Gwen snorts. "We did get some shouted proposals."

Nightbat Tony, no longer wearing the mask and still carrying Gwen's hoard of shopping, manages to sweep Gwen up and off her feet. "Marry me, Hemlock!"

"Exactly!' Gwen giggles. They disappear in a crush of sugary-sweet PDA. Just me and Adam now. Well, and a few hundred strangers.

"Cosplay is growing. You're very good at it." His cheeks color as he stares down at my boots. "You haven't broken character once all day."

"And you've been watching? Like, all day?" I'm done. I can't flirt in cosplay. I can't flirt out of cosplay. That's the way it should be. Has to be. I'm walking toward the exit, leaving my fantasies behind at the convention center, where they can be corralled in lost and found for all eternity.

Adam jogs a step to catch up. "You've been to Disneyland? You took a picture with a princess, right? It's the same idea. I bring the superheroes and supervillains to a fun, interactive, immersive escape room experience. My patrons get a piece of their fantasy, some bragging rights to the fastest times and pictures to post to their IG feed."

"What's your superhero fantasy?"

"Me?" Adam's eyes go wide, and somehow I get the sense I've missed something embarrassingly obvious. Maybe it's just been an epically long day, and his chill façade has worn through. In any case, he shakes it off and lands on his feet before I can figure it out. "I want a piece of the industry," he says. "I think I could make enough to pay my student loans. Look, Sabine. May I call you Sabine? You spent hours making this costume. You clearly love being in this character's skin. Wouldn't it be nice to get paid to do that?"

A Dark Morph Angel with feathered wings jostles me closer to Adam.

I put one of my gloved hands, complete with wired claws, on his chest to steady myself. He tries to steady me but overcompensates. And now I've got my other hand around his neck. It's either that or fall. But ooh, maybe there is not much of a difference.

CHAPTER FOUR

Adam smells really nice. Nicer than any man should after working a convention all day. The air inside the convention center must be compressed with sweat and stale nacho cheese. I'm sure the smell is permanently stuck to me, but not to this guy. This guy... He's exactly the type of clean-cut man that Mom would pick out of a church lineup for a family dinner invitation *because you need more friends, Sarah.*

Conventiongoers and cosplayers continue to shuffle past us to the exit. Sweat drips down my back. I feel uncomfortably clammy. The crowd clearly has conspired to push us closer. Now when I close my eyes, it will be too easy to imagine a casual—no, comfortable—hand resting on my lower back.

He's waiting for an answer, but I've temporarily lost my mind and am enjoying the pressure of his skin against my vinyl. I close my eyes, inviting the fantasy in, but instead, that idea of Mom inviting him to a family dinner IRL has taken hold. He'd say no. Everyone says no when they connect the dots of my last two years. *The whack chick who gets married at twenty-one and divorced at twenty-two and now lives with her mom—yeah, something is obviously very wrong with her. Steer clear of the sad, little crazy-pants. Don't make eye contact. Move along now.*

I don't live up to the cosplay IRL.

I try to catch my breath. "I'll pass." I nimbly duck and jostle my way through the crowded exit until I'm outside in the limitless ocean air.

Adrenaline shocks and seizes my tired body as arms and legs wrap around me from behind. "Catstrike!" Gwen sings out. "Where have you been? Nightbat and I are gonna get out of here. Save Abandum City. Wanna come?"

Gwen is too tipsy to scold. I gently but firmly unwrap her from my torso, like she is a Kids Clubber. "You're a villain," I say. "You don't save Abandum." Seriously, what this woman doesn't know about comics.

Gwen smirks. "Then I'll enjoy frustrating Nightbat's plans and every other part of him."

Ew.

Gwen pulls me aside. "It's Tony," she whispers with a giggle.

"You sure?" I steady my friend. "Maybe you should ask him to put his mask back on."

"Please." Gwen snorts. "This isn't my first rodeo." She sloppily twists a lock of hair in her fingers but pulls too hard and tangles it. "Ow. You wanna come?"

"And risk being identified by my boss? No, thanks."

"Suit yourself." She digs the key out of her bustier and hands it to me. "You can change at my place. Help yourself to a hoodie."

"Text me?"

"You know it." She gives me a quick kiss, which makes a few of the departing attendees cheer. "Enjoy your last few minutes of nerd ball. Don't leave a glass slipper or anything behind."

"You mean a sharp claw?"

"Sure."

Tony pulls up, and the two of them drive away.

"Hey, Catstrike! Say meow!" A dude with a selfie stick jumps in front of me.

I raise a single eyebrow and deadpan, "Meow."

"Classic!"

A yellow Camaro appears with a Lyft light in the window. I check the license plate against my app. "Are you my Lyft?" I ask.

A goateed man with a midlife-crisis stud in his ear reluctantly reaches for his phone. "Catstrike and Poison Hemlock?"

"Hemlock made other plans."

I reach to open the door, but the driver takes one look at my clawed fingers and screams, "Watch the paint job!"

"I got it," says a recognizable voice. Adam—Adam West McKinney—opens the car door. "I'm taking Poison Hemlock's place."

"Just make sure your girlfriend doesn't scratch the leather."

My shoulders tense. "I'm not his girlfriend." I slide into the car, my vinyl crackling against the leather.

"Whatever. Same destination, sweetheart?"

"Please, and thank you," I continue in my rough monotone. I'm not about to slip into anything genuine in front of Adam. Or Camaro Dude.

The driver puts the car in gear. "Pacific Beach it is."

Adam smiles. "So you're a local. That's great."

My eyes narrow. "What do you want?"

"I want you in my escape room. New characters mean repeat business."

As we drive farther away from cosplay mecca, I begin to feel more and more uncomfortable. "Cosplay isn't something a girl does in real life."

"Not even for a paycheck?"

"People do all kinds of stupid things for money that they regret in the morning." Like take a friend's dare and say exactly what you think to a guy dressed as Cicada-bro at a party. The memories of that stupid night are swirling too close to the surface. Especially now that cosplay and I are over for good.

"You had fun. I know you did. I had fun watching you have fun."

"This is getting uncomfortable," Camaro Dude mutters.

I scoff in frustration and also in disbelief. Really? I have to take heat from my Lyft driver? "Cosplay only works for Comic-Con. It's just weird outside of it. I'm weird outside of it."

"You look weirder than weird. You look plain stupid," Camaro Dude says.

I barrel on before Adam can defend me. Not that I want him to or think he would. I don't. "I have a real life. If people in my real life saw me like this..." Mom would force me to go with her to Bible study. Brent would make some awful joke about me getting married again. It would be open season on my terrible life choices and only a matter of time before Mom found out about my miscarriage. I'd never be trusted again. I'd turn into Mom's pet human. She might even make an IG account featuring tearful and public discussions about lost sheep and shepherds, replete with photographic evidence of my rehabilitation. I shudder. "No one would take me seriously. This is a stunt that's only okay for one day during Comic-Con. Nice girls don't get a pass to dress up like this even for Halloween."

"I could give you that pass."

"You're not listening," I say with more than exasperation in my voice.

"He's really not," Camaro Dude agrees. Again, I try to ignore his commentary. Momentum is important.

"I don't want a pass," I say. "I'm an adult. Adults don't do this outside of Comic-Con." Particularly if she is a loser who lives in her mom's office/spare bedroom.

Adam grows quiet. "Even if no one knew your true identity? If you were only ever Catstrike at my escape room?"

"Yeah, but you'd know." And the thought of this man ever seeing me for what I really am—a sad little divorcée whose life stopped before it ever even started—that is even worse than my mother spotting me in costume in the *Union-Tribune*. Oh gosh. I hope the *Union-Tribune* doesn't pick my picture for its article.

"Let's say I didn't," Adam says. He's tactfully staring out the window. Streetlamp reflections squirm in the water of Mission Bay below us. "Let's say there was a clause in our business agreement that kept your true identity a secret. You could write your conditions. What's your number?"

Camaro Dude snorts. "Smooth."

I stare at the back of his shaved head and then refocus on Adam. "Seriously?"

"Right," Adam says, pulling out a business card and a very sleek-looking titanium pen. "This is my number. This is my Fem Fantastic's number. She's one of my managers—my best manager. Call her. She will vouch for my character and operation. It's nothing but good, clean, superhero fun."

I pinch the card between my thumb and forefinger. "I doubt that."

"Yeah, me too," Camaro Dude says. "Anyone can carry around business cards." He swivels in his seat at the next red light. "But where did you get yours printed, man? I was thinking of getting some."

I indulge in a momentary fantasy of scratching swears into the pristine leather seats with my fake claws.

Adam goes on, "You can give me a call. We can work out a Venmo account for payment. I swear I'll never ask who you are, or ask you to take off your mask." His face flinches as if he's just forgotten something. For a moment, I feel his eyes bore into the back of my gloved left hand. "You're not worried because you're married or something? I mean—" He's floundering, rubbing the back of his neck. "My Cardinal Flame is engaged, if it makes you feel any better. She and her fiancé would be happy to talk..." His face is flushed. "Hey, man. Can you stop the car here?"

Our driver gives us some serious stink eye but pulls over.

Adam scribbles a second number on the card. "Give them a call." He slides out of the car. "Offer stands. Let me know."

CHAPTER FIVE

I don't know what I would have done if Gwen hadn't given me her key. What was I thinking? That I'd just walk back into Mom's house dressed as Catstrike? I was lucky to time my exit when I left for Comic-Con this morning. I didn't even think about how I would get home.

I borrow a hoodie, Lululemon top, and a pair of sweats from Gwen, shove my cosplay costume into the very back of her closet, and run home in the dark in her sneakers that are two sizes too big. No part of my run feels great after a day in boots, but maybe that's the point. My face burns with the memory of my arms draped around Adam. How they lingered. How I lingered. Shirley Temples, what is wrong with me? You don't get fresh with a random stranger when you're in cosplay. That way lies listing slightly-used wedding gifts on eBay to pay rent, while your husband plans one campout after another with his best friends Tiffany and Charlotte. It's temporary insanity that I never want to repeat.

And I would repeat it if I were dressed up again, and Adam were there. I mean the flirting, not the doomed marriage, but that's the problem. Flirting is a gateway drug. Just like comics and cosplay are a gateway drug. Hence my rules that will keep me far from guys like Adam with their charming confidence, winning smiles, and jaws so yummy you want to exfoliate your face on the stubble.

I need more rules. More running. That's my fourth rule. More running. Always running.

I'm out of my mind, and I'll run until my senses are restored, and I'm too tired to remember that Adam's middle name is West and that he has a dimple in his right cheek and eyes the same blue as the ocean before dawn.

You know what? I think I need to sprint the last mile.

It's past one a.m. when I get home. If there were crickets in our corner of San Diego County, they'd be chirping. Instead, I have the sound of next door's sprinklers ratcheting up and spraying the drought tolerance out of every square inch of the neighbors' back lawn. Irrigation aside, the air seeping in through my mom's little house feels quiet and sleepy. I might actually sleep until morning.

I creep into my mom's office/spare bedroom. Everyone has a place in their house where they dump the crap they don't know what to do with. My mom's is her office/spare bedroom. I fit right in with the homemade teacher-appreciation Pinterest gifts, old curriculum books, and filing cabinet.

I jump out of my skin when I see Mom's face lit up with the blue glow of her Mac.

"Mom! What are you doing up this late?"

"Playing solitaire. Trolling Twitter for Russian bots." She looks up at me, and I know I'm in for it. "Waiting for you."

I shove my pile of laundry across the floor and stretch.

My mom fixes me with her twenty-five-years-of-teaching stare over the frames of her glasses. "We need to talk, Sarah."

I groan and touch my head down to my knees in a deep stretch.

"Where were you?" Mom demands.

"Can we please talk tomorrow?" The run was a mistake. My feet and my spine will never be the same after a day in those absurd boots. I am not just sore. I am deformed.

"If you're going to live in my house, you're going to tell me." Mom's mouth is set into a thin line. Her day-old lipstick has bled into the whisper-thin lines around her lips.

"I was out for a run," I mutter.

"You've been out for a run since this morning? I get home with the shopping, looking forward to spending one of my summer Saturdays with my little girl, and you're not here. No note. No phone call. Am I supposed to just watch *Mississippi Bake-Off* by myself?"

"I'm sorry, Mom. I thought I texted."

"Where were you?"

"I was..." I hesitate. No way am I going to tell her I was at Comic-Con. The questions wouldn't stop, and then after we rehashed my irresponsibility yet again, she'd drag me to her therapist, and we'd sit on a too-small-couch and talk about trust for ninety minutes, followed by goals—all of them pointing directly to Bible study and other new hobbies, like spin class, with my mom and her Bible study friends. Pet human in tow. "I was at the gym. I was working."

"It wasn't on the calendar." Mom taps the dry-erase board above her computer. She insists my shifts be put in writing. It's the fifth-grade teacher in her.

"Someone called at the last minute, and I forgot."

She narrows her eyes at me.

"I worked a double shift, and then I ran home," I say, kicking off Gwen's shoes.

"I don't like you running alone at all hours of the night." She sounds exasperated.

I tug my knee up to my chin and close my eyes as my back adjusts. "I can outrun anyone."

"It stops. Right now. Do you hear me? I'm not staying up all night praying that my daughter isn't dead in a ditch somewhere because some DUI diva can't be bothered to slow down."

"Mom!"

She hands me a trifolded piece of paper. "This came today."

Oh no. My student loan statement shakes in my sweaty hand. "You opened my mail?"

"My last name and address were on the envelope. Excuse me for making an honest mistake. When were you going to tell me you defaulted on your loan?"

I reach around the stack of boxes in the closet and grab my fluffy winter robe. Yes, it is July, but it is one of the only clean items hanging in my closet—Mom's closet.

"You need to do laundry."

I try to close the closet door, but Daniel's boxes are in the way.

"And when are you going to do something about those boxes?"

I pause. Mom is almost hysterical. She's definitely more of a morning person. Unlike me. It's another source of contention that she'd love to talk about with me *and* her therapist.

I inhale, quietly and slowly, before turning around. "Mom, I'm sorry. You're right. I should have texted. I should have added the shift I was picking up to the calendar."

"And the loan?"

"I'm picking up extra shifts at the gym, aren't I?" True, but I'm also going to Comic-Con and pretending that I'm a different person, a caricature of a sexy, confident woman, which I'll never be. "And I'll do laundry in the morning. I'll be here till noon, and we can watch all the *Bake-Offs* you want while I fold—"

Mom puts a hand on her hip and stares at me.

Oh, right. "Never mind. You have church."

"Yes." Mom jabs the power button of her computer. "And an extra shift here and there." She shakes her head. "It's not enough, Sarah. You're barely making enough to cover your credit card payments."

I really need a better place to keep my statements than my mom's desk. I sigh and plunge my hands into the pocket of my borrowed hoodie. Adam's business card brushes against my fingers. "I know. I'm working on it."

"And the boxes?"

I stare at the three carboard boxes monopolizing the real estate of the office/spare bedroom closet. "Yeah. The boxes too."

CHAPTER SIX

Sure, there are divorced men who sell all their earthly possessions (save what can fit in the super-expensive backpack they registered for at REI while their fiancées are too busy addressing wedding invitations to notice) and take to the wide-open road and find themselves on the Pacific Crest Trail, where they manage to rescue the world's most pathetic-looking dog that suffers from anxiety, depression, and hip dysplasia. While hiking, and staying at the occasional spa, they post buttloads of pics with novella-length captions about how they found themselves, and really, it was the dog who rescued them. Then they decide to teach English in China with the dog and plaster their adventures, which consist of clubbing, eating, and being worshiped by all the adorable schoolchildren. Don't get me started on the gorgeous "friends" who pop up in their feeds and drape themselves across the divorced men and all the little IG squares with an abundance of beauty, grace, and flawless skin.

Daniel didn't sell all his earthly possessions. A lot of them he just couldn't be bothered with. "I'll get them when I come back," he told me. "I just can't deal with this right now."

So I got to deal with it. I agreed to hang on to his random stuff—

three full XL boxes that make it impossible for me to close the closet door.

It was the least I could do, right?

Bright morning sunshine streams through the kitchen window, making my mom's robust potted herbs chartreuse and glowy. I have half a mind to tell these herbs to fudge off as I wait for my comfort wellness tea to cool. Instead, I scroll through Daniel's Instagram feed. Mom stormed off to bed with threats of calling Brent after church to talk about dental hygienist school. Yay for picking up a morning shift at the gym. My thumb hovers over Daniel's stories before I remember that he'll see my views. I hit the home button of my screen.

I'm not stalking. My ex's Instagram is public. I'm not pining either. Daniel is a douchebag. But I *am* bitter. And sad. It's desperate to want to have something I can put on Instagram to show that I, too, can be a successful, fully-realized individual, even if I am not flanked by adorable children and gorgeous members of the opposite sex everywhere I go. But that's where I am. Contemplating muttering obscenities at the cheerful herbs in my mom's kitchen and looking to prove I'm not a pathetic cliché of a Gen Z.

I open up the photos on my phone, but there are no pictures, no evidence, of my cosplay and epic day at Comic-Con. I have nothing to post. The last photo I took was of where I parked my mom's car for my shift at the gym two weeks ago. My last post was of a nebulous ocean before dawn.

I'm a social media ghost who badly needs someone else to haunt.

I do a search for #SDCC #Catstrike and feel my face glow red. My picture is everywhere. Adam was right. I was popular. The details in my costume translate in the photos, but damn, so does my runner's body.

After everything that happened with Daniel, I did my best to avoid mirrors. I took to hoodies the same way I took to running. No one says, *OMG, are you pregnant, or did you just get fat?* when you are wearing a hoodie. No one pays any attention to your shape in a hoodie. It is the ultimate camouflage. But good gracious—my shape has changed. I don't even recognize me in the pictures. And it isn't just the figure-hugging costume. My face, my expressions—I never look that confident or sexy IRL.

I fish Adam's business card out of the pocket of my hoodie, punch in the number for his Fem Fantastic cosplayer, and compose a text:

Hi Stacey aka Fem Fantastic. Sorry to be random, but Adam gave me your number. I have some questions about his business, which frankly seems too good to be true. Would you be willing to meet me for a coffee and chat off the record? Sincerely...

Signing my real name seems way too risky, but signing as Catstrike feels like a commitment to the cosplay that I'm not ready to make in broad daylight. I need a step removed. So I use her alter ego:

Sincerely, Not Sabine Kennedy

And so here I am a few days later, in my favorite old Padres hoodie at the student union Starbucks on the SDSU campus, waiting with a venti licoricey tea.

"Sabine?"

I look up, and a tall, athletic brunette in jeans and a perfect gray tee smiles down benevolently at me. I'd told her to look for a girl in a Padres hoodie. "Sorry, are you Sabine Kennedy?"

I wince. Goldfish, this is embarrassing. "Yeah."

"Hey. I'm Stacey Frances." She shakes my hand and gives me a wink. "Or should I say Agatha King?" She sets her coffee on the table and takes a seat. "Are you a student here?"

"Um, well, I applied." Once upon a time, when I was still in high school. I tug the strings of my hoodie. The location was Stacey's idea. Something about study sessions and a looming philosophy final. "How about you?"

"Yeah. I'm a civics major. Captain of the swim team." This chick may look like Fem Fantastic's alter ego, Agatha King, but she's serving me AJ Comics' vintage Mary Sue heroine—confident, open, no-nonsense. I immediately respect her.

"That makes sense," I say. Stacey is warrior princess levels of #goals.

"How about you?" She sizes me up.

"I like to run," I say quietly.

"Of course." She smiles wide, and her teeth rival Brent and Jen's best work. "And you like to cosplay."

I duck my head, checking to see if anyone in the Starbucks is eavesdropping. Man-Bun in the back corner is tied up with his phone. The baristas are bickering over the lyrics of the latest Taylor Swift single.

"Girl, it's nothing to be that shy about," Stacey says.

"It's not like some sleazy sex ring, is it?" I ask.

Stacey Frances, aka Agatha King, aka Fem Fantastic laughs. Loud. Hard. "No. Everything is completely aboveboard, even down to the character licensing. It really is just photo ops and typical escape room operation."

I'm a dork, but I had to get that one out of the way. Fudge goes down in college. I can't be stupid about it. On to my next burning question. "Do people recognize you? I mean, you don't wear a mask."

"Not really. I mean, sometimes you get that vague, I-think-I've-seen-you-somewhere-before look, but that's happened only a handful of times." Stacey blows on her coffee and smiles. "It was honestly a lot of fun when it did."

Fun? Maybe if you're a goddess secure in your captain-of-the-swim-team status. Or maybe the security came from a happy, healthy relationship. The image of Adam and Stacey as a couple flashes in my mind. I don't know what my reasoning is—maybe I'm trying to drown out the image—but I swallow way too much hot tea and spit half of it back in my cup.

"You okay?" Stacey asks.

"Yeah." My tongue is pulsing with its own heartbeat, and from now on, everything will taste like hot licorice. "Does your boyfriend—"

"Girlfriend," Stacey corrects.

I apologize. I can and will do better with my assumptions.

Stacey smiles into her coffee. "It's okay."

I pick at the cuffs of my hoodie. "She doesn't mind?"

"Nope. Teases me a bit when I put on the costume. She's into different fandoms."

"And the customers are respectful? No inappropriate touching... or unmasking?"

Stacey looks thoughtfully at me, and I have to physically stop myself from squirming. "Adam has a lot of waivers before people can play. He also has been known to hire some pretty impressive security, who are not in costume." A crease forms on Stacey's perfect brow. "It's easy to spot the potential troublemakers, and they get tighter leashes."

"But you get hit on?" Goldfish, what is wrong with me? I sound like a creep. I stare into my tea.

Stacey laughs. "Where have you been cosplaying?"

"Adam saw me at Comic-Con. That's the only time I've cosplayed." Not true. Not true by a million billion times.

"People are pretty shy of gorgeous women towering over them while they're trying to escape from rooms. I say my scripted lines. I pose for pictures. I get paid a lot of money."

"How much money?"

"More now that I'm a manager, but let's see." Stacey grabs a napkin and scribbles. "My first weekend cosplaying paid for a semester's worth of books."

She shows me the figure, and my eyes bulge. "Is Adam a good..."

My cheeks redden as I search for the right word. My internal autofill makes my blush spread to my neck. "Boss?"

"He's a go-getter. Total professional. Sometimes a little aggressive when it comes to bookings. I worked every weekend winter semester. He respected my swim schedule, but if I wasn't in the pool, I was in my blue skirt and red bustier. Well, unless I was in the leotard."

"You wear different costumes?" I can't keep the dread out of my voice. Last thing I need is an excuse to invest in more cosplay.

"Yeah. Adam has the standard version, and then he has the vintage camp version that is more family friendly." Stacey's expression softens. "He's more than willing to buy the costumes, but then he wants a deposit, and it was just easier to get my own. I'm guessing you have just the one?"

She must have misread the panic in my eyes. Still, I shake my head slightly.

"You do have a Catstrike costume?" she whispers.

I nod. "Inspired by *Nightbat Returns*," I mutter.

Stacey bites her lower lip, probably to suppress her smile. "What's wrong with that?"

"I grew up with a mother who would tell me to change if my skirt was above my knee, and my cardigan was too tight." I press my lips together. "She doesn't know I cosplay. I don't want to find out what would happen if she did." Would she blame me for Daniel being a total douche? Or worse, would she blame me for my miscarriage?

"I get it. I wouldn't exactly want to walk out in that." Stacey brushes her hair back with a grin. "I mean, I would. Lots of fun, very kinky, but I don't think I'd want just anyone to know about that side of me."

"It's mortifying," I say. My entire story really is. Start to finish. Cooking up the idea of cosplaying as Cicada Nymph in a minidress and red wig to beat back boredom sophomore year. Agreeing to a doomed marriage that never had a spark of love in it. Accepting I am a pathetic loser and swearing off cosplay forever, only to do it again because my one friend in the world wants to go, and I don't want to lose that friendship. Potentially gleaning a side hustle from it. And considering it only because the man offering is... what? Confident? Articulate? Intriguing?

"How did Adam find you?" I ask.

"He was recruiting at the pool. Everyone knows swimmers have the best bodies." She eyes my hoodie. "Do you cross-train? You have great shoulders."

How can she tell when I'm wearing a hoodie? "I row sometimes." I leave out the part that it is on a machine.

"Right. Adam pitched his business, and someone outed me. Told him I'd dressed up as Fem Fantastic for Halloween. He got me and Frankie. Vlad and Hector too. They're polo players. Sweet guys."

"So everyone knows everyone?" Oh no.

"I mean, now we do. Adam poached Christian, Mike, and Jessica from a drama club." Stacey smiled widely. "It's cool that we're getting a Catstrike. I mean, if you sign on. Adam's been looking for one for ages. Don't know why he's been so picky about it. Frankie and Vanessa have volunteered before, but he likes to rotate them as Cardinal Flame, Fair Play, and Poison Hemlock. Fem Fantastic, too, on the nights when I have a swim meet."

"What about the guys?"

"Christian and Mike usually play the villains. Sometimes they do Burst and Emerald Broadsword. I think once Adam asked Mike to play Fledgling, but he threatened to quit. Vlad and Hector rotate between Nightbat and Magnificent Man and some of the lesser-known heroes."

"Like Soar? Cyborg-man? Black Morph?" I ask.

Stacey stares at me. "Yeah. It can be a lot of fun. Everyone loves it. Adam's a cool guy. Eye for talent too. I never would have picked me or Frankie out as Fem Fantastic or Poison Hemlock, but we kill it every time."

"If I do this, you won't ever mention that we met in real life? I mean... you wouldn't tell Adam about me? What I look like?" I get that Adam doesn't know me, and doesn't know my past. But I know me. I know I don't live up to the cosplay, and for whatever reason, I'd rather not have Adam clued in to that sad little detail.

Stacey's brow furrows. She takes a swig of her coffee. "I'm the last person in the world who'd ever out another girl in any way." She flips over her phone. "I've got to run. I've got a study date. It was nice to meet you, Not Really Sabine. I hope I see you at work sometime. It's a good hustle, especially if you're going to be going here in the fall." She winks and leaves.

My hands shake as I grip my transcript, but I know me. If I don't do this now, who knows if I ever will?

I walk into the administration building, hopelessly lost but determined. Any open door will do at this point. I duck into the nearest.

"May I help you?" A woman with dyed, red hair looks up at me over her frameless glasses.

"I'm here to talk to a counselor or an academic adviser." Really anyone who can help me figure out a path forward.

"Do you have an appointment?"

I smile my most winning smile. "I'm a walk-in."

The woman folds her hands and takes in a deep breath. "I'm sorry, but all our counselors are busy. Would you like to make an appointment?" She wrangles her mouse into cooperation and clicks the computer into submission. "We have an opening at four thirty."

"I'm working then."

She blinks twice before continuing. "You can, of course, book your own appointment through the campus portal."

I laugh nervously. "I'm a transfer student. Or I hope to be a transfer student. I just need to talk to someone—"

"It's very simple. You can access our appointment page by logging in with your student ID."

I grip my transcript tighter. The row of F's and W's wink up at me. "I don't have a student ID yet. If you only knew the hoops I had to jump through to get my transcript printed out at the student center." I feel my dream sliding away from me. I feel like I can't breathe, and I have eight more miles to run before I reach the halfway point.

A door pops open, and a woman with dark black hair and a friendly smile steps out. An insulated cooler covered in kawaii lemons with rosy little faces is slung over her shoulder. "I'm off to lunch," she says around bites of her granola bar. She stops and does a double take when she sees me. "Sarah?"

It's Janet Stephens. Her son Evan is a regular at the Kids Club. "Hi, Mrs. Stephens. How's Evan doing? Is the teething still going strong?"

"So bad that he's been skipping his naps every afternoon, except the days when we get to the gym. Do you run a pint-size boot camp in there?"

"I don't think so, but we've collected and hatched a lot of dragon eggs recently." Evan is obsessed with dragons, and I've learned if we pretend we're dragon catchers, he will not scream, throw things, or color on the walls. "We've had to outrun a lot of fire-breathing hatchlings." I sound crazy, and my frantic energy isn't helping.

"Ah, our post-gym errands are starting to make more sense." She takes another bite of her granola bar. "You need some help?"

"But your lunch break," my friend at reception says.

"It's fine, Clare."

Clare looks scandalized. If she'd been wearing pearls instead of a gaudy gold chain, she would have clutched them.

Janet props her office door open wide for me. "Come on in, Sarah."

Janet brushes granola crumbs off her tweed pants before gesturing to the chair opposite her desk.

"I brought my transcript." I've managed to crinkle it in my sweaty hand between here and the student union.

"Let's take a look." Janet marches over to her desk. Meanwhile,

I'm dumbstruck by her gorgeous view—blue skies with big fluffy clouds framed by palm fronds.

"So you're hoping to transfer, or you already have?" Janet grabs the glasses perched on the top of her head. The faint smile on her lips disappears when her finger lands on my sophomore year. "Seems like you hit a speed bump."

I try to swallow, but my throat is too dry. "I had some health stuff followed by some personal stuff." Or was it personal stuff, then health stuff? How do you sum up your unexpected pregnancy, miscarriage, and depression without saying anything about any of it?

"And life got real," Janet says, looking up from my transcript.

"Yeah. I lost my scholarship and... dropped out." One of the fluffy clouds rolls across the sun, and the light dims. "But I'm working now. And I think I can afford—I mean, not all at once. But I think—"

Janet smiles. "Have you applied for admission?"

"I was accepted at one point, a few years ago, but ended up somewhere else. My plan is to apply this year, but I was hoping to take a class or two this fall. You know... ease back into it." Somewhere in the distance, a leaf blower starts up. I twist the strings of my hoodie around my fingers. "I just needed to know, what would it take?"

"What would it take financially, academically, or timewise?"

I stare down at my torn-up Asics. "All of the above."

The leaf blower wails louder as Janet clicks around on her computer screen. She swivels her monitor so that I can see it. "Have you heard of Open University?"

My mouth is once again bone-dry, and my tongue will not move to form intelligible words. "Uh. Um."

"It's $281 per unit. The good news is, you don't have to be admitted the old-fashioned way. The bad news is you get lowest priority when it comes to enrolling in classes."

"But the credits?"

"Would be added to your transcript."

"And I could retake some of my failed classes or W's?"

"If there is availability." Janet grabs a toffee from her dish and unrolls it. "You know, based on your grades freshman year, you'd qualify for a scholarship."

"What about all my F's and W's from sophomore year? Won't they haunt me forever?"

"Not if you retake them and pass. We do course forgiveness here. If you earn an A the second time around, we drop the F like it never happened."

My mouth opens, but nothing comes out. Janet swivels the monitor back around.

The cloud rolls past, and the office is once again bathed in afternoon sunshine. I find my voice. "Do I need to retake my failed classes through Open University or somewhere else before I apply?"

"What's your major?'"

"Business."

Janet smiles and shakes her head. "You'll be fine, but let's see what kind of damage control we can do now while you're applying and waiting to be accepted. You failed four classes and withdrew from two classes the fall of sophomore year and then retook but failed a class that winter and took another two W's."

"I could retake my GEs," I say.

"If you get lucky and a spot opens up. I mean, with the physical fitness course, sure, there's a lot of room in the independent study fitness courses, if you're not choosy. That's definitely an option to look in to. Let's check this econ course. Aha! That's your best next step. Econ 101. We've got at least 10 different sections. And our Econ 101 is equivalent to this bad boy on your transcript. There's a section that meets every Wednesday from one to four p.m., with an optional lab Friday morning. That, combined with an online physical fitness class and an English class next term, should solve half of your transcript problems. If we can find you a marketing class and an equivalent for this geology class next semester..." She looks up and smiles. "You'll only have three W's left to deal with. And they're nothing to worry about."

"They're not?"

"A few withdrawals never stopped anybody from getting a scholarship."

"Are you serious?" Two part-time semesters, and my transcript could be in scholarship-worthy condition.

"If you're interested in attending through the summer months, you could snag a scholarship sooner."

"I can really do this."

"Yes, you really can." Janet leans back in her chair. "Working through school can be challenging. Many students struggle to balance the demands of work, classes, and their social life. It's important to be honest with your friends, family, and employers about what you're trying to do. Hopefully, they'll understand and be supportive."

Janet scribbles something on a Post-it Note. "This is me and my contact email. Come find me if you need anything, and definitely if you hit another speed bump."

"Thank you." I stare at the pink Post-it. "I will. Come find you, I mean. I'm not going to hit another speed bump." I'll make sure of it.

CHAPTER SEVEN

I stare at Adam's number on the front of his business card. I ran by his escape room on Garnet Avenue this a.m. And maybe every morning I've had off since Comic-Con. It looks legit. I mean, it is a door between a dispensary and a bar. The stark white lettering looks nice against the dark green paint of the door, and the transom window above is clean.

I thought about showing up with Gwen some random night, but Gwen with the fire-engine red hair and larger-than-life personality matches too easily to the Poison Hemlock at Comic-Con. And from my searches on IG, Poison Hemlock and Catstrike were seen everywhere together. Connecting the costumes would be too easy if I show up with her.

I could go alone, or better yet, I could show up with my mom. No one sees a twentysomething when she goes anywhere with her mom. It's like acknowledging that anyone could be that pathetic is too painful. People actively repress the experience for you. Even while you're standing right there.

After snooping on Adam's website, it is clear I am not going to be showing up at all on the customer end. Holy burning wads of cash,

Nightbat. Who has $$$ they can just drop on an escape room? Not me. Every penny of my gym paycheck is put toward student loans, credit cards, and my phone bill.

If I want $843 for a three-credit class this fall, plus book and gas money, I need a side hustle.

I turn the card over and over. If I did this... if I cosplayed every weekend at Superhero Escapes, I could pay for a semester's worth of civics books in one weekend. That's what Stacey said. I mean, yeah, civics. Not talking STEM majors, but still. If I did this, I could pay for Open University classes. I could pay for books, and for Lyfts and Ubers to class, and photocopies at the student union when my phone dies, rather than just begging them off of nice boys. I might even be able to pay for a new pair of Asics.

If I cosplay every weekend, I might actually have a second chance at a real life. Not some sad, pathetic, limp-noodle life that involves living in my mom's home office, trying to outrun my demons, and scrolling through Daniel's IG feed in the middle of the night.

Although, last night I was scrolling through Adam's. Interestingly, he hasn't posted any of the pictures that he took with me at Comic-Con. It doesn't bug me. I just want to know why he posted pictures of himself with other cosplayers and not me.

I set up a Google Voice number so Adam can't trace me to my actual phone or real life. Separate spheres. Never the twain shall meet. And it has to stay that way, because I'm serious about avoiding speed bumps, and Adam is definitely speed-bump material.

I can do this. It's what Stacey said. It's a good hustle. I need to hustle if I want to afford books and someday a car and the life of an independent, fully-realized adult.

Adam picks up on the second ring. "Adam McKinney."

Holy fudge goldfish. I hadn't even thought of what to say. *Hi, this is Catstrike* is nothing that would willingly come from my lips.

"Hello?" Adam's voice is clear through the connection.

I close my eyes and jog my memory with how it felt to be in the costume. A sexy, rough voice seeps out of me. "Adam..."

He instantly recognizes me. "Catstrike! I was hoping you'd call." A brief pause. He's excited, but is he excited for the same reason I'm smiling? That flirtatious I'm-calling-you-back-and-it-means-something giddiness? Or is this just about business? "Would you mind if I called you Sabine? People around me are staring at the grown man talking to the unseen superhero."

"Hmmm..." I purr. Holy fudge goldfish, Nightbat. Who purrs on a phone to a man they shared a Lyft with once? The same woman who falls asleep remembering what it felt like to have his arm around her vinyl-ensconced shoulders—but that was from being swept up by cosplay. It wasn't the real me. "I'm in."

"Fantastic."

"But I have conditions." See? The real me is pragmatic.

"Name them." Adam sounds confident on the other end.

"I never take off my cowl. Not for customers. Not for you. Not for any of your other heroes or villains."

"Done."

"Fem Fantastic told me that she sometimes wears different costumes for different events."

"Yeah. I meant to talk with you about that—"

"I need full and complete control of my costume choices."

On the other end, I hear a female voice whine for Adam. "I thought you liked the vintage-camp Catstrike." There is a beat and what sounds like a hand over the phone and Adam's muffled response before he continues, "We sometimes try to expand our demographic, and yeah, on those nights, I encourage retro and camp costumes. Look. Why don't I book you for some classic '90s realism beats, and you can see how you feel about branching out after a month or so?" Adam's voice sounds playful. "Might be fun to play around with your character."

Tacky ripped leather pants come to mind, and I shudder. "I doubt it." I hear more voices and Adam asks for five more minutes in a muffled voice. "Is this a bad time?" I ask, and my spine arches as I imagine a girlfriend hanging on his arm—only because I'm getting into character. I have to be to keep up the sexy voice.

"No! No. Please continue." He doesn't sound a bit embarrassed. Amused, though.

"I only work Fridays and Saturdays—"

"Our busiest nights. Done. Easy. Next."

"And you provide me with a back door where I can plan my entrance and exit."

Another beat. "Should I be worried for my safety?"

"No, Adam. No one is asking you to parade around in a thinly veiled dominatrix costume for their own personal gain."

"Stacey said you were cool when she explained it as modeling. People wear all kinds of silly clothes for modeling."

"My conditions."

"Fine. Whatever you need."

I take a deep breath. It's not enough to only sound confident. I need to be a mad boss lady. Like Gwen. Every day, she brings it. Now it's my turn. "You pay me in advance for the next three months. And I don't pose for pictures."

I hear shuffling on his end and voices. It sounds like a party, but it's ten a.m. on a Saturday and way too early for typical young-people revelry. At least in my limited experience. "Pictures are prohibited inside the escape room. Phones, too, so you won't have to worry about any candids. However, part of the Superhero Escapes experience is a celebratory photo op at the end. Bragging rights and the accompanying hashtags are good for business. I'm afraid this is nonnegotiable. I can have a handler in addition to the photographer out with you when it's your turn to pose. With your mask and a closed-mouth smile, you should evade most facial recognition software, if that's what you're worried about." I hear more shuffling and loud voices on his end. "As far as being paid in advance." He half sighs, half groans. "Perhaps we should settle on a wage before I commit to advances?"

I squeeze the arm of my chair till my knuckles are white. I've run my numbers. If I'm going to do this, it has to really make a difference for me. "I want double what the other cosplayers make."

"You're not serious."

"Stacey told me you've been looking for a Catstrike for ages. Said you were very selective. But we both know you were pretty obsessive when it came to finding... me."

"Sabine, Sabine, Sabine. Okay. Sure." He names a figure.

Nope, not double. I need more than just my inner Gwen. I need Catstrike herself. I focus on my character's scrappy badassery. My spine arches and rounds. My lips curl into a pout. "Stacey told me she bought an entire semester's worth of books off the wages of her first weekend alone. Don't play games with me now."

He groans. "I'm pretty sure that was a Labor Day weekend, and Stacey worked Friday through Monday."

"Your escape room isn't open on Mondays."

"We make exceptions."

"I want fifty dollars an hour."

He laughs. "Oh, you were serious?"

I plop down on my bed and begin folding my laundry, smug at my negotiating and adulting skills. Look, Mom! Clean panties AND money for classes.

"Jeez, Sabine. You're not kidding about this. Look, the average wage for my cast comes to about thirty dollars an hour."

I smile. "So find someone more average."

"Forty-five dollars, and I can pay for the first month up-front. But if you so much as breathe a word about your advance, it'll be the end of me and my business."

"Relax, Adam. I'll keep our secret."

"So you're in?"

"All in."

CHAPTER EIGHT

Gwen was kind enough to give me a ride to the gym.

"Does Tony know you got a second job?"

"Of course not. No one knows but you."

"So you told your mama—"

"I said I was working out and then spending time with you."

"Oh no. I'm not your alibi. I mean, sure, this one time, but if this is a regular gig, you're going to need a better story than that."

"I'll... I'll say I've got study groups and homework."

"Or you could just tell everyone that you found a gig that is paying for classes."

"Things went really south, really fast the last time I cosplayed, remember?"

"I thought things went well at Comic-Con."

"I'm talking about the time before."

"I met one of my exes at a drag party. It was fun while it lasted, sharing shoes, shopping each other's closets." Gwen sighs wistfully.

"Yeah, but you didn't end up married."

"No." Gwen glances at me with a smile. "Though I did swear off dating any man who is a smaller dress size than I am."

I try to keep a straight face. "So you understand my position completely."

"Oh, they're totally equivalent, hard-won life lessons," Gwen teases.

"I have to avoid all speed bumps." I reach for one of Gwen's hair ties that she hoards in the center console, but they're gone. In fact, Gwen's car is devoid of empty pickle packs, stray sandals, and the other jetsam of her life.

"I'll go really slow if we come to a speed bump, but there aren't many from here to PB."

"No, I have to avoid the things, aka the speed bumps, that made me flunk out of school before. No parties for me. No cosplay. And definitely no boys. My rules have never been more important."

"I see a problem with this. Do you see a problem?" Gwen asks.

I roll my eyes, but there is a satisfied smile threatening to break free too. "That I'm getting paid to cosplay and said pay is the reason why I can go back to school?"

"That would be *a* problem. I was thinking of another problem. A cute, tall, square-jawed, blue-eyed, blond-haired problem."

"Adam has brond hair, not blond. And it's fine. Adam is fine. I'll keep things between us strictly professional. I'll only cosplay for work. It will be the one and only exception to my rules."

Gwen raises an eyebrow. The gesture is worse than any counterargument.

"Work is work," I offer. "Work isn't a party."

"Definitely not a party," Gwen says.

"As far as the social stuff and the boy stuff. Those I have a pretty good defense against, thanks to living with my mommy."

"Right." Gwen brushes a speck of glitter from her dashboard. "People can see that too—that you live with your mom. From a mile away. Just by looking at you."

I know what she's trying to do, but I have to stay focused. "No speed bumps. I can do this. I can cosplay and get paid and go to school and stop being a sad little failure who is obsessed with running."

Gwen pulls up in front of the gym. "I don't think you're ever going to stop running."

Gwen's right. I love running. "Probably not." And before she can refute anything else I've said, I grab my bag and shoulder open the car door. "Wish me luck?"

"Oh no, I'm coming in to watch. I'll run interference too. I have a feeling you might need it." Gwen drops me off and leaves to circle the block for parking.

My catsuit is shoved into the bottom of my gym bag. Under my towel. Under my shower flip-flops. Under my bottle of shampoo/conditioner. Under my makeup bag. It is there in all its shiny-black-vinyl-and-boots glory. No one knows. I mean, besides Gwen. So why do I feel so embarrassed? My face is beet-juice-fast red when I walk into work at the gym.

"You read my mind," Tony says by way of greeting. "Kate canceled. I need you to work tonight."

"I can't work tonight." I also can't look Tony in the eye. "I have plans."

"You never have plans!" Tony falls against the counter of the front desk and starts doing stress push-ups. "Why are you even here?"

"I want to work out before my plans. Is my favorite treadmill open?"

Gwen must have found parking close, because she's just walked in.

Tony looks dazed, like an hour-long hot yoga session stretched into ninety minutes. "A quick workout is calming. I get it. Can you cover for any part of tonight?"

I end up covering the front desk until Tony can phone in Julian. So much for my comfort run.

I duck into the women's locker room and breathe silent prayers of thanksgiving that one of the private changing cabanas is open. This is risky, but it would be impossible to do at home. I strip down to my black lacy knickers and begin by whiting out my face. I mean, not *white* white. Really, not much changes, because I'm pretty pasty. You'd think with all the running I've done, I'd have a tan, but I don't tan. I burn, and I peel. It gets old fast, so I'm devoted to my sunscreen, visor, and sunglasses. I rummage in my makeup bag and find my contour pad. And while I'd never contour in real life, chiseling my features is nonnegotiable for cosplay. These are costumes. Restraint means you stand that much more of a chance of being recognized. I hastily stain my lips a dark berry red. The false lashes are next before I layer on the mascara. I pause to stare at myself in the changing cabana's full-length mirror. My winged cat's eyeliner looks fierce and my blue eyes electric—and worlds apart from their normal dull denim color. My cheeks are chiseled into a high relief that makes my face look heart-shaped.

Shimmying into vinyl isn't easy. Particularly when you are trying not to smudge the plaster mask of makeup on your face or muss the false eyelashes. The invisible side-zipper that I added in my mom's bathroom the morning of Comic-Con is the only reason I can get the corset on by myself. I tug on my cowl and fasten it.

There's a tap on my cabana door. "Coast is clear," Gwen calls softly.

I step out, and Gwen freezes when she sees me. "Holy hell!"

I put a hand on my vinyl-ensconced waist. "You've seen me cosplay before." I tug on one of my clawed gloves. I've had to blunt the tips of wire, but they are still absolutely ridiculous.

"Yeah, but that was Comic-Con. You expect to see lions at the zoo. Seeing one walking around in real life is—"

"Ridiculous?"

"Freaking awesome. Have you seen yourself?"

I turn to face the full-length mirror in the locker room and am stunned when Catstrike blinks back. She mirrors my movements. I stretch, and she does too. She's taller than me in the black lace-up boots. And skinnier than I've ever been. Is that what running away from the damn memories does to a woman? I've done my best to avoid mirrors ever since... well, even before I got married. I don't think I've forgotten what I look like, but I certainly don't look like a supervillain/antihero/sexpot.

"Obsessed." Gwen tucks in the ties of my corset from the back. "I mean, if he isn't already."

Not that it matters, but a satisfied glow starts up somewhere inside. With my corset squeezing my insides, I'm not sure where inside. But somewhere.

I shove my gym bag into my locker, just as LouAnne, one of our senior patrons, shuffles out of the shower, stark naked. Gwen must have forgotten to check the showers. LouAnne has no qualms about modesty in the locker room. She once stopped me to talk for fifteen minutes with not even a towel in her hands. *Deeply disturbing* doesn't even begin to do our little chat justice.

Can I fit in my locker? I'm mortified. But Gwen smiles good-naturedly. She intercepts LouAnne, and catches her with her back to me, before she turns the corner to the lockers and discovers a fully-realized Catstrike. "How's it going LouAnne?"

"This gym needs a pool," she says.

Gwen nods seriously. It's all the encouragement LouAnne needs to launch into her good-old-days stories of competitive swimming. I mouth my thanks to Gwen and dart out.

I double-check to make sure the hall outside the locker room is empty. I think for a moment about giving myself a pep talk. A *you got this, you're a professional, everything is hinging on being a huge success.* But there is no time. Getting ready took longer than I thought it would. I really need to find a different pair of boots. The laces alone are ridiculous, and the heels are definitely not my sweet spot.

I grabbed my whip before streaking to the yoga patio out of panic, or maybe despair? I'm sure that this qualifies as the most insane thing I've ever done.

The yoga patio is not a big space, but it is predictably underutilized. And more important, it butts up against the back alley. A block wall and some jasmine vines are all that separate me from the quiet backstreet, which conveniently joins up with the alley behind Garnet Avenue and thereby the back door of Superhero Escapes. Stacey texted that the emergency exit door would be unlocked for me. I just have to get there. I stand on the teakwood bench and try to heave myself up onto the top of the block wall.

Nope.

"Come on. What's the point of all those planks if I can't even get up a block wall?" I mutter.

I try again to scramble up the wall, but this time I fall, landing on my butt. I growl in frustration and lie there, staring up at the thick branches of the eucalyptus tree. They stretch and spread effortlessly over the block wall.

I take my whip and throw it over a branch. It's not graceful. It takes me more than a couple of attempts, but when it lands, it is the leverage I need to scale the wall. I straddle the top triumphantly, but before I can swing both my legs over and scamper away into the dark alley, I hear a door creak open. Panic freezes me in place.

The back door of Stu's Donuts, a Pacific Beach institution if ever there was one, is propped open. Stu himself, a stooped-over grandpa with a cigar habit, stands in the alley, holding a bag of trash and staring at me atop the block wall.

I feel my face turn the same color as Stu's famous cherry filling. I swing my legs over and land in the alley with a thud. "Hi," I say, straightening.

Stu says nothing but has dropped the bag beside him. He's not going anywhere.

I try to tug my whip out of the tree. It doesn't budge, but a shower of eucalyptus leaves do.

Stu keeps watching. He pulls a cigar out of the front pocket of his shirt.

"Probably the weirdest thing you've ever seen in your alley, right?" I say, brushing the stray leaves off of me.

Stu considers. "No."

I try awkwardly one last time for my whip, but the tree has eaten it. Instead, I grab the bag of trash from Stu and quickly toss it in his bin. "Don't tell anyone?"

I don't wait for him to answer but tear down the alley. Running in heels would be satisfying if Stu wasn't watching.

Stacey is a saint. She's left the emergency exit door to the alley unlocked as promised. I heave it open and collide with Adam. "Goldfish," I yelp.

"You're late," he says, peeling me off him. "I wanted to show you the room before we got started."

"I—" My eyes lock onto him. When you've met someone only once, you forget pieces of what they look like. I remember how delicious Adam looked at Comic-Con, but I thought that was because he looked so normal in an ocean of bizarre, loud, and (at times) obnoxious. Adam looked familiar in a sea of bewildering. Now, in a completely ordinary stairwell, surrounded by nothing but faded taupe paint and fluorescent lights, I am immobilized by the many details I missed. Like how quietly blue his eyes are. How they carry an intensity and energy to them that is hypnotizing, even if the color is subdued. How his hair is a darker shade than I remember and falls across his forehead in a way that could haunt me if I don't actively remind myself of my rules and no-speed-bumps plan. Even so, I want to hold his face still and look for faded freckles. I want to press my cheek against his jaw and imprint his stubble on my skin as I inhale.

"No speed bumps."

His eyes narrow. "You okay? You're not backing out, are you?" Something flashes in those stormy blue eyes. What is it? Fear?

"And miss seeing you panic every weekend when I'm a few minutes late?" Holy fudge. What did I just say? I start up the stairs. "You coming?"

He brushes past me. "This way."

He pushes open a door on the second floor. "Welcome to Superhero Escapes."

I step into what looks like the back room of a comic book store.

"What's with all this stuff?" I ask.

"People'll buy it. So I stock it. Back this way."

I follow Adam behind the counter to the computer. He taps it awake. "We've got a party of six in the Mystery at Osric Manor Room. Four cameras in each corner of the room to monitor the progress. Audio feed is here." He toggles the digital control on the screen.

I watch as the people on the screen tap walls and scramble around, looking at things.

"Essentially, there are five puzzles in this first room. Weight-loaded lock. Heat gun. Water reveal. Hidden key. And sequential-word riddle."

"Nightbat was a detective before he was a superhero," I say.

"Exactly." Adam smiles. "They solve these puzzles, the door opens to the second room, which has five additional puzzles. Ten puzzles total. We figure five minutes per each puzzle and ten minutes to celebrate."

"So what do I do?" Goldfish, I sound confident. But it's one little computer and walls of puzzles. Why would I be worried?

"On this one? Nothing. You haven't been trained. But when you are, you hang out in the control room with a feed like this, monitoring the audio and making sure that the team is on the right track. You'll hand out clues as needed."

Stacey, in all her Fem Fantastic cosplay glory, appears. "We've got quite the queue outside."

Adam's eyes sparkle. "Right, Let's get our Catstrike set in Malum Escape and get this party started."

I follow Adam down the corridor. A dull thudding vibrates the walls. "This is all above the bar?" I ask.

"The bar, the restaurant, and two dispensaries. I convinced the owners that renting their upstairs real estate to me was a better invest-ment than using it for storage." Adam opens a small door, and I am staring at a jail cell with padded walls. "Escape from Malum Asylum is more quintessential haunted house than escape room. We've got live actors in each room. The escapees will enter your cell through this door." He taps on a panel of the padded wall, and it swings open before he pushes it shut. "You say your line, hit the strobes with this remote, and get out of their way. They fumble around in the semi-darkness, looking for this button that unlocks the small cell door." He gestures to a switch under the cot.

"Wait! I'm locked in with them?" I'm not feeling so confident anymore.

"Calm down," Adam says evenly.

"I would, too, but you're still smiling."

Adam looks perversely amused. "You have options. You can get out the door they came in, which is ideal. You can slip between the bars here." Adam gestures to a wider gap between the faux jail bars and wall. "Escapees tend to think literally, so it's a safe option. Last option: You can stay put and heckle them." Adam checks his phone. "If you'd gotten here on time, we would have run through it. Congratulations on making it this far."

I fold my arms across my chest. "Thanks?"

Adam laughs. "No, that's your line. And then you say, 'But you'll never make it past me. Now can you see in the dark?'"

"Wrote that just for me, did you?" I say in my soft growl. I take a sauntering step closer to Adam. Even with the dull echoes of the bar seeping in from below, my boots still make excellent little accents of sounds.

Adam's eyebrows arch reflexively. "Feel free to punctate your lines with Catstrike laughter. Almost forgot. You hit the strobes with this." He hands me a palm-sized remote, which I immediately click on. "The room goes black for a count of three before the strobes pulse. You exit while they feel around in the dark for the key."

I click off the strobes, and the stage lighting is on once again. "What if I can't get out in time, and they end up feeling me?"

"Relax. We've got you on camera, we've got them on camera. The 'wardens' patrol the hall too. You'll do great. Jerry is stationed tonight in the cell before yours, and Vanessa is in the cell right after yours."

Adam checks his phone again and swears. "Sorry, there isn't time to introduce you to everyone. Click the remote again to reset the strobe and slide the cell door shut before the next group arrives. If there is an emergency, you look into the video camera in that corner and say, 'Deputy Chief Eden.' Then hold down all the buttons on your clicker. It sets the houselights on the entire wing. People come running. Only for emergencies, got it? Questions?" He slides open the cell door, leaving me alone in my white padded cell.

I wrap my clawed fingers around the bars. "Plenty."

"Ask me later. We only have one video camera in this room." He gestures to the corner where I spy a small red light. "It's been enough for now, but I'm working on getting a second added. Just in case." He pauses and looks at me. An odd smile curls on his face.

"What?"

"You look like a Jane Lee still. Sit tight. First group is due in five." He slides the door shut and disappears.

They're a group of accountants on an informal team-building excursion. The brunette screams when she sees me in the room. I say my lines, push the button. The strobe starts. I escape out the door they came in.

And then I do it again with a group on a double date. And again with a sorority. And again with birthday partiers.

It's easy. And kind of fun, I have to admit.

Before the next group cycles through, a woman in a Fair Play costume comes into the room and stands outside my cell. "Hey, you holding up?" she says. "I'm Vanessa, BTW." She reaches her hand through the bars, and I shake it. "Don't worry about another group coming in just yet. There was an incident in Mike's room, and it'll take longer to reset."

"Incident?"

"Some guy started filming." Vanessa grins. "I'd like to say it happens all the time—just to mess with you—but it's pretty rare."

My supervillain voice slides into more normal territory. "How does Adam book so many parties so close together?"

Vanessa laughs, and it is immediately apparent why she was cast as Fair Play, AJ Comics' female version of Badpun. She sounds completely unhinged. "Malum Escape isn't a real escape room. It's a haunted house, but it gets people coming back because it's easy enough to change it up. And sure, there are a few puzzles. Mike's room at the end is a crowd favorite. Although, from what I'm hearing, you're not bad."

"Who's Mike?"

"The guy in the purple suit and creepy clown makeup."

Adam has a Badpun. Of course.

Vanessa stretches and pops her neck. "Where'd Adam find you? He's been looking forever for a Catstrike."

That's the second time someone has said that. Why? "Comic-Con. You?"

"The Haunted Hotel. It's the best gig in town, but it's seasonal, you know? This one comes in a close second. Adam went through it and said I had the best timing out of everyone in the place. Asked if I'd seen Halifax Sisters' latest villain misfits flick. Wanted to know if I thought it'd be fun to flirt with the psycho side of the comic book world. When is it *not* fun to flirt with the psycho side, am I right?"

Then she laughs again. Gotta admit I want to take a step back. I mean, this girl is intense. But I hold my ground and smile widely. "Is it always this busy?"

"This is for you, girl. Everyone's here tonight to see Catstrike. You didn't see the posters out front? 'Coming Friday, August Fifth: Catstrike and all-new villains to Malum Escape.'"

I swallow. Oh, goldfish. Is one of my Comic-Con photos plastered all over PB? I feel sweaty. Nervous and sweaty. "I came through the back door."

Vanessa adjusts her blue-and-red-streaked pigtails. "Hey, as a heads-up, watch the high schoolers. Especially during photo ops."

My eyes go wide.

"But you've done this before, so you know how to handle yourself."

I open my mouth to say *of course*, but the words get stuck in my chin strap.

Realization spreads like a rash on Vanessa's face. "Ha! You're a newb. Oh, honey, tell me you've at least had some crowd-control experience. SeaWorld, Petco Park, something, anything."

I shrug. "Stacey said people aren't bad."

"To Stacey. She's a goddess. No one is going to try anything with her. She'd crush them."

I put a hand on my hip. "And I wouldn't?"

A wide grin spreads across Vanessa's face. "Now we're talking. What's your name?"

"It's Not Sabine Kennedy."

Vanessa narrows an eye. "Yeah, okay. Look, here's how you do it. Don't touch them, ever. The second you do, they get braver. Don't drop eye contact unless it's to pick on someone else in the group. And whatever you do, don't replicate."

"Replicate?" What the fudge does that mean?

"Villains, reset!" Adam calls over the sound system.

"Good luck. See you for pictures." Vanessa winks and leaves.

"Wait!" I groan and pace my cell. I can't look like a newb. Too much is riding on this. Replicate... Maybe Vanessa meant this is going to be a long night if I just stand in the room and smile with my eyes, Tyra Banks style, at each group of Malum escapees? Apart from the padded cell door and the door in the jail bars, there is a cot with the button on the underside to unlock the cell door and a fake window also covered in bars in my cell. It's not much to work with, but if all these people are here to see Catstrike, it isn't enough to say my line, push the remote for the strobes, and exit the room.

I look up at the video camera positioned in the corner. Adam is on the other end of that lens. He is watching, and his Catstrike is here at last. He's waited a long time for a Catstrike who meets his specific criteria, so this Catstrike needs to deliver.

I give the bars across the faux window a tug, take a deep breath, and, hoping they'll hold my weight, dangle from them. When the door clicks open a breath later, I push off and land in a crouch before springing up to a stand.

"You've made it this far," I say to the wine-tasting, well-dressed set collected in my cell. "But can you make it in the dark?" I press the remote, activating the strobes.

I duck past them for the exit. Outside, I nod to Mallard, an older actor and exactly the kind who might play Santa at the mall if he put on a fake beard. He is for sure the monocled, well-dressed, well-groomed mob boss Mallard variety. "Are you new too?" I ask.

"Yes and no. Adam had me playing Pluto Gorgo before." Magnificent Man's distinguished archenemy—I can see that. "Nightbat's butler, too, sometimes. I'm Jerry." He makes a small bow without rising.

"Not Sabine. Do you like the work?"

"I get paid to read the paper." He turns down the front page of his *Abandum Advance* to reveal the *Union-Tribune*. "If I finish a column, and they're still in my room, I give them a clue."

"You've got an actual puzzle in this one?"

"The keypad on the opposite wall. Punch in the right digits, the door opens."

A latch clicks in the cell outside Mallard's.

"Time to reset. Quack, quack."

I do. This time with my arms through the fake jail bars. It's a group of bar-crawling girls. Probably my age. After, when I exit to Jerry's room, he says, "Watch out for this next set. They sound rowdy."

I nod and step back into my room to reset.

For this set, I'm lounging on the bed, saucy vamp style, when the group comes in. "Nice job, but you'll never escape." I rise and saunter closer to the trio of high school boys. "Now then. Can you see in the dark?"

"I don't know, can you?" One lunges at me before I can beeline for the door. Had I been ordinary hoodie-wearing me staffing an escape room, I would have been surprised and scared. Flight or freeze would have kicked in. But tonight, I am cosplaying. I'm Catstrike, and I'm all fight. My knee goes up, straight into the guy's stomach. My fist comes down on another's head. If I had my whip with me, I'd crack it. Instead, I hiss.

"I don't play with boys." That's right. I hiss. "Now find the key and get out."

So maybe I break Vanessa's rule and shove them as I return to Mallard's cell. I don't care. I am not about to let a group of dumbass boys push me around.

When I exit into the other room, Adam is waiting, and Jerry is still reading the paper.

"I'm breaking you," he says.

I raise and lower a shoulder. "I'm fine."

"I'm breaking you anyway. People want pictures."

"Fine." I saunter with my chin tilted up and my shoulders back. "Thanks for the heads-up, Jerry."

Jerry doesn't look up from his paper. "Don't mention it."

Adam grabs me by the arm and steers me through his labyrinth of Malum cells. We pass Vanessa, who is still laughing maniacally, and the high schoolers, who are stuck in Mike the Badpun's room. "What were you doing?" Adam's voice is soft, controlled, but also full of suppressed rage.

No way is he pinning what just happened on me. "I was defending myself. You lied to me. You told me everyone would be on their best behavior, but those boys made a grab for me." I was lucky Jerry warned me TBH, or I might have gotten even more carried away. "What kind of escape room are you running, Mr. Adam West McKinney?" I jab his chest with my finger.

"Look," Adam hisses, ducking into a small storage closet and pulling me in after him. "Not everyone has the skill set or the patience for a real escape room. And the people who are into the real rooms, don't come for the live actors. The atmosphere sure—"

"Now you're demoting me to set dressing?"

"No! What I'm saying is you should have hit the house lights. You should have called for help."

I'm not sure what Adam stores in the boxes all around us, but I do know that it's tight in here. I'm only inches away from him. "And risk the wrath of Deputy Chief Eden? Do you think he's the jealous type?" I slide one of my claws up his arm before leaning against a wall of boxes.

"Just smile for their Insta Stories. Say meow. If you're not happy, we'll talk later."

Adam takes a deep breath before opening the door and beckoning me to follow him down the hall.

"There he is. Job well done, Adam!" a grizzled man calls out. He's from the same group I dazzled with my flip off the wall. Well-dressed, a tad snookered, expensive-smelling perfumes.

A woman with an Hermes scarf tied casually around her neck pats Adam's shoulder. "Quite clever, harnessing the appeal of haunted houses and creating an application that can be utilized year-round."

"Thanks, Dr. Withers."

Who are these people? His professors? One of the gentlemen shakes Adam's hand.

"But it's not just the business model," a second woman continues. "Adam has a keen eye for talent."

"I'll say," a red-nosed gentleman with salt-and-pepper hair chimes in.

I bristle. I don't like the way Salty Red Nose stares at me. No doubt he's done more than just taste wine tonight. Probably downed a bottle or two.

"How about a picture?" Adam forces a smile. "Look, Nightbat is here." He ushers a very au courant Nightbat cosplayer into frame.

"Wonderful attention to detail, Adam. So atmospheric," Dr. Withers says as we shuffle in front of the camera.

"Should we squeeze in?" Salty Red Nose puts his hand around the small of my back, and I flinch.

"Looks great," Adam says from behind his photographer with the *Daily Post* press badge. He studies the frame. "Professor Jackson, how about you trade places with Linda? That's it. Much more balanced now."

The old guy has to move away. Linda has the decency to keep from squeezing my vinyl with her hand.

The *Daily Post* photographer snaps a picture, then several more using everyone's phones.

"Lovely," Adam says. "If you use the caption #superheroescapes when you post this picture to your Twitter, Insta, Facebook, Snapchat, or TikTok, you'll receive 25% off your next adventure here at Superhero Escapes."

"That's clever," Linda says. "You seeing good results?"

"Oh, yes. All detailed in our next earnings report." Adam walks out with the group.

So they were Adam's investors. No wonder he was so uptight.

I pose for more pictures. I meet Nightbat. I stick it out for more Malum escapes and have to swat away only a few more extroverted, possibly inebriated, individuals. Our last group comes in at 12:48 a.m. I find Vanessa after they roll out.

"Replicate?" I ask. "'Whatever you do don't...'"

"Yeah, don't replicate. You can't do the same thing every time. You got to change it up. Keep it fresh. But you knew that. You're a natural."

Don't I know it.

Adam finds me as I head out the back door. My feet ache, and my stomach is sore from hours of wearing a corset, but seeing Adam waiting for me... It's like I get a second wind.

"Big night," I say, leaning against the wall. Adam looks a little on edge until I offer, "We stayed open nearly an extra hour."

He looks absolutely relieved. Was the meet and greet with the investors a surprise after all? "You should have seen the line." He pulls out his phone and taps out what sounds like a text.

My phone vibrates in my thigh pocket. I pull it out to find a notification from Venmo. "What's this?" I ask.

"Your advance." I'm one swipe away from depositing it in full, when Adam places a hesitant hand on top of mine. "I need you to promise you'll be back. Look, I'm sorry about what happened with the group of high schoolers. Usually, our crowd isn't quite so rough." His brow furrows, and once again, he's staring at my boots. "Once you're no longer a novelty, we can train you in hosting one of the other escape rooms. But for now, I need you in Malum Escape."

"You need me?" You bet I'm going to make him say it again.

"I need you, Sabine."

Of course I show up the next night.

Of course I show up the next weekend.

Of course I think about Adam's electric-blue eyes dicing my insides as he tells me he needs me each and every day.

CHAPTER NINE

Somehow, when you give men the opportunity to wear a mask and cape, they think they have permission to be a rogue, douche, and idiot. Usually simultaneously. If I had known Customer Cosplay Night at Superhero Escapes was going to be this much work, I would have shortened my marathon run this morning by half.

Most of the costumes so far have been good. Clearly, San Diego has a resident wealthy-nerd populace actively searching for opportunities to show off their expensive gear. Comic-Con comes but once a year, and with the marine layer finally bowing to the August sun, no one has Halloween on their mind. But Customer Cosplay Night at Superhero Escapes? The entire San Diego metro area will be there. Happily sweating through their custom-made getups as the AC tries and fails to keep up with an escape room filled to capacity.

I'll give Adam this: He knows how to keep the nerds coming. I wish he were here tonight. I know heart-eyeing your boss is the textbook definition of pathetic, but whenever I catch him staring at me, my ego soars. I could string my ego up and fly it higher than the banners the planes drag over Law Street Beach on Saturdays. My stomach gurgles as the image of "Free appetizer with every entrée!"

scrolls through my head in yellow letters. I need to change up my running route on Saturdays.

There is, of course, no lasting effect from Adam's double takes and glances. My ego deflates when he isn't around. I crawl back to Earth and remember I'm in a costume just like the sign flippers wearing furries on street corners. Humiliating, desperate, and so very weird.

The door outside my Malum Asylum cell opens. A gust of welcome cooler air and the hum of the crowd outside press against me until Stacey snaps the door shut behind her. She hands me a water bottle. "You hangin' in there, Not Sabine?"

Stacey manages to look completely resplendent in her warrior princess leather skirt ensemble. It might be that she is a literal goddess among us mortals, or it might be that her costume is breathable. My vinyl is probably permanently stuck to me at this point. "It's hot in here," I drawl, and then in a more authentic voice, I add, "I think I've sweated off all my makeup." I must have raccoon eyes and Badpun lips.

Stacey brushes her thumbnail against the edge of my lip in a no-nonsense big-sister way. "There. You look great."

Vanessa, who is rocking a far more gritty and realistic Fair Play look this evening, joins us, beaming. "This is the best night ever! I think I literally made a guy pee his pants."

I have never been more jealous of a woman's bare legs. I need to make finding a more comfortable, breathable Catstrike costume a priority.

Stacey hands Vanessa a water bottle. "Don't tell Adam I let you swing a bat at a paying custumer." She gives Vanessa a once-over. "Cute shorts. Where did you find those?"

"My *abuelita* made them for me. I told her I had to up my game following this badass." She points at me with her thumb.

My lips curl into a smile. "They save the best for last."

Vanessa preens.

Stacey checks her phone. "We've got another hour queued up for

Malum, easy. Can you hang in there? Adam says we can pay double
for every half hour we stay open past midnight."

"Adam's here?" I shouldn't be excited by the idea, but I am.

Stacey shakes her head, and I deflate. "Phoned it in," she
explains.

Sweat slides down my back. I am desperate for a cool shower, but
with classes starting next week, how can I say no to extra Lyft money?
"I'll stay."

"I'll rotate you out with Frankie for photos."

"You do, and I won't have it in me to get back in my cell," I say.

"You sure?"

I hand back my empty water bottle. "Absolutely."

By a little miracle, I make it through the next hour of escapes.
Only twice do I have to slap some punk's hand away before I say my
line. "Nice work. But can you see in the dark?" rattles in my brain
until it is etched onto my tongue. I'll be saying it in my sleep,
mumbling it in the shower. It'll take an hour of rowing before I can
exorcise it from my being.

I swear I could stand in the gym shower for hours. Forget the cold
shower. My muscles are so sore, I'm ready to break into the locked
closet where they keep the on-demand water heater and turn the
temperature up to boiling. I slowly clomp my way toward the photo
op. My boots feel like a million pounds of bad idea right now.

"Sarah!" someone hisses.

Adrenaline floods every inch of me. Did I slip out of character?
Did my mask fall off? I run my gloved hand over my mask. It's still
there, gripping my cheekbones.

Adrian in the *Daily Post* press badge snaps a picture. The bright
flash makes my eyes water.

"It's me! Gwen!"

I blink and turn around. Gwen is standing next to me in some
sort of anime costume, complete with pastel wig. "Gwen? What are
you doing here?"

She swings her white-blond-and-pink-striped curls behind her shoulders. "Some of the girls from the office wanted to try out an escape room."

"Were you in Malum?" Had I really been so out of it that I'd missed Gwen and her two pastel-dressed anime colleagues? "Who are you supposed to be?"

"We're ponies!"

I note the tails attached to their shorts and skirts. "Of course you are. If you want a picture, please make it quick."

"Whoa. Calm down." Gwen and the other ponies trot into frame. "Are you grouchy because Adam isn't here?" Gwen whispers through her dazzling teeth.

How does she know Adam isn't here? "Of course not."

"Because you know if you are, that only proves my theory. That you're doing this because—"

I cut her off with a hiss.

I may have mentioned to Gwen that seeing Adam, and especially seeing how his eyes linger on my shiny vinyl, is a perk, a modest perk, for all the trouble of climbing over the yoga wall twice a night.

"I'm grouchy because all the dressed-up dudes have been a little too comfortable draping their hands over me during the victory photos."

Stacey appears. "Sorry to break up the fun, everyone. Catstrike has one more party to see through Malum."

She drags me away, and I am practically dead weight. "You're kidding."

"It's the last for the night, I swear," Stacey says, sliding my cell door open. "Mixed group. Über well-costumed... I couldn't say no." She gives my cell bars a tap. "You've got this."

Über well-costumed? Okay, maybe that got my attention. I may not be seeing Ben-Day dots in my waking hours, but you can't take the comics out of the girl. I take my time staring them down when they enter my cell. An on-point, devastatingly-real Badpun with his arm around an equally disturbingly attractive Fair Play stumble into my room, followed by a '90s Nightbat with prom dress Penny Price on his heels. A vintage Mallard and Catstrike trail in behind them. A double take on my part reveals a gender swap—that's Lady Mallard in tails and a male Catstrike. Totally adorable.

I say the same tired line with as much sass as is left in me and twirl my little black whip. I carry a small one on me now. It helps to have a prop. Also helps to be armed. The strobe light flashes, and the room plunges into complete darkness as I beat my well-worn path of retreat through the door to Jerry's room.

I nearly scream when I see the '90s Nightbat blocking my path.

I look for Jerry, but he and his *Abandum Advance* are gone. "You've lost your party, Nightbat." My voice is rough from a night of cosplaying.

"Sometimes you find what you're looking for by waiting."

Sensitivity to strobe lights means that occasionally guests hang back in this particular room. Had Nightbat stepped out while I was admiring the other cosplayers?

I check the security camera in the corner of the room. The red light winks back at me, ever vigilant. I have nothing to be afraid of. But even if I did, I'm too tired to be afraid.

Nightbat's lips twitch into the briefest of smiles. He moves closer, and while it isn't easy to size up a man in cosplay of this magnificence, it is very easy to get carried away. I do the Catstrike equivalent of catching his eyes before blushing and looking down, which is to say I smirk, arch an eyebrow, and keep staring.

His eyes are inked behind the holes in his cowl, and in the dim light of the escape room, their color is indistinguishable. His chin is shaved clean, but something about him is very familiar. He's definitely not my brother. Brent has a Dermot Mulroney scar on his lip from a surfboard accident, and the Nightbat standing before me has no scars on his lower face. Not a one. He also isn't my ex. Daniel could never pull off a mask like this with his weak chin. Besides, his IG feed had him sporting a goatee in Shanghai this morning.

"And what are you looking for?" I drawl. Oh, but I'm getting good at the sexy, femme fatale voice.

"You."

"Easy, Ash. There's a lot more to me than you realize." Turns out I'm not tired at all. I feel slightly panicked but also heady. I've watched *Nightbat Returns* enough to fantasize about a moment like this. My favorite Nightbat comics are organized by which have the best Nightbat/Catstrike kissy-smoochy scenes. And in a moment like this—when I'm supposed to remember that I am Sarah Miller, who not too long ago was Sarah Miller Jonson, and the looming cape-clad gentleman is not really the millionaire, tortured golden child Ashley Osric of Abandum City, or any city, but probably a pathetic psycho with a paunch behind the sculpted rubber—I can't remember. Cosplay is about playing. And goldfish, I want to play.

"Tell me." He says the words urgently and gruffly. He stands closer and presses a hand to my waist. I feel that ASMR tingle crawl up my spine. He brings his other hand to my shoulder.

"I'm tempted," I say. Shirley Temples, I am more than tempted. My brain explodes into fireworks. I hear the muffled shouts of a successful escape from my room. I bring a claw up to his lips. "But I'm not about to ruin poor Penny's evening. You're safe from the strobe light. Good luck escaping, Nightbat." I shrug out of his arms and leave through the other door.

"Hey," Stacey calls, jogging toward me. "Everything okay? We lost audio, and the feed cut out." Stacey's brow furrows. "Nightbat didn't try anything—"

"I'm pretty sure he was just sensitive to the strobes." I wrap my hand across my waist, resting my hand where Nightbat held me seconds earlier. "The cameras went out?"

"I'm going to check them now. They might have overheated. Or someone might have powered them down early. It's been a crazy night."

My voice is desperately authentic. "Yeah, I, um, I'm going to head out."

"You sure? Frankie and Vanessa are planning quite the after party."

"I can't afford to miss another training run." True... as long as she doesn't ask what I'm training for.

"Say no more." Stacey places a hand on my shoulder. "You sure you're okay? You sound out of breath."

"Yeah, it's hot in this costume." I roll my shoulder, turn, and catch a glimpse of the last group posing for the camera. Badpun and Fair Play are laughing with their arms around each other. Penny Price, male Catstrike, and Lady Mallard are posing *Charlie's Angels* style. And '90s Nightbat is gone.

"Hey, Stace?" I ask.

"Yeah?"

"Were there three parties of two in that last group?"

Stacey checks her tablet. "Two parties of three. Penny Price, male Catstrike, and Lady Mallard were a group, and then Badpun, Fair Play, and Nightbat were the other. They wanted to be separate, but they agreed to be combined because of the time."

I nod. "Cool." My knees feel like they are about to buckle out. So Nightbat didn't come with Penny. He came for me. And that should be terrifying, but it isn't.

My spine warms over, and I have a new flush of delicious pinpricks. It was Adam. I'd bet my next two Venmo deposits on it. He's the only man who makes my cosplay kitten come out and purr.

I leave through the emergency exit and am not at all surprised to see the dark silhouette of a gorgeous caped cosplayer standing in the alley.

Hello, Adam.

I stare him down as I strut toward him. I know my costume photographs well, but it also moves well. The shine of the vinyl catches in the dim light with each of my steps and exaggerates the modest curves of my runner's body. Time for a game of cat and mouse. "Look, I'm flattered, but I don't need a stalker. Thanks."

A sea breeze, cool and pensive, catches his cape for a moment. "It doesn't seem very safe, does it? Back alleys."

"They're better than front doors."

"You could get hurt."

His words don't feel like a threat. Then again, they feel dangerous in a very different way. A hit-a-speed-bump kind of way. "You're the only man I've met out here so far, and you don't scare me. Now..." I turn sharply and start my two-block walk to the gym. "What do you want?"

"Why do you do it?" he asks. And he is really nailing the Nightbat voice. There is an edge—and a whole lot of that yummy sexy growl too.

The marine layer has already rolled in, obscuring the moon, making the streetlamp the only light in the alley.

I stop and stare hard under the yellow halo of the halogen bulb. Adam usually sports scruff, but tonight his chin is shaved clean. For as long as I've known him, he's been this easygoing, chill kinda guy. The confidence is still there, but tonight... Ooh. Tonight, there is something else, something a little frantic in his eyes, something that makes me super aware of my beating heart.

The sea breeze gusts again, and my sweat-soaked body shivers. He wants to know why I do it. Why I'm dressed up like a freak and sneak out the back door. Because let's face it, there are easier hustles. I saunter closer. "If I tell you, do you promise you'll walk back inside? You won't follow me?"

"If you tell me," he says.

He stands close, but I step closer. Black cat boot to black bat boot. I slide my clawed hands up his arms. I wrap them around his neck and press my lips to the corner of his mouth. I feel his arms wrap around me, confidently, comfortably. He pulls me off the ground, and my boots skid for a moment against the pavement that is perpetually dusted with beach sand. He holds me tighter as I kiss his chin. And then, because of temporary insanity and the fact that he smells yummy, like cardamom or anise, I full-on Catstrike-lick his face. And right when he is ready to open his mouth and come unglued, I let go and walk away. No turning back. I can't concede an inch of confidence.

I hear the creak of the emergency exit door at Superhero Escapes as it opens and shuts. Well, how about that? Nightbat kept his word. But if I'm being real, Adam has just as much reason for pretending this never happened as I do. The thought makes me feel... sad.

I walk the two blocks to the back of the gym, take out my whip, loop it around the branch of the tree on the yoga patio, and scamper up the block wall. I sit on that wall long enough to make sure no one is watching before I pull off my cowl and my gloves and toss them down. I unlace my boots and unzip my corset and toss them down to the pile below. Black vinyl is certainly a strange getup for yoga, but if you were tired and bleary-eyed, I just might pass as a late-night yogi at the twenty-four-hour gym. At least this is what I tell myself as I collect my effects and dart toward the women's locker room.

I strip, shove my costume into my bag, don my flip-flops, and jump into my steaming-hot shower. The water skids over me, and I hiss in both pain and embarrassment.

What the fudge kind of answer did I give Nightbat Adam? I dress up as Catstrike so I can duck into dark alleyways for furtive make-out sessions with similarly costumed men where the majority of the kisses involve tongue baths?

My skin turns lobster shades of red. Adam is probably right now disinfecting his face. I grab my face and moan at the idiocy of my life choices.

But wait a hot second. Adam is just as guilty of gut-wrenching embarrassment. He wanted me. He was waiting for me.

I pump the dispenser on the wall until pink soap pools in my hands. I'm out of shampoo, and this will have to do.

Nightbat Adam wanted me. What does that even mean? He wanted the vinyl and claws? Or does he have some sort of fetish over the secret-identity angle? I lather the soap into my hair. I wish the water ran hotter.

Maybe Adam just wanted a no-strings, tonight-only make-out session with the craziest, hottest of hot messes at the party?

He said I was what he was looking for.

Well, not in so many words.

I stare at the water pooling down the drain. An awful thought hits me. Maybe it wasn't Adam in the bat suit. He can't say anything even close to what Nightbat said to me while I'm his employee, right? Not if he doesn't want to be sued. Besides, Adam isn't the cosplaying type. The nights he's managing the escape room, he never wears a costume. He sports an ID badge that says Deputy Chief Eden, when he remembers, but wearing a lanyard doesn't count as cosplay.

But I wouldn't have kissed Nightbat if I wasn't sure he was Adam. Oh goldfish. I grab my head and groan as water beats against my back. I didn't kiss. I licked. What kind of insane person licks another person's face?

Fudge, I wish this gym had a pool. I towel off, wrestle into my workout clothes, and grab my hoodie. I'll row for the rest of my life if it means I can live this down.

CHAPTER TEN

It's Tuesday night, and I am at Gwen's place in Bird Rock, telling her everything. Well, almost everything.

Gwen blows her mint-green nails dry. "What I want to know is, is Nightbat a good kisser?"

"I don't know. I didn't really give him a chance." I pick through Gwen's collection of nail polish and settle on an elegant light pink. "He was certainly a willing kisser." I wince. I can't bring myself to tell Gwen about the feline nature of my Nightbat encounter. "I walked away before it escalated."

"Moron."

I roll my eyes. "Speed bumps, remember? How are things between you and Tony? Are you on again or off again?"

"Off again, which is why I'm so mad at you." Gwen throws a pillow at my head. "How can I live vicariously if there is nothing to live vicariously for?"

"Can you stop with the pillows? You're going to ruin my mani." My fingernail stubs look almost pretty in the subtle shade.

Gwen walks on her heels to the kitchen and grabs a Diet Coke. "Kind of surprised Adam cosplays, actually."

"If it was him," I mutter.

Gwen slams her fridge door shut. "What? It might *not* have been him?"

"I don't know. I mean, I think so. I thought so. I don't know."

"Woman, you are playing with fire." But she's not mad. She's more marveled. Which is kind of funny.

I giggle in spite of myself and speed bumps. It's not easy to surprise Gwen.

She clinks her can open. "*If* it was Adam, you know he went out and found a '90s-era Nightbat suit just so he could match you."

"Ha-ha," I deadpan.

Gwen flops down on her sofa. "And then he spent all night hiding, watching you work, waiting to put his carefully-crafted plan into action."

"You're making him sound more than a little creepy now."

"And now that he has, he's spent the last three days sick in bed because he can't puzzle out if you know it was him or not."

I laugh and grab my head as if I have the worst case of brain freeze and do my best imitation of the Nightbat voice. "But if she knew it was me and kissed me, does that mean..."

Gwen nearly sprays her Diet Coke, she's laughing so hard. "Does she like me for me, or does she like me for Nightbat?"

She sounds more like a caveman than Nightbat. I laugh until my sides ache. "Are you sure it is necessary to paint your nails before the first day of class even if you're only taking one class?"

Gwen throws another pillow at my head.

"Again with the pillows?" I say, ducking.

"You told me you were taking two Open University classes. Did you chicken out?" Gwen demands.

The smell of the nail polish makes me dizzy. Or maybe it's the last-night-of-summer jitters. "No. But online courses don't really count. I'm only going to campus one day a week."

"Online courses do count, dummy. And yes, I'm sure that painting your nails is absolutely necessary." Gwen beckons me over to inspect my work. "You have to start the new school year off right." She grabs a wooden dowel, twists cotton around it, dunks it in acetone, and deftly swipes at my cuticles until they are lacquer free. "Don't suppose there's any chance I can persuade you to wear something other than a hoodie?"

"Nope."

She blows on one of my nails. "We'll take what we can get."

Gwen isn't the only one concerned about my wardrobe choice.

"Is that what you're wearing?" my mom asks the next day, minutes before my first (again) day of college departure. A frown tugs her lips down. Her eyebrows knit together. She is a portrait of dismay.

I look down at my slouchy jeans and old Padres hoodie. "What's wrong with it?"

"Honey, I know you've been self-conscious about your figure ever since you gained that sophomore fifteen before your wedding—"

"Mom, please!" I yell. "I'm going to be late."

"But you are such a beautiful girl, and you've worked so hard at the gym. You don't have to hide in these oversized, old clothes."

"Bye, Mom. Love you." The words come forcefully before I am out the door, keys in hand. It's nice of Mom to let me borrow her car, but if the true cost is a monitoring of my wardrobe choices before class, I'm going to need to budget more money for Lyfts. If only the trolley were done by now.

Lucky for me, traffic isn't yet snarled. I've got more on my mind than just reacclimating to student life. Gone are the days when all I had to worry about were academics. Running your tush off and working two jobs will do that. Especially if one of the jobs has you dressing up in a catsuit and kissing strange men in dark alleys. Yeah, I'm still chewing on that. Maybe it doesn't count. Maybe it was a mistake. Maybe it is still fun to think about.

I arrive at SDSU and find my way to the Nasatir lecture hall, where I choose a seat at the top in the very back.

Minutes later, a cliché of a college professor walks in—horn-rimmed glasses, white hair, bow tie. If it were cold outside, I'm sure he'd be wearing a tweed jacket with patches on the elbows, but September is the hottest month in San Diego. Professor Burnbalm opens up a PowerPoint. His name and face illuminate the giant white screen. The professor is flanked by a row of what I guess are his graduate students. I'm glad I'm sitting in the back where no one can see my lip quiver. I focus hard on not crying by twisting Dad's old wedding band around and around on my thumb. It's too loose, but I can't stomach the idea of having it resized.

I had no idea I was going to be this emotional. The last time I sat at one of these desks... my life was ending.

Thankfully, life is different now. I'm at a different school. I'm not married, or about to be married. True, I am divorced, but no one on this campus knows that. I work at PB's Fit Gym 24. I have already defaulted on student loans for an education I haven't finished. I have a second job playing Catstrike in Adam McKinney's superhero-themed escape rooms.

And then, as if I conjured him up, here stands Adam McKinney in front of the lecture hall. That shock stops my weepiness cold.

What the fudge?

I grip the strings of my hoodie tightly. I blink again as I slouch lower in my chair. Oh my fudge.

"Afternoon," Adam says. "Sorry I'm late, Professor."

The professor waves his hand in one of those no-worries gestures but insists that Adam introduce himself.

Adam slides one of his hands through his dark blond hair. "I'm Adam McKinney. I did an internship this summer with Halifax Sisters. I've got one more semester left in my MBA. I'm writing a thesis on entertainment-driven consumerism, specifically the intersection of superhero pop culture, merchandising, and experiential entertainment."

My jaw is practically unhinged from the rest of me. Holy smarty-McSmarty-pants, Nightbat.

Dr. Burnbalm interjects, "Adam is being modest. He's also an entrepreneur and the only undergrad in the history of our department to attempt a raspberry blancmange at the annual bake-off."

A whoop sounds from a girl two rows in front.

Adam laughs. "'Attempt' being the operative word."

"Yes, we take our potlucks very seriously in the Econ Department. My Victoria sponge is responsible for half the talent you see up here." Dr. Burnbalm gestures to his TAs and garners modest chuckles from my fellow students. "Adam is one of the TAs for this class and will be heading up the Friday morning lab. Make good use of him."

"Early and often," another TA says.

"Easy," Adam says good-naturedly.

More TAs introduce themselves. Meanwhile, my jaw continues to sway. How is this happening?

"All right. For a class of this size, we're going to assign you all TAs." Professor Burnbalm clicks to the next slide. The alphabet is fragmented on the screen above. He clears his throat. "We thought it would be best if we use the rest of this lecture for you to get to know your TAs as they explain the course requirements, assignments, and grading system of Econ 101."

I can't decide what I want more—for Adam to be my TA, or for him to not be my TA. I can't bring myself to glance back up at the screen and learn my fate.

"Last names ending in J through N to the back of the hall," Adam yells, pointing to my corner of the lecture hall.

Holy fudge-covered goldfish. M comes before N. What's my last name? Miller? Shirley Temples. I pull my hoodie up and bury my face in my sleeve.

"Hey, Hoodie, wake up." Adam is inches from me. Holy empty chair, Nightbat. He's taken the seat right next to mine. I wish I wore five hoodies. The cluster of students now around me could not have filled in the seat next to me?

"So, J through N," Adam begins with a smile. "I've already been introduced. But you, of course, haven't. Let's go around the huddle. Tell us your name, major, and what you did this weekend."

"You go first," a pretty brunette in eyelet shorts says to Adam. Fudge, but her legs must be as long as my entire body.

"Again?" There's a laugh threaded through Adam's voice. He passes out the syllabus. "Sure. I'm Adam. I graduated with a major in economics two years ago. I'm getting my MBA."

"What did you do this weekend?" Long Legs asks, and I swear her legs grew longer as she spoke.

Say it. Say you went to your own escape room dressed as Nightbat and snogged Catstrike. I'm melting with embarrassment, like plewds of sweat are stippling my forehead over an entire tier of palpable mortification, but I keep my eyes on Adam.

"I was in LA," he says. "Meeting up with some of the contacts I made during my internship this summer. You next, Hoodie."

Goldfish, who the heck did I kiss in a dark alley?

I pull down my hood sheepishly. "Hi," I squeak. "I'm Sarah Miller. I'm a business major. I worked this weekend."

"Where do you work?" Long Legs asks. Jeez, she's pushy.

"I—" I falter. In a parallel universe, I say it. *I work for Adam, actually. In fact, why don't we talk to the professor now, because you probably shouldn't TA one of your employees? And by the way, did you come down late Saturday to catch the last round of escapes? Because I made out with a Nightbat who I would have sworn was you.*

"I work at Fit Gym 24," I mumble.

Long Legs snorts.

"Yeah? Do you teach classes?" Adam asks good-naturedly.

"I mostly staff the Kids Club."

"Ouch," Long Legs murmurs.

I text Gwen in my Lyft to work.

Me: I've hit a massive speed bump. Like, caught air and landed in a ditch on the side of the road. Adam is my TA. I'm never going back.

Gwen: WHAT? What do you mean you're not going back?

Me: I don't know how it could be any worse. He doesn't recognize me. I probably kissed a married pervert of a man last Saturday night. I've got a loser nickname.

Gwen: What's your loser nickname?

My cheeks flush, and I have to do a face palm.

Me: He called me Hoodie.

Gwen: Oh, babe. That's adorable. They only give you nicknames if they love you.

Me: How can he love me? He's only just met me. And I'm like worse than a second-class citizen. He's my TA!

Gwen: He's a student. You're a student. I really don't see the problem.

Me: You don't fall for someone you TA.

Gwen: Did you spend the first twenty-two years of your life under a rock? Have you never heard of hot-for-teacher fantasies? Did you even have sex with your ex-husband?

Me: Of course we had sex. He knocked me up. Shotgun wedding. Remember?

Gwen: But after that?

Me: He said having sex with a pregnant woman was gross. So, no.

Gwen's texting goes super quiet. I know she's trying to think of how to even respond to that.

Gwen: Oh, Saire.

She adds an emoji with a single tear.

On my run home after my shift at the gym, I am able to get a grip on the situation. Yeah, Adam being my TA is a speed bump, but I am not going to stop attending class because of him. I'll keep going. We don't know each other outside of Superhero Escapes. Pretty face aside—and goldfish yes, he has one—he is just a guy paying for school like everyone else. Everyone TAs at some point. He happens to be mine. It's no big deal. I've got this. I'm not messing around.

CHAPTER ELEVEN

I remember enough of my previous college career to know that the labs are not optional but essential. My other classmates bemoan the early lab hours, but I am there that first Friday at seven a.m., ready with a draft of my essay and two of my homework problems that made absolutely no sense.

Adam is there, too, maybe not quite as ready as I am. Honestly, he looks like he just climbed out of bed. His eyes have that soft focus to them, and goldfish, they're a pretty shade—like the ocean on a gray morning. "Hey, Hoodie," Adam says, punching in the code to the lab door.

"Good morning, Adam."

A smile twitches up a corner of his mouth. Is he pleased that I remembered his name? "Just rolled out of bed in time for lab hours?" he asks.

"I've been up since four, thanks."

He chokes slightly on his coffee. "What on earth have you been doing since four a.m.?"

"HIIT. Sprints, mostly. I like to run when I can't sleep. Did you roll out of bed just in time for lab hours?"

He stops sipping his coffee. "You don't strike me as a runner."

I bristle and drop my book bag to the floor with a thud. "What the fudge is that supposed to mean?"

"Whoa, calm down. You want to talk economics?"

"I want you to read my essay." I pull out my copy.

"I don't proofread essays," Adam says. And he's cockier in real life than when I see him at the escape room. Is that because of stress? But how is TAing more stressful than running a business? Unless...

"Why? No one else is here yet." It's just me, Adam, and the fluorescent lights down here in the econ lab.

"Fine." He grabs my essay and manages to dribble coffee on the first page. Yeah, we're off to a great TA-student start. "This reads like an email."

"Can you give me some actionable feedback?"

He reads on. He reads the entire essay before handing it back to me. "It's good. Your tone strikes me as being"—he seems to be sifting through his thoughts for just the right word—"informal. I mean, it makes it all very accessible." He looks at me over the top of his coffee cup again. His gaze wavers. "But that's not always the idea in academia."

"You want me to change my tone?" More formal. Okay, that's fair feedback. Maybe this will work, him being my TA. I decide to dial it down. Nobody's their best first thing in the morning, right? I scribble a note in my magenta-sparkled notebook. It has a unicorn and the words *Believe in your dreams* on the front. It was a gift from Gwen, and I use it ironically.

"Yes. No. If you want." Adam sighs. "It's a solid essay." He rubs the back of his neck. "High-intensity interval training, huh?"

"Clears the mind," I say.

"You wrote this essay afterward?"

"I revised it."

He swallows, and I swear the negative space between us radiates for a moment with stippling. "Do you have any other questions?"

"Plenty," I say.

He does a double take.

I stare back at him. Goldfish, his eyes. And a white T-shirt again. Yum. I feel like I am actively resisting a magnetic field. I've been this close to Adam before, but not in my real skin. There's always been my Catstrike outfit between us. Without a mask on... I don't know. It feels oddly intimate. Just him, me, and the hum of the fluorescent lights.

Another student walks into the lab, and the spell breaks. Not that there was any magic in the first place.

Adam rises—well, he digs his knee into the table, winces, and then hobbles upright. "Cool. Brenda will be in soon. She's great with, erm, questions."

For the rest of the lab, I focus on the academics. I'm making this new beginning happen, no matter what. And Brenda does turn out to be great with, erm, questions—informative, succinct, even if she is a little brusque.

Later that day, actually all through my shift at the gym, I let myself go back and chew on what Adam said. What did he mean I don't look like a runner? Was it the hoodie?

Tony is typing into his computer at the front desk when I decide I'm done chewing. "Why don't I look like a runner?" I demand, slamming my hands on the counter.

Tony startles. "Are you asking me?"

A groan escapes me. "This guy—"

Before I can get another word out, Tony has a hand up. "No," he says. "No, don't bother explaining. I'm not getting involved with any personal drama. I have no opinion."

"But what am I supposed to do?"

"I don't know," Tony says, grabbing his empty titanium water jug. Seriously, the amount of water this man drinks. "Circle back to the source," he mumbles. "Just leave me out of it."

"Thanks, Tony."

It's a slow day. It's not much of an excuse, but I reach for my phone all the same. I double- and triple-check that my email is sending from my school account and not from the one connected to my Venmo Sabine Kennedy alias.

SarahMiller@sdsu.student
    to AdamMcKinney@sdsu.student
    Dear Adam,
    What do you mean I don't look like a runner?
    Sarah aka Hoodie

It's minutes before my phone buzzes with a new email notification.

AdamMcKinney@sdsu.student
    to SarahMiller@sdsu.student
    Dear Hoodie,
    Runners don't wear hoodies unless they are Rocky Balboa. And then they're actually boxers.
    Adam aka Your TA

I send the next email without thinking.

SarahMiller@sdsu.student
    to AdamMcKinney@sdsu.student
    Dear High-and-Mighty Adam aka My TA,
    This runner wears hoodies. They come in handy when you run at four in the morning and it's cold

outside. **Why don't you meet me for a run next Friday before lab, and I can show you what I mean?**

Sarah, the runner who wears a hoodie

It's not even two minutes before I get the next email.

AdamMcKinney@sdsu.student

to SarahMiller@sdsu.student

Dear Hoodie,

No, thanks. I'll be sleeping then. Too bad you can't do the same. Why don't we go for a run after lab, and you can not wear your boyfriend's ratty old hoodie, and you'll see what I mean?

Adam aka Your TA

I'm not even pretending to work anymore. I'm so enraged.

SarahMiller@sdsu.student

to AdamMcKinney@sdsu.student

Dear Adam,

It's not my boyfriend's hoodie. It was my dad's. Fudge you. I'll see you for that run, and we'll see who's a real runner.

Sarah

My phone buzzes almost as soon as I put it down.

· · ·

AdamMcKinney@sdsu.student

   to SarahMiller@sdsu.student

   Jeez, Sarah,

   I'm sorry. Now would you calm down and please never wear that ratty hoodie again?

   Adam, who will probably never be a TA again after these emails

I was an idiot and forwarded every email to Gwen in real time.

   Gwen: DON'T RESPOND! For the love of all the swears, DON'T RESPOND!

Gwen is, of course, right.

   Adam is a no-show at the escape room this weekend.

   But after Wednesday's lecture, another email pings in my inbox.

AdamMcKinney@sdsu.student

   to SarahMiller@sdsu.student

   Dear Sarah,

   Are we still on for that run after lab on Friday?

   Adam

"Can he do that?" I ask Gwen when I see her at the gym. "Can he seriously go for a run with me?"

   "You tell me. You're the one who made all the rules about speed bumps," Gwen shoots back. She's working hard on the Jacob's Ladder Climb.

   "Isn't there an ethical dilemma?"

"Ethics went out the door the minute you didn't tell him you're the chick who works for him in a catsuit, IMO."

She is right.

"So do I wear the hoodie?"

"You did grow up under a rock. Yeah. You wear the hoodie. And then you let him watch you take it off after the run."

"I have to do more HIIT. You're fast, Hoodie." Adam collapses on the intramural field.

"I can't believe you came with me," I say, smiling. Sweat runs all over me. I peel off my hoodie and toss it on the grass.

Adam whimpers. "Clearly, you don't work just the Kids Club at your gym. Which Fit Gym 24 is it? I'll come, and you can train me."

"Nice." I sit next to him and stretch out my legs. "But I'm not a trainer."

"Perfect, then I don't have to pay you." He throws an arm over his head but winces with the movement.

"You gotta stretch it out, Adam. You're going to hurt all over if you don't."

"Too late." He groans. "So come on. Which one is it? It's gotta be somewhere local."

"How would it look if my TA turned up at my gym?" I'm enjoying this.

"It'd probably look like a coincidence. La Jolla? Fashion Valley? Hillcrest?"

I lie down to stretch out my back. "Pacific Beach."

"No way. My escape room is in PB. Have you been?"

"Which one is it?"

He tries to catch his breath. "Superhero Escapes."

"Like Cicada-bro?" This is fun.

He gets that pained expression whenever anyone brings up

Amaze Comics. "Nightbat, Fem Fantastic, Magnificent Man. You should come."

I move into a downward dog to hide my smug smile. "I usually work nights."

"Then I should come visit you. Do you work weekends?"

I can't help but smile. He's cute when he's panting. "Yeah." Oh swear words. So many swear words. I answered without thinking. I can't have Adam come visit me at the gym when I'm working at his escape room. He's smart enough to start putting it together.

I reach for my hoodie. "Weekends are too unpredictable. Either we're mobbed, or we're empty. Either way, you'd get me in trouble."

"How could I get you into trouble?" We walk back to the lab, where Adam punches in the code to unlock the door.

"You'd monopolize my time, and it would be painfully obvious to my manager. Come on a Tuesday. It's always steady on Tuesday. I'll get you on track so you don't look like such a sissy the next time you say a girl can't run."

"That's not what I said." Adam's eyes lock with mine. "And I'm not a sissy."

"Says the man who couldn't keep up with me when we were running the bleachers."

He flashes me a smile that I return before mouthing, "Sissy," one more time. I slip my hoodie on, grab my book bag and water bottle, and leave.

I usually really look forward to my Friday and Saturday cosplay nights, but now I'm more excited for my evening shift at the gym on Tuesday.

But Adam doesn't come Tuesday. He doesn't come in at all. I know. I check the guest logs.

And I am humiliated. What was I doing? Flirting? Dating? I've gotten so used to not counting my time in cosplay against my rules that I carried some of that impunity over into real life. I am sickened that I'd jettison my no-speed-bump plan so easily.

I double down on my no-speed-bump rule.

I get to class seconds before the bell rings—in my hoodie, no less —vanish during the breaks, and leave immediately when the lecture is over. I can't even look in Adam's direction. And rather than attend another early-morning Friday lab, I email Brenda and ask for clarification on the problem that I need to double-check.

Economics isn't complicated.

Then an email from Dr. Burnbalm drops in my in-box.

CHAPTER TWELVE

Dr. Burnbalm rises when I tap on his door. "Sarah, come on in. I was hoping you'd be able to stop by today. You know Brenda?" He sweeps his hand to gesture toward Brenda, one of his graduate students. She has jet-black hair and a penchant for piercings.

"Have a seat," Dr. Burnbalm says.

I do, but I cannot squelch my nerves. Professors don't send out personal emails inviting undergrads to office hours. Most of my professors up to this point in my academic career haven't even been in their offices for office hours.

"How's your semester going?" Dr. Burnbalm asks, smiling widely. "You're an Open University student?"

"Yeah, hoping to transfer." My hands are sweaty, and I hide them inside the sleeves of my hoodie.

"You adjusting okay? Ocean air and all that?"

"Yeah, I grew up here." I leave out the part about how I wish I'd never left for Michigan State.

Professor Burnbalm clears his throat. "I'm going to let Brenda take the lead here since she's head TA."

Brenda, who seems to prefer dressing all in black and probably has been to every grunge concert in San Diego since birth, gives me a you-sad-stupid-undergrad face. "As you know, Econ 101 is graded on a curve." She waves a hand quickly. "We've got a classic conflict of interest, as I'm sure you are aware of."

I stare back. I blink. "Conflict of interest?" Is this because I failed my last econ class so spectacularly? "I know my transcript doesn't change until I pass this class, but I'm okay with that." I'm okay with any second chance. "I don't plan on failing twice."

Professor Burnbalm looks up from his computer. His glasses reflect back what looks like the *Mississippi Bake-Off* show's website. "It's not your transcript, Sarah," he says gently. He grabs his silent phone. "I have to take this call. Excuse me, please."

Brenda moves into Dr. Burnbalm's chair before the door closes. "We're talking about your relationship with Adam McKinney," she says, not at all gently. Bluntly. Brenda is the queen of blunt.

I feel myself go bright red. Juice-fast, beets-for-breakfast bright red. I try to swallow, but my throat is dry. "What relationship?" Gold-fish. If the next word out of her mouth is *cat*, I am going to change my name, change my major, dye my hair, and run for the next three weeks straight.

"Your flirtation," Brenda clarifies.

Shirley Temples. I blink. "My flirtation?"

"Since he is your TA and is responsible for not only assisting you in learning the material, but also helping to assess your efforts, any sort of nonprofessional relationship creates a conflict of interest for you both. In other words, you have an unfair advantage and are screwing everyone else with a crappier grade. Aren't curves fun?" Queen of Bluntness is actually saying these words. I'm not hallu-cinating.

I manage to speak at last. "I thought Professor Burnbalm did the grading?"

"A class of this size?" Brenda snorts. "Get real." She leans forward, her arms clasped comfortably on Dr. Burnbalm's desk. "We saw all the hoodie emails."

"Those emails were harmless." And embarrassing.

"We've had a complaint from another student that you stripped in front of Adam during Friday lab hours."

Fudge brownies. "I took off my hoodie outside after a run. I had a top on underneath. I'm sorry if removing outerwear is against the Econ 101 syllabus." I am about to mention that this happened after lab hours ended, but I shut my mouth. This couldn't be more humiliating. Maybe if I was wearing the catsuit.

I try hard not to lose it and burst into tears. "I'm sorry if I caused offense to Adam, or to the other TAs, or any of my fellow students."

"That's nice, Sarah. But it doesn't change the conflict of interest," Blunt Brenda says.

Oh goldfish. My heart races. "How do we fix that?"

"You could drop the class," Brenda suggests. "Start fresh next semester."

My heart thuds fast inside me. I can't drop out of school over another stupid boy. It took everything I had and then some to get back to this point. "Please, there's got to be another option."

"Drop the class."

"No," I whimper. "I can't drop the class."

Brenda, who seems altogether too happy with my panic-stricken face, rolls her eyes. She drums her fingers on the desk, and I feel cornered and terrified.

"Please," I beg.

A smile surfaces on Brenda's dark purple-stained lips. "We have openings in the Tuesday-Thursday section. I'd be your TA, and you wouldn't be associating with Adam any further."

I can tell I'm past beet red. I've drifted into pasty, almond milk territory. I swallow. "Can't I just switch to a different TA in the Wednesday afternoon section? I can't miss two days of work every week." Scheduling at work is difficult enough these days with me requesting every Friday and Saturday night off. You can volunteer for the early mornings and afternoons only so often before everyone gets wise. And then jealous. Plus, I don't know if I can financially swing another missed shift.

"Sarah..." Brenda butts into my thoughts. "I'm trying to moderate a situation that could quickly escalate into allegations of harassment—"

"Because we went for a run together after lab? Adam could have said no."

Brenda folds her arms across her chest. "He felt he couldn't when you brought up your late father."

Holy fudge. I feel ill. Worse than ill. I'm scared. I didn't trap Adam into a run, but is that how he felt? "This is a nightmare. Fine, transfer me to the Tuesday-Thursday section." I wince. "What about Friday labs?"

"I could never tell a student they are not welcome at Friday labs. However, as head TA, I suggest that you make use of the last twenty minutes of lab hours to avoid any awkwardness."

That's right. Adam mentioned needing to head out early on most Fridays for a lecture or something. Still, twenty minutes isn't going to be much help. "Are there any other lab hours?"

"No." Brenda preens like a peacock. A goth, blunt peacock— okay, maybe peacock was the wrong analogy. But she is smug as ever.

I swallow and collect my things. "This is all a really big misunder- standing." I am trying desperately not to cry, which means tears are brimming in my eyes and threatening to overflow down my cheeks. If I bite my tongue really hard, will the tears stay put? "I never meant to make anyone feel uncomfortable, and I definitely didn't mean—I didn't want..." But I can't say the words. I did mean to flirt. I *did*, past tense, have intentions. Playful, harmless intentions. I should have stopped, because I was clearly headed for a speed bump. When will I grow up? "Thank you for helping me transfer sections. I'm glad I don't have to start Econ 101 over again."

"About that," she says. "We feel—"

"Who is we?" I ask.

"The TAs. Dr. Burnbalm too. We feel it is important to eliminate even the hint of bias or favoritism that may have played into your assessments when Adam was your TA. It would be unfair to the other students not to. All the assignments affect the curve, after all." Brenda shifts comfortably in the professor's chair. "We'd like you to resubmit your course work from weeks one, two, and three. Please use different topics and essays, as we understand that Adam provided substantial feedback—"

Substantial feedback?! My legs itch for a run. My head pounds with the need of it. I have to speak quickly to avoid sobbing in front of my new TA. "Yeah. Um. Yeah. That seems fair. How long do I have to do over the first three weeks of my assignments and turn them in?"

"You can bring them to me at lab hours on Friday."

"This Friday? Two days from now?"

Brenda smiles.

A knock at the open door is accompanied by the lean silhouette of a man in a white-T-shirt and jeans. Oh no. "Dr. Burnbalm, do you have time to look at my data sets—" Adam looks up from his stack of papers and sees me—hoodie-clad, red eyes, tear-streaked cheeks—and goes completely pale.

I shouldn't have turned to look. I should have just cowered in my chair.

"Dr. Burnbalm headed out to take a phone call," Brenda says. By the glint in her eyes, you'd think she was giving a victory speech.

Adam wavers for a minute before disappearing down the hall.

"Any questions, Sarah?" Brenda says dismissively.

I shake my head and swipe at the tear that slides down my cheek.

She leans back in the chair. "See you Thursday, then."

CHAPTER THIRTEEN

"So we hate Adam now?" Gwen says.

"Passionately," I say, picking my head up from my notebook. Rewriting miserable essays to even more miserable Econ 101 prompts is the worst. Doing it in long hand, because the only computer you have access to is being monopolized by your mom as she prepares for parent-teacher conference week, is insane. Gwen said she'd let me borrow hers if she had one. I took her up on the offer to study at her place at least.

"Is it the sexy hate or the disgusted hate?" Gwen asks.

I sniffle. "What's the difference?"

"Sexy hate is like Demi Lovato's sorry-not-sorry 'I'm going to do my best to make sure you never forget how bad you want me. You're going to want me always. I'll enjoy watching you suffer.' If not Demi, then Musetta and her 'Quando m'en Vo' from *La bohème*."

"What?"

"Here." Gwen casts an opera scene from her phone to her TV. "Laura Giordano's version is my favorite."

"Disgust hate," Gwen continues while the aria plays in the background, "is like literally throwing up on him if he were ever to kiss you again. That's the acute case. It dulls into just wishing he no longer existed and peters out into never wanting to see him again."

"Sexy hate means wanting to see him again?" I clarify. The beautiful woman on the TV is standing on the counter of a bar and singing opera to an enthralled crowd.

"Yeah, it means wanting to confront him with what an epic cock-up he made and knowing he'll regret it every time your paths cross."

"I disgust-hate my ex," I say. Truer words were never spoken.

"Yeah, me too. But Adam?" Gwen asks. The aria is coming to a gorgeous climax.

I look up from my paper and mouth, "Help me." Gwen scoots my books out of the way and places a pint of rocky road ice cream in front of me.

"Adam lives and breathes #sorrynotsorry." I groan, reaching for the spoon she offers me. "My life is getting really complicated."

By some miracle, I manage to write and type three essays with different sources on efficiency, equality, and incentives. I have to use the computer and printer at the gym to print them out. It helps that Gwen came with me when I asked Tony for the favor.

The Santa Ana winds are bumping the temperatures into record-breaking territory. And while a hoodie would be comforting, it would also be ridiculously hot. I settle on a white dress that appeared in my closet after one of my mom's thrifting excursions. Nothing says *I've been treated unfairly* like a cutesy white sundress. It is demure and sweet and the furthest thing I have from a Scarlett O'Hara red-sequined number, black catsuit, and well... hoodies.

Clearly, my hoodie days are over if I want to fly under the radar.

It still bugs me that Adam shared those emails with everyone. Why couldn't he have just talked to me? Okay, maybe that is hypocritical. But still.

I have to park in a different lot and beat an entirely different path to lab hours. Arriving bright and early on Friday mornings meant getting a good parking space. Coming during the peak of morning rush means wasting time circling for a parking space or walking miles. I'd run, but then I'd risk being mistaken for a slut if I show up again in athletic wear.

I trudge down an unfamiliar set of stairs to the basement of the econ building. As I make my way down the bleak corridor with buzzing lights, I hear shouting coming from an open office door, and it takes me a moment to realize the voices are familiar.

"What the hell, Brenda?" Adam shouts. "She didn't do anything wrong! She didn't change a word of her essays, despite my one meaningless comment. Why would you make her redo all her work?"

"You're lucky I stepped in to handle this," Brenda screeches. She sounds completely pissed.

"Lucky? Lucky? You could have ruined her life. You could have gotten her expelled!" Adam sounds scary levels of angry. Rabid animals come to mind.

"You could have lost Dr. Burnbalm as your chair for something this stupid."

I lean against the wall outside the office door, well out of sight. Not that it matters. "I said I would handle it," Adam says. It sounds like he's pacing now.

"Handle it how? By volunteering to be the first one here on Fridays so you can be alone with her?"

"I get here early because I have to leave early for my elective—"

"So how do you explain the nonstop staring during lecture? People were noticing."

"And by 'people,' you mean you. I told you. I have a girlfriend."

Girlfriend?! My mouth is gaping open. Shock much?

"Oh, yeah. The Comic-Con princess—"

Oh my fudging goldfish. Adam told Brenda that I was his girlfriend? I've heard enough. "Hey," I say, knocking pointedly on the office door.

Adam and Brenda both look up like the guilty little monsters they are. Brenda slouches down in her office chair. It's her turn to go red, and it doesn't go well with all the black. Adam, who was slumped against the office wall, straightens and pulls his hand out of his hair. He must have been grabbing fistfuls of it while he was stomping back and forth, because it is sticking straight up.

"Brenda, I'm glad I caught you." She said she'd be in the lab, but here she is in the graduate students' office. With Adam. Yelling about me. "I have my course work you said you wanted redone."

"You could have emailed it to me." Brenda stares at her computer screen, which she then turns on.

I try hard to remain civil. "I'll remember that from now on."

"I'm going to have to mark this as late." Brenda glances up with an arched eyebrow. "The assignments were due last week and the week before, respectively."

She has to be kidding, but when her lips purse with extra bitchiness, something fuses hard and fast inside me. "Hmm. Well, obviously, that is something the two of you need to discuss, as well as the nature of your"—I gesture between them—"*relationship*. I wonder if you've been in yet to see Professor Burnbalm. He seems preoccupied lately with the idea that everyone in the Econ Department is being strictly professional."

I slam my folder of essays and rewritten homework questions on the closest desk. "Or maybe I should give him a call now, and we can hash this all out together." Brenda looks like she might be physically ill. I'm too mad to hazard a glance at Adam. "Brenda, Adam." I sound like my mom chiding naughty schoolchildren. "Can you please leave me out of your Shirley Temples the next time you want a go at each other?"

"Sarah," Adam calls as I turn to leave.

I turn around and stare him into silence. I then round on Brenda. "If you for one minute think you're going to screw me with a B grade, you've got another thing coming, Brenda. You're going to have every single one of your fudge brownie TAs give me a blind score on my essays from here on out to make sure that no bias is creeping into my grade or throwing off the sanctity of your beloved curve. Have fun explaining that one."

I snap my bag closed and head back up the basement stairs.

Outside, the dry Santa Ana winds catch my skirt, whip my hair back, and feel good for once.

"Sarah!" Adam jogs toward me, breathless, face flushed. Goldfish, he looks good. I mean... if I was looking.

"I'm not supposed to talk to you. And I'm not about to rewrite another essay on Adam Smith."

"I just—"

I hold up a hand. "Why don't you not and save me some trouble?" I slip on my sunglasses and walk away. Okay. Maybe I saunter just a little.

CHAPTER FOURTEEN

"Tony," I say in the nicest, most respectful voice I can muster. "I have a favor to ask."

"As long as it's not a scheduling favor." He doesn't look up from his computer.

Shirley Temples. I should have asked Gwen if they were on again or off again before I attempted to ask for another two scheduling miracles.

"I had to change my econ class to Tuesday and Thursday afternoons."

Tony groans.

"My Wednesdays are free. All of them. Every last bit of them. I can swap someone a Wednesday for a Tuesday, right?"

"Sure." Tony pulls up the schedule with feigned patience.

"That just leaves the question of a Thursday shift, yeah?"

"Let's just see who I can switch you with. You want to take Kate's Saturday night shift?"

I press my lips together. "Is there anything else?"

His patience is wearing. I can tell by how tightly he grips his mouse. "How about Henry's Friday night?"

"I'll do any graveyard. Any other morning or afternoon. Any other night except—"

"Sarah, I want to help you out. And I definitely will do my best to make sure you make your study groups and classes, but my hands are tied this month. I'm already getting enough flack from the rest of the crew as it is for never scheduling you Friday and Saturday nights. You know what everyone is saying, right?"

"They're saying that my study group is mighty convenient."

"Mighty too convenient."

I wince. "Which would make me more friends?"

"Friday night."

Fine. "I'll take it." I don't know how I'll afford my phone bill, but I'll take it.

Sometimes I wonder, mainly when I'm delirious after sixteen-mile runs, if I should wear a part of my suit when I call Adam about Catstrike stuff. Standing in my yoga pants and Lululemon top and purring into the phone seems... wrong. Fun, but wrong, I think, licking the chocolate amaretto gelato off my spoon. Mom's been making vegan ice cream every night since the Santa Anas started.

"Sabine," Adam answers cautiously. Not cautiously—that's me projecting our basement-of-the-econ-building-party-with-Brenda-baggage into this phone call. He answers professionally. No bias. No feelings. No caution. All professionalism. I can be professional too.

"Adam. Things have... changed," I say suggestively in my yummiest Catstrike voice. What? I'm a professional cosplayer. Owning my character's flirtatiousness is professional in this instance.

I can hear the smile in his voice. "How so?"

"My Friday nights are no longer available."

He groans. "This is not my day."

I want to make a flirty quip about his nights but stop myself just barely. The discrete panels of my life, separated by careful margins of white gutters, are starting to bleed together. "Maybe it's time to find another Cat—"

"I need another night, Sabine. Thursday? Can you do Thursday?" He sounds slightly frantic.

I check my schedule, which Mom has on a whiteboard. "For now."

"Great. We'll start next week. I'm going to need a different costume from you on Thursdays. You ready to go camp for me? I don't care what color your hair is—"

"Okay."

"Okay, you'll do it?"

"Okay, I've got an idea."

"Will you give me a hint?"

"Maybe. If you ask nicely." I hang up before he can say another word. Shirley Temples, I have to finish my other costume.

It has been so long since I've worked a Friday night at the gym, I've forgotten how long and endless and boring it can be. I mean, working the escape room in a catsuit isn't a giggle a minute, but working with Adam... It is stupid, but the nights he manages are always fun. Not that I waver from character and not that we say all that much to each other. Goldfish, I'm sounding sad and desperate. It beats a slow night at the gym, is all.

Nathan, a co-manager, and Alice, one of the personal trainers who occasionally picks up a regular shift, are the other employees scheduled with me for the night.

"You need a break?" Nathan asks.

I twist my dad's old ring around my left thumb. "Maybe in another forty. You take yours. We got this. Right, Alice?"

Alice is with a gym member but gives me the thumbs-up.

Nathan leaves for some air and probably a cold drink. The Santa

Anas are setting records all across San Diego County. My performance polo can't wick sweat fast enough in this heat.

"Why don't you go staff the floor?" Alice says. "I can handle the front desk."

"You sure?" I ask.

"The air is better up here, and you are too young for hot flashes. I am sure. Go do some stretches and mind the cobwebs."

Alice is right. It is a tomb. The Kids Club closed for the night ages ago. Everyone is at the beach, in a pool, opening their freezer drawer for the seven hundredth Popsicle. I'd sleep in a freezer tonight, if it were an option.

I am so tense. I didn't have time to stretch after my run this morning. And more than anything, I want to stop sweating. Glancing quickly around the empty gym, I peel off my sticky polo and grab the TRX bands and lean hard into them. In my neon green sports bra, I feel mildly better. The fan oscillates air over my sweaty body. Maybe on my break, I can run down to the pier and dive into the ocean. I loop the bands onto my feet and rotate into a supported downward dog of sorts. I groan appreciatively as the stretch finally settles into my back.

Alice's signature red sneakers come into my line of sight. "Sarah, this member has some questions about the free weights."

I notice a pair of Vans sidle into view. "And those straps she's using," says a familiar voice.

I wince and freeze. More like I wince and fall on my shoulder.

"You okay?" Alice asks.

Adam helps me back to my feet before I can bark at him that I'm fine. "Yeah. I'll show Adam around."

"Oh." Alice's eyebrows dance up. "You two know each other."

Adam says "Yes" at the same time I say "Not really."

Alice nods but looks smug as she walks back to the front desk.

I grab my sweaty shirt and pull it on. Goldfish, of all the days to wear a neon sports bra. "What do you want?" I say, glaring at Adam.

Trying to glare. It's hard to glare at anyone when you know they've just seen your belly button.

Adam ignores the question. "So... you really do work here."

"Of course I work here." I refasten the straps to a higher bracket and hand them to Adam. "Take a step forward."

He does. "I came to say I'm sorry—"

"Lean back," I command, pushing his chest. "Arms straight." What is wrong with me? Why am I finding excuses to touch him?

"—and ask if you'd like to grab a drink with me after work."

It's my turn to ignore him. "Pull yourself up. Ten reps. Quick as you can."

"How about that drink?" Adam asks on rep seven of his TRX pull-ups.

"How about never?" I pull the bands and adjust them. "Side squats."

"I don't need TRX bands for squats," Adam says.

I take personal offense at that. I toss a band back and adjust the height of the single band to my size. I slip my right leg in and squat low, with my right leg swinging straight out in a perfect right angle. "You try," I say, handing him the band.

"How about a movie? Dinner? Another run?"

"Are you trying to get me expelled?"

"I'm trying to tell you that I'm no longer an Econ 101 TA. I switched with a buddy. I'm helping out with Econ 450, if you want to find me there."

I am slightly grumpy that he can do the move. Not effortlessly like me, but he can do it. "Other leg," I tell him.

"How 'bout it, Saire?"

I'm trying to process what he said. He switched sections. Did he do it for me? Did he do it to avoid further ugliness? How do I even feel about this?

"Saire?"

There is a very short list of people who call me Saire, and now Adam is on it. Goldfish, he's cute when he's struggling. "I'm working till eleven." And movies, dinners, and runs all fall under my no-speed-bumps, no-dating rules.

"Then come to my club."

"Your club? Oh right. Your superhero escape room? So I can meet your other girlfriend? The one Brenda mentioned, from Comic-Con?"

Adam's face reddens. And yeah, it could be from the second set he's just started, or I could have found his weak spot.

"Look." He pulls himself to standing. Is he really that much taller than me? I guess I've never really stood beside him without the platform heels. "I don't have a girlfriend. Brenda is just mildly annoyed that I never invited her to cosplay at my escape room. She's a megafan of the industry with a bad habit of reading other people's email and assuming the worst. I told her I met someone at Comic-Con this summer because I did, but I'm not dating her. She works for me." He pauses awkwardly. "You can ask her yourself."

"I'll pass, thanks."

"About meeting my cosplayer, or going out with me?"

"Both."

"Why?"

I glare at Adam. "Have you ever been called into your professor's office because you were accused of an inappropriate flirtation?"

Adam smiles and leans a hand against the weight set. "As a matter of fact." He's got that look again—the one-with-the-universe, cheeky confidence that makes my spine melt.

"Well," I say, trying hard not to remember running my tongue across his face. If it was even *his* face. Oh goldfish, I hope it was his face. "I wouldn't have if it wasn't for you."

"Look. I'll make a deal with you. Go on one date with me—"

"And what?" I cringe at his sales-pitch tone. It is too hot, and I am too upset to play more games. "You'll change my mind, and suddenly I won't think you're a pushy, rude, self-entitled Shirley-Temple-for-brains." I push him as hard as I dare in the chest. "Let me help you out, Adam. You're not entitled to any second chances.

You're not entitled to first chances. I don't owe you a qualified no. I don't have to give you the benefit of the doubt. And I sure don't need to spend any more one-on-one time with you to know my mind. Get. Lost." My chest rises and falls, like I'm approaching heaving-bosom territory. I somehow manage to be standing close enough to Adam to... well, close enough to feel him breathe in. Long and slow.

Nathan struts back to our corner of the free weights. "Hey, Sarah. Everything okay back here?" I swear he growls at Adam.

"Fine, Nate," I say.

"I was just leaving." Adam carefully tucks the TRX straps back into place. "Good night, Sarah. Thanks for showing me around."

Piles of raw beets and grapefruits cover the kitchen counter. Mom is doing a juice fast again. Experiments like this happen often in the summer. I wonder if all schoolteachers recover from burnout in equally interesting ways. This year, some of the experiments are bleeding into the school year.

Mom appears from behind her industrial-sized juicer. "We can't all be twenty-two with a metabolism that won't quit," she says.

Quit. The word spins circles around me. I should quit. I am in over my head. I've already sent Gwen a bunch of texts from my Sabine Kennedy number by accident. It's only a matter of time before I mix them up with Adam. And I don't want to get mixed up with him. I don't want any more speed bumps. I don't want to lose my second chance at my business degree because of a boy. Even if this boy is so much yummier than the stupid first one. No more speed bumps! No!

The fact remains: I need the Superhero Escapes side hustle. I need it now more than ever with tuition, books, and rides down to SDSU twice a week since Mom is no longer biking to work and needs her car again. I can't quit.

Mom hands me a glass of dark burgundy juice. "Try some, honey." It looks terrifying.

"No, thanks, Mom. I've got study group after class tonight and weights that won't lift themselves. Cross-training, you know?" Lies. I have a gig dressing up as Catstrike and claws I haven't yet finished sewing onto my new costume. At least the part about class is true.

Mom pours some of the juice into a glass pop-top bottle. Mom doesn't believe in plastic anymore—another summer adventure that stuck. Thank fudging goldfish, Mom is back in the classroom. I don't think I could handle any more of her summer fun. "For the road," Mom insists. "Now off you go. Don't forget your books."

I make it through class and manage to finish my costume by skipping dinner and a workout. And after a couple of hours of escapes, I am desperate enough to reach for the bottle of beet juice in the break room.

"What are you drinking?" Adam asks, shutting the door behind him. He's a stickler for maintaining the atmosphere for the customers. No behind-the-scenes glances allowed.

"The blood of my enemies," I all but growl. It's not bad, like citrus and dirt. Okay, maybe it's bad.

He pauses. "Is my blood in there?"

"Should it be?" I set the bottle down. The clink rattles off the walls in the quiet break room. "What have you done?"

His eyes wander over me. I am in my new gray suit complete with gold belt—Catstrike from *Nightbat the Animated Series* come to life. It's a campy compromise, but I get to wear my mask and head cap, which means I don't have to wear a scratchy wig over my wispy, fluffy blond hair every Thursday. There is no way I am going to show more of myself than I have to. But this costume is definitely more camp than dominatrix. #missionaccomplished.

"I don't know," Adam says, opening then slamming the fridge door. Is he annoyed that I am still wearing a cowl? "What happened to the vintage-camp idea?"

I walk over closer. This set of boots doesn't give me the same height as my other pair, but it is closer to my sweet spot. I still have a good three inches on my five-foot-five frame, which gives me a different angle to admire Adam's excellent jaw.

No, I still can't say for sure if it was him in the alley on Customer Cosplay Night, but I like to pretend it was. I run a hand confidently up Adam's right arm. "You don't like my new look?"

A gray catsuit with just a bit of sheen shows a lot more of my body's contours than my previous costume. The gold medallion belt sits low on my hips. My matte black leather gloves, tipped with black acrylic claws that, though pointed, are nothing that would scare a car-happy Camaro owner, embolden me.

"I like every square inch of you." Adam puts his hand on my waist.

I press my bright red lips to the stubble on his neck.

Adam shudders. "The square inches you're comfortable showing, that is."

He slowly brings his other hand up my arm. "What are you doing?" he asks.

I gently drag my nails across his jaw. "You need a shave. I liked you better with a clean jaw."

I have Adam pinned against the door of the break room, and I am fully prepared to have some fun. Fudge speed bumps. It's time for answers.

Adam's voice is tight. "I don't know what you're talking about, but please keep talking." His touch is light. Maybe he thinks he'll spook me if he holds me too close.

I purr in his ear. "Hmm. Dark alley. Dark night. Maybe it was someone else." I pull ever so slightly away. Do I want to kiss him? That would make sense, right? You are supposed to want to kiss people you have feelings for, and I definitely have some strong feelings for Adam. None of them bending toward the sweet, lovable, Maybell June variety. I mean, once you kiss someone, you can never unkiss them. All that first-kiss energy vanishes. And while I did enjoy whatever it was I did that night a few weeks ago, it certainly wasn't kissing. It was like Bollywood kissing. Yeah, it'll make you blush, but my lips never locked with his.

My lips brush the bottom of his ear. The fringe of his dark blond hair tickles my cheek. He swallows and shuts his eyes.

"This is messed up." Adam says the words like he is trying to convince himself. He pulls my arms away from him. Goldfish, he is pushing me away. "The new costume is great, Sabine. Really." He leaves me. I'm once again alone in the break room. And once again, I am fudging furious.

CHAPTER FIFTEEN

No one walks through life without acquiring scars. We all develop Achilles' heels. Rejection is mine. One of mine. I've got lots. Goldfish, I should see a therapist. Mom took me to one in fifth grade. The woman asked me about school and about Dad's death as Mom sat on the couch next to me and blinked fast and hard throughout the entire forty-five-minute appointment. Brent was at Judo. "It takes time," was all Dr. Branson had said. Shirley Temples, you think?

Do I want to talk about my shotgun wedding, my miscarriage, my divorce, my job at the gym, my econ class, or the fact that I want to make out with my boss while cosplaying, but never want to see him in real life? Do I want to sit on an overstuffed couch, with a box of tissues conveniently available on the coffee table, while I explain how mortifying, embarrassing, and angry being pushed away feels, even when I am parading around in a sexy superhero-fantasy costume? Do I want to explore why I am willing to even put on the mask and catsuit in the first place?

No.

Nope.

Time to review my no-speed-bumps rules over a ten-mile run.
No, let's make it fifteen.

I'm still nursing my bruised ego next Tuesday when Stacey finds me
in the Student Union Starbucks. I made fudging sure to ask the
barista to put my wellness and comfort tea in a reusable ceramic mug.
I am over my mom's guilt trips for using disposable cups.

"Hey, is this seat taken?" Stacey asks.

I look up from my econ book. "Stacey! Hey!"

A normal human being would have slumped into the chair next
to me, but Stacey is magnificent both inside and outside of cosplay.
The chair across from mine might as well be a throne.

"How's the swim team?" I ask.

"Yeah, it's good." Stacey smiles.

"And the girlfriend?"

She looks enviably wistful. "Monique's good. We're good. What
about you? Dating anyone?"

I look up and catch an uncharacteristic blush on Stacey's face
before she winces then squints her eyes shut. "What's going on?" I
demand quietly.

"Look, don't be mad. I won't say anything if you're not comfortable with it. Adam asked me to ask you. He's worried you're married
or dating someone. He's worried you're 'taken'"—she uses air quotes
—"and that's why you're so paranoid about staying in costume."

I feel myself turn bright red. I refuse to process this. I sense not
just a speed bump but dangerous off-road territory. I retreat to safer,
albeit unrelated, ground. "He told me Frankie was engaged."

"She is. In fact, you're invited to her bachelorette party, if you
want to come in your real skin. She can't wait to regale you with all
manner of tall tales about our fearless leader and his merry band of
cosplayers. None of which are ever true." Stacey narrows an eye on
me. "But we're not talking about Frankie."

"But we could be." I all but squeak.

I can tell Stacey wants to laugh. Instead her lips press together and her head tilts to the side. "How well do you know Adam?"

"I know he's an MBA student here at SDSU and TAs Econ 450."

Stacey stirs her coffee. She seems to be struggling for the right words. "Backstory always gets complicated, especially when it's not your own."

"Come again?"

"I don't know the specifics. I don't even know if it's true." Stacey takes a deep swig of her coffee. "He was serious with someone who was unavailable, is what I understand. He didn't know she was unavailable until it was too late. Look, Adam is a great guy, and despite how douchey it looks asking me to ask you if you're single, I think it's only because he is determined not to repeat history."

"Stace. I'm not... That is, he's not..." I'm not even sure how to finish this sentence. I could lie and say he is not my type. But you don't fantasize and plot how best to drive a man nutty if he isn't your type. And I don't know him well enough to know if I am his type.

"Look, I'm not going to say anything. I won't even tell Adam we met. In fact, I wasn't going to even ask you. It's just I happened to see you today. Cute dress, by the way."

I stare down at my navy A-line. It appeared in my closet after Mom took a pledge last weekend to only thrift-shop, for the sake of the environment. She was already doing a lot of thrifting over the summer. The environment and I both are grateful. Although, I did hide the sequined tuxedo pants in the linen closet.

"Thanks," I mumble.

"I'll send Adam a text to grow a pair and do his own dirty work. Either way, I'm glad I told you. Now you won't be caught off guard."

The door to the Starbucks jingles open. Adam walks in. Classic.

"Look who's here." Stacey waves to Adam.

"Don't do that!" I slouch down in my chair, aware that cross-hatching should be inked on my cheeks they feel so obviously red.

"It'd be weird if I didn't. Don't worry. I won't blow your cover."

"Hey, Stace." Adam gives Stacey a one-armed hug. "Hey, Sarah."

Stacey looks from Adam and then to me, completely puzzled. Then a cheeky grin spreads over her face. "How do you know *Sarah?*" she asks.

I shake my head. I try hard to communicate with my eyes, to beg Stacey not to ask.

"I was briefly Sarah's Econ 101 TA," Adam explains.

Stacey licks her lips and chuckles into her coffee. Then it turns into an outright laugh.

"Why are you laughing?" I ask as calmly as I can manage. Which isn't calm. At all.

"So it's true, the last story Frankie told me?" Stacey laughs until she cries.

"What did Frankie tell you?" Adam asks.

"Don't say it," I say, packing up my books.

"Oh no!" Stacey rises, towering above me. "Look, I'm sorry, Sarah. You don't have to pack up. I'm leaving."

"Wait, how do you know Sarah?" Adam asks.

I open my mouth, but no words come.

"I've been trying to recruit Sarah for the swim team." Stacey winks.

Saved. I hope my eyes telegraph my undying thanks. "I'm too small for the swim team."

"As you can see, I haven't convinced her yet. I'll leave you two to work out how Adam and I know each other." Stacey taps the back of her chair twice in parting. "Ask him about his escape rooms." She leaves us, laughing.

"You and Stacey met at your escape room?" I can't bring myself to look Adam in the eye.

"Stacey is my best manager at the escape room, cast member too. All my staff are superheroes." His eyes look so warm right now.

"So she's, like, Captain Amaze?" I do enjoy knowing how to hit him where it hurts.

He winces. "Licensing was tricky enough for AJ characters.

Stacey's a killer Fem Fantastic. Nearly the best cosplayer I have in there."

"Who's your best?" I take a sip of my mint tea.

Adam clears his throat and tugs at his collar. "I guess it's a matter of personal preference. My Badpun gets rave reviews."

Fair enough. Mike is totally committed to being a psycho. Also, not bad-looking. He's starring next week in the campus production of *Much Ado About Nothing*. I totally want to see it, if I can get off work.

"How's Econ 101?" Adam asks.

"Well, thanks to you, it's now part of my life twice a week." I flip over my unicorn-encased phone and finger the crack on my screen. It's a nervous tick, one Brent tells me will only further damage my screen.

"You headed over there now?"

I drain the last of my tea and rise with an, "Mm-hmm."

"I'll walk with you. How's the tea here? I always mean to try it, and then I get distracted by the coffee."

"Minty," I say, bussing my mug and collecting my things.

Outside, the air still doesn't feel like fall, but I don't mind. Turns out you can attend class in sunshine-and-sandal weather too.

"So..." Adam says, kicking a stray pebble. "You were absolutely right, and I'm really sorry about being pushy and rude and an idiot." He stops in front of the econ building. "I've got a bake-off coming up with some of the other grad students. I was wondering if you—"

The warm wind swirls, and I have to swat my dress down. We are garnering looks. "Email me. Are you allowed to do that?" I ask.

"Yeah. Yeah, of course. Okay." Adam smiles widely. "I'll email you. Enjoy the lecture. Opportunity costs. It's a good one."

He does email, but I'm busy, and even if I wasn't, I've got my rules, and they aren't made to be broken.

CHAPTER SIXTEEN

"Bye, Mom," I say, grabbing the keys. Mom is home for her lunch break and for more beet juice. A perk of living less than a mile from her school.

"Where are you off to?" she demands.

Can she ever just *ask*? "To Thursday lecture and then study group." Study group being my cover for working for Adam on Thursday nights now. "Remember when I told you my schedule changed?"

Mom looks dismayed. "What about Brent and Jennifer's dinner? They're taking us out to the Fishery tonight. What about book club afterward? We're talking about what's-her-name's book. The one who homeschooled herself, and her brother's pants caught on fire." Mom gets flustered when seafood hangs in the balance. The only thing she loves more than a fresh seafood dinner is a family dinner. The only thing she loves more than family dinner is a family dinner followed by dessert at book club.

"I've got study group after, for econ."

Mom's eyes narrow. "The calendar says it was a study session for your health class midterm."

Was that what I put on the calendar? Shirley Temples, keeping track of my excuses is more complicated than keeping track of my real life. "That one meets Saturday night."

Mom gives a great big huffy sigh.

"I must have written it down wrong. You want me to get a Lyft?" I ask.

"You'll have to. I'm not missing my lobster dinner."

I get an ear full about how next semester I need to schedule my time better, blah blah blah, while I'm waiting for my Lyft to arrive. "Maybe if you got a better job or a second job," Mom suggests.

"Lyft's here. Have a great dinner, Mom. Tell Brent and Jen I say hi! Hope the lobster is good." I grab my very stuffed gym bag and fly out the door. If Mom only knew I was headed to my second job after lecture... Well, she'd probably tell me I should hustle out a third somehow.

Having screwed up colossally, epically, at my first attempt at college, I've become the kind of student who shows up to class fifteen minutes early and turns off her phone during lecture. I don't even use airplane mode. When you're shelling out your own dollars that you earn through sweat, tears, and humiliating costumes, the stakes change. And while I'm sure Mom would have appreciated my new serious academic nature extending to my wardrobe, most days I can't get past my hoodies. Especially not on the days when my catsuit, boots, and makeup bag are all crammed into my gym bag along with my books.

I sit in the second row now, on the end. I take notes. I even ask the occasional question, if it spares me time on the week's problem set. And at the end of class, while a few students always mill around, waiting to ask Dr. Burnbalm some questions, I turn on my phone.

Today when I pull out my phone to turn it back on and open up my Lyft app, I find a text from my brother filling my screen:

Brent: Hey. I wanted to make sure you heard this first from me. Jen and I are pregnant. Fertility treatments were worth it. Wanted to tell you tonight at dinner, but Mom says you've got class and study group.

I blink. I stare at my phone. I flick the screen off. I swipe it back on. The text doesn't disappear. My brother and sister-in-law are having a baby.

Dr. Burnbalm logs out of the computer while the last of the students head out the door. Turning off the projector, he sees me frozen in my chair. "Any questions, Sarah?" he asks.

I hold my head in my hands. Tears slide down my nose onto the laminate square of my desk.

I can't speak. It's all I can do not to heave loud, ugly sobs.

I should be happy for them. I love Brent and Jen, even if their perfect smiles and perfect lives make me want to punch holes in walls. I should be happy. But I'm not. What is wrong with me?

My quiet sobs bounce and echo in the empty lecture hall.

Dr. Burnbalm says something about grabbing a TA to help him count quizzes or lock up before quietly leaving. I am alone in the lecture hall. Fudge brownies, I am always alone. I was alone at the hospital. I was alone after the hospital.

I cry harder.

The door of the lecture hall opens, and Dr. Burnbalm returns with someone. I'm sure it's Brenda. "You sure you can manage locking up?" he says before retreating.

That's right. Run away. Everyone does. I press my hands to my hot, wet face. Even me.

"Hey, Hoodie."

I look up, and there is Adam. The smile falls from his face. "Sarah?" Concern now floods his voice as he takes a seat next to me. "Hey, it's okay."

"What are you doing here?" I wipe the tears and snot from my face with my sleeves.

"Dr. Burnbalm flagged me down upstairs." Adam scoffs and shakes his head.

"And what?" I say accusingly. I can't play head games now. I have zero filter and no chill.

"He said he thought he left a stray essay up here and needed some help." He peers at me again. I must look absolutely disgusting, because his face twists into the most pained expression I've ever seen. "Come on, Sarah. You've been in this room for hours. Let's get some air."

"Goldfish, I don't need your pity." I sob, burying my face in the sleeves of my hoodie.

"Sarah, please." Adam pulls me up, and I am going to turn and run away. I swear I am. I am going to grab my bag, hop over the first row of chairs, and run. Forget the Lyft. I'll run back home with my bag slapping against my stomach.

But instead, I grab on to Adam's shirt and sob into his chest. He holds me. His hands on my shoulders and back wring words from deep inside me.

"I wasn't allowed to be sad about it. Everyone was relieved." I sniffle. "And maybe I was too. But I was also sad and scared." And alone.

"It's okay," Adam says quietly.

"It's not okay," I say, pushing him away. "It's never going to be okay. Everyone makes stupid mistakes. And people say, 'It's okay. That's what life's about. You learn from them. Try, try again.' But I made stupid mistakes, and I'm still paying for them. I'm so sick of still paying for them."

I grab my bag and push my way past Adam. I make it exactly five feet outside the lecture hall before I lean my head against the wall and slide to the floor. I hear the door close behind me. I hear keys in the lock. I hear my bag shifting off the floor. And then Adam's hands are around my own, strong, gorgeous hands. He's kneeling in front of me, and I don't deserve his tenderness or his concern. "Let me take you home," he says.

"No!" I cry harder. "I'm not fudging it up for Brent too!" How can I smile and say congratulations and ask all the questions that under the right circumstances are congratulatory but under the wrong circumstances are accusatory?

Adam lifts me to my feet, and I cry hard into his chest again. I need a run, but for the first time since the divorce, I have no run left in me. My snot- and tear-riddled sleeves are pressed against Adam. I hold on to him as I sob. "Please don't make me."

"Okay," he says. The word barely registers above the pounding of his heart. "Let's go somewhere else. Come on."

He leads me out an emergency exit to a small faculty parking lot. "It was my fault," I sob.

Adam buckles me into the front seat of his black sedan like I'm a child who can't be expected to do it myself. He's not wrong. "You don't have to talk about it if you don't want to," he says.

But when he gets around the car and into the driver's seat, the words spill out of me like vomit. "I was twenty-four weeks. Daniel was on some stupid camping trip when it started." I shudder now with my sobs. "I thought I was cramping because I went for a walk and carried home groceries. I went to bed, and when I woke up—" I sob. I can't even begin to count how many three a.m. runs I've been on to try and forget the blood clots and the cramps that just kept getting worse. "I should have known I was in labor, but I didn't." I desperately try to wipe the tears away. "I didn't know what to do."

"Sarah, it's okay." Adam's voice sounds desperate. He swerves onto the highway.

I grab my head and groan. A migraine digs in behind my eyes. The swerve of the car makes me feel sick. "The baby would have made it. My baby would have made it. She was perfect." I wish I could stop crying. "It was my fault. I took a nap instead of calling the hospital when it started." I shake with sobs. "An 'incompetent cervix,' they called it. There are things they can do for that. I could've saved my baby, but I didn't. I napped." I napped! Having to admit that to Daniel... "I bought this little dress. It was pink with a yellow snail on it." Newborn size, with matching shorts. Small enough to fit a doll. "Oh goldfish," I bury my face in my hands.

Adam puts a hand on my neck and rubs. "Hey. Hey, it's okay."

I cry in Adam's car. I cry as he leads me up an old flight of stairs. And then I cry on his couch until I fall asleep.

I wake up as the sun dips down into the Pacific, the last little piece of it flashing green. My dad claimed Grandma went blind because she watched the sunset every day, looking for the green flash. My eyes are so puffy, it's hard to see. I squint as my mind reboots. My eyes land on a flat-screen TV, and I bolt upright. I'm on Adam's couch. I'm at his place. I...

"Hey," Adam says. "I was just about to run out to pick up dinner. You want anything special?"

"Life Savers," I say without thinking.

The corner of Adam's mouth twitches up. "Come again?"

"Could you get me a tube of the green, minty Life Savers?"

"Yeah, back in a few." Adam grabs his keys. "Don't go anywhere?"

I shake my head. The minute I hear his car start, I lunge for my bag. I phone Gwen. *Pick up. Pick up.*

"As I live and breathe," she says in greeting. "Is this my long-lost friend Saire? I thought you got trapped in the internet and were reduced to just phantom texts that periodically came through at odd hours."

"I need your help, Gwen. I'm in deep." My voice is enough to rattle even the most unflappable of friends.

"What's going on?" Gwen asks. All business. That's why I called her.

As fast as I possibly can, I explain the triggering text from Brent, and Adam coming to my rescue, and the fact that in less than an hour, I have to be cosplaying. "Or it's all over. He's going to put it all together."

"Holy cabooses. Just tell him the truth," Gwen says.

"Are you kidding? After all the sobbing and snot and—"

"Yeah, okay. Take a shower and then tell him the truth. Wet hair and tears—every man's kryptonite."

I take a deep breath and squeeze my swollen eyes shut. "I need you to cover for me."

"You need me to what now?" Gwen demands.

I squeeze my aching forehead. This is a bad idea, but when has that stopped me? "My mom is out tonight at dinner, and then she has book club. I need you to go over there, grab my other catsuit, and cover my shift for me. Please, Gwen! I've already told Adam the most pathetic aspect of my life today. I really don't want to hash out the runner-up territory. Please, I'm begging you."

I hear Gwen take a deep breath. "This is a bad idea."

"I know."

"I'm only doing this once."

"I know."

"What time do I need to be there?"

"Quarter to seven. The costume is in the suitcase under my bed. The spare key is under the red flowerpot." I finger the fringe of one of the couch pillows.

Gwen groans. "You're going to owe me your life for this one."

"I know."

"Breakfast at the very least."

"We'll meet up for omelets, and I'll debrief you just as soon as this is all over." Although, by the way my heart is racing, it's hard to believe that *this* will ever be over.

"Okay," she says. "How's the other part? You doing okay?"

"No."

"Take a shower. Trust me. It'll help."

"Thank you, Gwen."

"Thank me later. I've got a catsuit to liberate."

I do what Gwen says. I take a shower. Only after, in Adam's towel, do I discover my wardrobe issue. I don't have a change of clothes in my gym bag other than my catsuit and spandex running gear. I'd die before putting either on. I mean, the spandex would have been okay if my hoodie were an option, but that is at least one wash-and-rinse cycle from being wearable.

I hear a car pull into the complex. Shirley Temples, it's Adam. I slip on the black leggings and rummage through Adam's dresser until I find—what else?—a hoodie. I pull it on over my sports bra and return to the couch, but not before I stuff my vixen boots down deep under the snotty hoodie and zip everything closed.

"Hey," Adam says, setting his keys on the kitchen counter along with two bags of takeaway boxes. "You're still here."

"I took a shower. I hope that's okay."

"And you helped yourself to a hoodie."

"I did."

A smirk flickers on his face—a nice smirk, not a douchebag smirk. Do guys like to see women in their clothes as much as we like to wear their clothes? I swear the patriarchy extends to thread counts and fibers. "I didn't know what you wanted, apart from the Life Savers." He reaches into his pocket and tosses me the green tube. "So you can choose. Thai, sushi, or street tacos."

"Yes," I say, rising. "To all."

"Good girl." Adam brings down a couple of plates from the cupboard. "I know I said you didn't have to talk, but we need to talk. Who's Daniel, and who's Brent?"

"Brent's my brother. Daniel's my ex."

"Does your ex-boyfriend live around here? Because if he does, I personally would like to tell him—"

"Ex-husband. And no. He lives in China now."

He sets down a couple of glasses heavily. His brow furrows, and for a moment, I think he's scrambling for a way to change the subject. His eyes find my own, and I wonder if it's my own pain or something entirely his own reflecting in them. "That's really rough, Sarah."

The words come easily, especially after a few bites of Thai food. "We hooked up at a party, and while lots of people have one-night stands and nothing happens, I got pregnant. He panicked and told his daddy, who is Michigan's most conservative lawyer. Daddy Ray told Daniel to do the right thing, and before the semester ended, we were married. Both of us were miserable. And the baby was coming... until she wasn't."

"What happened?"

"Daniel would go on camping trips. He'd take our car. It was a wedding present from his dad, so whatever. He'd leave me home, and I read all the stupid marriage and parenting books people gave us for our wedding. It's so obvious now. *I* needed to be all in. *I* needed to show my love and appreciation for Daniel. *I* needed to make sure my marriage was strong for the baby. Never mind that Daniel was off camping and sharing his sleeping bag with Tiffany, Charlotte and Dixie. I spent most of my days puking, so I was slow on that one. Anyway, I walked to the store on Friday, walked back with bags of groceries to make his favorite meal—mac and cheese, breaded chicken tenders, and apple pie with ice cream. I prepped it all for the next day. I was exhausted and sore, so I took a bath, went to bed... I had no idea."

"How far along were you?" Adam asks.

"Twenty-four weeks. Incompetent cervix. Daniel blamed me. He said that only a fudging idiot would take a nap instead of call the hospital. Okay, fine, that was stupid, but I didn't know it was a miscarriage. I mean, yeah, I figured something was wrong when I woke up bleeding..." I trace the seam in Adam's granite countertop with my free hand. At the Kids Club, I've added strips of Velcro to the bottom of our homework tables for the kiddos who need more fidgets and sensory input to focus... calm down. "He even blamed me for my body, said I was 'clueless.' That if any part of his anatomy were incompetent, he'd have known about it and would have been vigilant." I take in a deep breath. "Responsible."

"Not knowing you were miscarrying wasn't your fault either, Sarah."

"Doesn't mean it doesn't feel like it."

"Not. Your. Fault. None of it. Period."

I shrug. My head knows, I guess. But my heart...

"So I take it Brent had some news," he says.

"They're pregnant. Yay." And then I'm done. I am done and desperate to change the subject. "Do you live alone?"

"What? Oh, yeah." He looks around, a little pride creeping onto his face. "It was my motivation. I told myself all summer that the hours would be worth it in the end. I'd have my own space."

"Nice space." I am jealous.

"Obnoxious roomies?" he asks. He slides the box of tacos toward me.

"No, but no privacy... No chance at watching what I want on Netflix."

"You want to watch something? They just put up a new season of *Mississippi Bake-Off*."

"What is it with everyone and that show?"

He digs the remote out from the couch cushions. "I dunno. Dr. Burnbalm got me hooked on it. Everyone in the Econ Department watches it. Naturally, we have the best potlucks. It's why I majored in econ as an undergrad."

Somewhere between the fourth episode of *Mississippi Bake-Off* and Adam's hilarious story of a failed brioche, I feel it—an inescapable twist inside me that makes me want to bury my head in the sleeves of my hoodie—well, Adam's hoodie—and whimper.

I've made a huge mistake. And while it would be so easy to tell myself that it was my sobfest, followed by bare-naked honesty, it's not tonight's events that are eating me up inside.

I should never have lied to Adam. That first day in econ, I should have come clean. I didn't, and now I don't know if I can.

If I tell Adam right now, *Hey! Surprise. I'm the cosplay freak who licks people she doesn't know. BTW, hope it was you, and you liked it,* then one of two things will happen.

One, Adam runs for his life. *You're an insecure, out-of-control crazy-pants. Now that I can connect the backstory dots, it all makes sense. Smell you later.*

Two, he says, *You're crazy, but I love crazy. Let's do this!* Happily ever after, the end.

Option two sounds the most appealing. But it's a fake, a dupe, a false choice. It would be the end of my second chance at college and independence. Mr. Speed Bump is here to distract me and make sure I don't have a fudging prayer of thinking about anything even remotely academic. Because the quality of the guy is not the real problem—Adam is great. The real problem is me. I'm the one who gets carried away.

I can't let that happen again.

CHAPTER SEVENTEEN

Not that it's been a particularly rowdy Saturday night, but my feet ache. I've forgotten just how high my lace-up boots are. Forget the gym. I'm calling a Lyft and soaking in my mom's tub just as soon as I get my catsuit and makeup off.

"You headed out?" Stacey calls from the registers. She's fisting money from one hand to the other as she counts but pauses. "You want someone to go with you? I didn't like how those last guys were looking at you."

I drag my wired claws over the counter before retracting them into a tight fist. "Guys don't look at me. They look through me." I don't know why I am so grouchy. No, I do know. Adam has perfected the art of walking down a hall and not making eye contact with anyone. *Yeah, check your phone right as you pass me. Call out to Vlad when you get too close.* It shouldn't matter, but tonight it did. I arch my back, desperate for a good stretch, but my corset has other ideas.

Stacey shoves the money into a deposit envelope and slams the register drawer shut. "All the same, why don't I call Vlad or Ernie to walk you to your—"

"I'll be fine," and I am out the emergency exit and into the alley before she can ask where my fictitious car is parked.

I make it half a block before I hear them.

"Here, kitty, kitty."

A trio of frat boys is tailing me. They look vaguely familiar and probably came through the escape room tonight, but by now I've seen the equivalent of Petco Park filled to capacity filter through my padded Catstrike cell. Everyone in San Diego looks familiar at this point.

"Hey. Slow down," one of them calls.

I don't. Three drunk boys in a badly lit alley in Pacific Beach. I'm not stopping for anything.

Fog has rolled in, and the air is salty with sea spray. The noise from Garnet Avenue is muffled in the alley.

"Hey, did you hear me?" a boy shouts. He sounds offended. I'd say he sounds angry or belligerent, but if I admit that, I might get scared.

"Cat's got her tongue," one of his buddies says.

Drunken laughter echoes in the alley.

They run toward me. I'm still two blocks from the gym. I won't even make it to the nearest side street, not in these stupid heels. I grab my phone and press buttons. Any buttons. All buttons.

"Hey. We just want to talk." One of the boys grabs my arm and, either by design or accident, knocks the phone out of my hand.

Fudge.

Three guys—a big one, one almost too drunk to stand, and a shorty.

The big one reeks like he's bathed in gin. Not bathed. That implies hygiene choices that were clearly eschewed.

"Don't touch me," I growl, twisting out of his grip.

More drunken laughter.

"Kitty's got claws," the drunkest one says.

"Claws," I say. "A Taser. And a very big, bad boyfriend who

knows exactly where I am and will kill you if you touch me again."
Lies. My heart races, and my limbs feel rigid.

"Hey, hey, hey," the short one slurs. "We just want to be friends."

My eyes narrow. "Oh, is that all?" I'm sassier than I have any
right to be.

"Depends. What do you look like with that mask off?" The goob
reaches for my mask, and I struggle.

My heart hammers as everything inside me twists and knots. Maybe
I can buy them off. I manage to pull away. "Let me buy you boys a drink
first, and we can see where the evening goes." I will go directly to the
nearest public space, where I can scream for help and then run.

"I'd rather find out here," the big one says, grabbing me before I
can bolt.

Car lights turn into the alley. I flinch. Not just lights, but high
beams, blind us.

The biggest boy's grip tightens on my arm, and I squeal, but not
in pain. I recognize the car. Fudge goldfish, am I happy to see
that car.

Adam steps out and slams his door shut. "Get in the car, Sabine."

"I dropped my phone," I say.

"Cracked the screen too," Shorty snickers, and the big one holds
me as tightly as ever.

"You think this is funny?" Adam asks, a dangerous edge in his
voice.

The big boy speaks. "Dude. We were just—"

Adam exudes alpha male, which in its own way is terrifying. He's
never exuded alpha male around me before. Confidence, yes. But this
dangerous, testosterone-drenched alpha standing next to me is no one
I've seen before. Adam takes me firmly by the elbow and pulls me
away from the drunk boys. They let me go. "Pick up the lady's
phone," he says to them.

"Hey, man. We were all just having some fun." Shorty reaches to
pet me. "Weren't we, kitty, kitty?"

I shudder as his fingers dig under my chin.

Adam steps in front of me protectively. "The hell you were. Pick up the phone."

"Come on," the drunkest of them says. "We'd let you watch."

Adam bares his teeth, and then his fist is in the jerk's face. My boot falls on the big one's foot, and my elbow is in his stomach. He doubles over. Shorty attempts to run, but Adam catches him by the neck of his shirt.

"Dude. Are you crazy?" the frat boy gasps. His buddies have already recovered somewhat and are stumbling away.

Adam grabs the idiot, hauling him up by the shirt. "I see you or any of your friends anywhere close to around here, there will be trouble. Do you want more trouble?"

"No."

"No," Adam agrees. His phone flashes bright as he takes a picture of Shorty's face. "Apologize to my friend."

"Sorry," he slurs. "Really, really sorry."

"Run."

And I have the satisfaction of seeing the last of my would-be assailants disappear.

Adam shakes out his right fist and squeezes it a few times.

"Thanks," I say, turning. The gym, my shower, and a good hard run on my favorite treadmill are less than five minutes away. I'll just stay at the gym until the sun comes up.

"Where are you going?" Adam says, his voice still edged with anger.

Shirley Temples. Adam is seething, and my mouth parts in disbelief. Adam is mad... at me.

He shoves my phone into my hand. The screen still has just the one crack. Thank fudge, because I have zero funds to replace it. "Get in the car, Sabine."

My shoulders tense, and I have to force them down. "Fine. I don't feel like walking just now anyway."

"What the hell were you thinking?" he shouts when we're both in the car, speeding down the alley.

"I go out the back door every night."

"You're lucky I answered my phone. Luckier still that I stayed on long enough to realize you were in trouble."

"I—"

But Adam doesn't give me a chance to speak. "What do you think would have happened to you if I hadn't?" he snaps.

He swerves, and I slam into the passenger door. "Can you watch the road?"

"You can't leave out the back anymore. You can't arrive or leave in costume again."

"The hell I can't. We have an agreement."

"Yeah, that was before your safety became a concern."

"If I can't come in character, I can't work."

"Fine! Save me the cost of extra security."

"What?"

Adam glances at me as if I am a customer who has failed to escape the simplest room. "I'm going to need extra security now for you."

Unbelievable. "Yeah, and what about you? What do you need if you go around beating up drunk frat boys?"

"What, now you're defending them?"

Adrenaline pumps through me. Fight or flight, and I needed flight. I need to run for the next three days straight. "Where are we going?"

"I don't know!" Adam yells.

"Take me back to the alley," I demand.

"No!" Adam shouts.

"Stop the car! Stop the fudging car!"

He swerves across a lane of oncoming traffic and skids into a parking space on Garnet.

Garnet Avenue is glowing in neon pinks, blues, and greens. It is a sophisticated, twenty-first-century scene, unrecognizable from the time warp of bubble-gum-stained sidewalks and fast-fashion dives that I knew back in middle school.

Adam white-knuckles the steering wheel. "I don't know you. I don't know where you come from or where you go after work, but I do know that everything has to change, because it's not safe. You are not safe."

"Those boys were drunk. They were idiots. But they weren't murderers or rapists. Things were fine." I say the words to reassure myself as much as Adam.

He lets go of the steering wheel, and I swear the car whimpers. "Then why did you call?"

Because I was scared. I'm still scared. I couldn't call anyone except you because anyone else might turn me into a Sunday school lesson. A cautionary tale of why women do not parade around in sexy cosplay.

My mouth twists up in a practiced Catstrike smirk. "I missed you."

Adam stares at me with his gorgeous, ocean-gray eyes. My heart careens, and I feel more terrified than I did in the alley. Shirley Temples, he's beautiful. "You're fired," Adam says.

"The fudge I am." I grab his face and kiss him. Hard. And when he kisses back, I climb into his lap, the vinyl of my costume crunching and crinkling with the movement. I kiss him. He kisses me. It is wonderful but not enough. I catch his bottom lip between my teeth and pull until he yelps, but he doesn't stop.

I kiss him, and forget that I'm wearing a mask and he has no clue who I am. I kiss him, and I'm in his hoodie, lying on his couch with wet hair. I kiss him, and it's me, not the sexy, cosplaying, Catstrike me, but all of me. Me with the pathetic past, me with the hoodies in econ, me running, always running, trying to escape my life.

I've wanted this since Adam held me, snot bubbles and sobs, outside the lecture hall when my world was falling apart, buckling under grief that felt as fresh as the day I miscarried. I've wanted this since white T-shirts and escape boxes. Since I picked up comics and dreamed of a man who would fight with me, for me.

His arms are at my back, across the laces of my corset. Moving up, pulling me closer, until he gasps for breath.

"I can't do this," he says.

His hand glides gently down to my elbow, where it rests. Can't, huh? I'm not convinced. "Why not?" I purr. "Don't you want me?"

"I want you." His fingers trace the lines of my mask. "But not like this."

I pull away. My muscles tense up, and my neurons, which were doing the equivalent of a Fourth of July firework spectacular just moments before, screech to a cold stop.

I'm off him and out of the car in one motion. I lean in before shutting the door. "Call me if you change your mind."

"I won't—"

I'm so furious, my voice comes out in a rough growl. "I mean about work."

I slam the car door and disappear into the night.

CHAPTER EIGHTEEN

I still don't do well with rejection, and I think tonight I might have broken the rowing machine.

Now it's early-morning hours at the gym. My Catstrike suit is buried under my towel and shower flip-flops, and most of the sane world is sleeping. I, on the other hand, am swearing up a storm at the rowing clips that have my sneakers in their unyielding grip.

I wanted to kiss Adam since he took me back to his place and let me cry myself to sleep on his couch. And when I woke up, sure, I felt panic, but I also felt that warmth. That radiating, cozy, safe feeling only grew—that wasn't because I was eventually wearing his hoodie. It was first-kiss energy, the chemistry, the build-up, the understanding, the communion.

Maybe not communion. *Communion* is a fudged-up word.

But the feeling was there. And why the fudge didn't I do something about it then? Why did I wait until we were shouting at each other in his car, and Adam thought I was a different woman?

I licked Nightbat Adam (if it even was Adam) because I was cosplaying and fooling around. I kissed Adam tonight because—

That slow, warm creep starts up again inside me. It's the kind of feeling that comes from watching too many happily ever afters and hoping that someday it's going to be you nibbling on Prince Charming's bottom lip. Fudge brownies. I wrestle my sneakers out of the foot clamps and stumble over to a treadmill, where I punch buttons until it beeps back at me.

Tony hits the emergency stop button. "No. Not that treadmill. That one's scared of you."

"It's a treadmill," I say. I should have said, *Leave me alone if you value your life*, but that would have meant more words. Fudge words.

"It is a treadmill—one that you've worn the belt out on. Twice. Move to the next one and pound it into submission."

I do what Tony says and start my run at a sprint. The better to clear my mind. The harder I work my body, the easier it is to let the dangerous thoughts slip away and realize I'm mostly angry with myself.

Tonight, I got carried away by cosplay yet again. Simple as that. Adam and I aren't anything, and I certainly don't have any real feelings for him. That kiss was adrenaline and latent comic book fantasies. Being acquainted in real life has nothing to do with it. So we know each other, big deal. We can keep things in the friend zone indefinitely. My rules allow for the friend zone.

It's four thirty a.m., and the sky is already lightening when I head home. My phone rings.

"Hello," I answer.

"Hey, Sarah. How's it going?" Holy blast from the past. It's my ex-husband.

I groan. This night...

"Listen," Daniel says, and his insufferable voice, honeyed with arrogant privilege, makes me cringe. "I'm writing my memoir."

"Your memoir?"

"Turns out I have a lot more life experience than our peers. You know, having been both a husband and a father. I have you to thank for that."

I am speechless. But not in a good way.

"Listen, my dad seems to think that I need your consent to publish this. He asked me if I'd run it by you. Always thinking like a lawyer." He laughs, but my blood freezes and throat constricts. The first time I met Daddy Ray, he told me all about the surge in custody cases his enormous, well-respected law firm had taken on. He described in detail how simple it is to bend facts to grant a father full guardianship of a child when the mother outright refuses to marry.

"He drafted some papers that you need to sign. You don't mind, of course."

He presses on before I can say anything. "I already wrote the first two chapters, sent it off to Molly. She's an editor, friend of the family. Molly loved them. Wants to see more. Says she can't wait for my Africa chapters."

"I thought you were in China," I say.

"Yeah, but Africa is on my radar." He sounds exasperated.

"Daniel," I say. Nothing gets his attention like his own name. "Why can't you do what everyone else does and change the names and call it a novel?"

"Authenticity, Sarah. The unauthentic life is not worth living. I learned that from you."

Is that supposed to be deep?

"Listen, my dad drafted up some waivers and stuff, basically just saying you're cool with everything. He sent them to me to sign, and now I have to mail them to you for your countersignature. When you get them, I need you to sign both and then send the original back a-sap." There's a pause and then snickering. "You can keep the other copy for your legal team."

I'm tired and still have to walk all the way up Yost Drive. "Sure. Send me your chapters, and I'll read them and—"

Daniel's whiny laugh on the other end of the call makes me bristle. "You're not reading my manuscript."

"So I'm supposed to agree that you can say whatever you want about me, our marriage, and my pregnancy? Go to fudging—"

Daniel tsk-tsks half a world away. "Still can't swear like an adult."

"Grow up, Daniel."

"I have. See, that's the difference between the two of us." His sigh is grotesquely self-indulgent. "I grew from our journey together. That's why people need my memoir. That's why Molly wants to publish it. I have so much wisdom. What happened was just as hard for me, but I chose to learn from life's hard lessons. Not run away from them."

My shoulders sag, and I feel sore, stiff, completely worn out, and defeated. "Let me think about it," I squeak.

"What's there to think about?" Daniel presses. "Some docs show up in your mailbox, you sign them, send one back, and then we never have to speak to each other again."

Goldfish, I hate him. "Sure, whatever. Mail them to me." Anything to get rid of Daniel forever.

CHAPTER NINETEEN

My mom's dwarf Meyer lemon tree is magical. Somehow it is always, without fail, bursting with lemons.

I didn't appreciate my mom's lemon tree for what it is—a miracle. Soft, juicy lemons. An abundance of them, a *reliable* abundance from the day we moved in. And what did I do with this treasure? I occasionally pulled off a lemon and rubbed it on my hair when I was desperate for highlights. I rolled my eyes and complained whenever Mom asked me to head out to pick lemons. I begrudged the little tree its thorns.

Sure, there was the one summer when I did the lemonade stand every weekend and ended up buying a season pass to SeaWorld. That was before the whole *Blackfish* documentary thing. It was also before people like my mom bought stainless-steel straws. Not that SeaWorld was ever the paradigm of cool. Okay, maybe when you were finally tall enough to ride the roller coaster, but still too little to drive a car, and realized that the gift shops were filled with junk you could never afford.

I thought of that tree every day when I was stuck in that crappy apartment in Michigan, sick, pregnant, and alone. I craved lemonade.

Craved it. And not the store-bought kind. And not the kind you make from the thick-skinned yellow rocks that cost a dollar at Walmart.

Two cups of fresh lemon juice, one cup of sugar. Fill Mom's heavy glass pitcher with water up to the base of the neck. (I finally got around to measuring, it's eight cups.) Add a cup of ice. Stir. Magic in a glass. Every single time.

Now that I have access to the magic tree and can appreciate the culinary virtues of the humble lemon, I realize what a numpty I was all those years. Who cares that the house we moved into after Dad's accident had only two bedrooms and one bathroom? It had a back-yard with a Meyer lemon tree.

I grab a glass and a stainless-steel straw from the cupboard and pour myself an enormous glass of fresh lemonade. Making a pitcher and sipping on it after a hard run might be my new favorite form of recovery. Because while my life may be seriously fudged up, stretching under the shade of the jacaranda tree while sipping on lemonade makes everything seem okay.

My phone pings, and the email icon lights up my screen. My lips twitch into a smile, and my heart pulls all taut as I bend deeper into my kneeling quad stretch. I am blushing. To be this excited over a man's email is embarrassing, even when I am completely alone. I shake my head because I am a colossal idiot, but I flip over onto my back and read Adam's email.

AdamMcKinney@sdsu.student
  to SarahMiller@sdsu.student
  What are you doing this Friday?

I toss the phone down and move into a downward dog. A breeze whips my hair across my beaming face. And I'm totally confused. I feel like squeeing. Adam was the one to reach out, right? That's got to mean something. But maybe this is the post-run euphoria and lemonade. I glance down at my phone. Shouldn't my wounded ego and bitchy streak be surfacing about now? Shouldn't I be furious, annoyed, irritated at the very least? And seriously, who uses email in place of a text?

People who don't have other people's numbers.

People who avoid giving out their numbers for fear that their alter ego will be discovered with an inadvertent pocket dial. I've accidently called Gwen with my Google Voice number a number of times. I get my head back and remind myself that in real life I've never made out with this guy in a car. He never pushed me off him and then fired me. I pound out a reply.

SarahMiller@sdsu.student
    to AdamMcKinney@sdsu.student
    Studying.

AdamMcKinney@sdsu.student
    to SarahMiller@sdsu.student
    You want to study in my car on the way to and from Leto Con?

SarahMiller@sdsu.student
    to AdamMcKinney@sdsu.student
    I don't know. Do I?

AdamMcKinney@sdsu.student
    to SarahMiller@sdsu.student
    You do. Pick you up at 9:00 AM?

. . .

SarahMiller@sdsu.student
　　to AdamMcKinney@sdsu.student
　　I've got work that night.

AdamMcKinney@sdsu.student
　　to SarahMiller@sdsu.student
　　I'll get you back in time.

It's no big. Because we aren't anything. We aren't going to become anything. Like I'd be interested after the other night. I have my pride. I mean, maybe we're friends. But that's fine. We don't need to be more. And a friend would go with another friend to a convention. I mean, it would be suspicious if I said no.

SarahMiller@sdsu.student
　　to AdamMcKinney@sdsu.student
　　Okay. Sure.

AdamMcKinney@sdsu.student
　　to SarahMiller@sdsu.student
　　Text me your address.

SarahMiller@sdsu.student
　　to AdamMcKinney@sdsu.student
　　I've got a better idea.

⌇

I ask for a table on the patio. It is a gorgeous Friday morning with just the right amount of marine layer to make sunglasses unnecessary. The ocean lolls below me in a sedate, untroubled way. Sometimes, especially at Law Street Beach, the Pacific looks downright lazy.

I've read Frank Herbert's *Dune* enough to know I'm asking for trouble sitting with my back to the entrance, but I don't want to watch for Adam. I don't want to know what it feels like to see him smile as he walks toward me. What if something happens? What if my heart explodes, and some stupid pop song starts blasting in my head about how he *could be the one*, and there is no denying my feelings? Nope. I'm not doing that. I'm not taking the chance that I choke on my water because he's even sexier than I realized.

All the same, my neck tingles with that ASMR buzz when I hear Adam walk in and ask for me. "I like the way you think, Hoodie," he says when he finds me.

Goldfish, his voice is delicious. I force aside a shiver as goose bumps flush over my skin.

Thankfully, Adam slides into the chair opposite me and doesn't notice.

"Sarah," I correct. "You're not calling me Hoodie all day."

"Sarah," he repeats with a smile. His Ray-Bans are tucked into the neck of his cobalt blue T-shirt. "Come here often?"

The fairies ate my sandwich is printed on the front of his shirt, and my eyes linger. "I've always thought about it after my half marathons. It smells so good when I run by. Every good con begins with food, right?"

The Green Flash is the type of place my mother would come to with her buddies for brunch. But this early, it is decidedly more chill.

Adam folds his arms on our table and leans forward. "So this was entirely about breakfast and had nothing to do with not wanting to tell me where you live?"

"Because I'm homeless," I say, smiling over my orange juice.

"Because you don't sleep but run all night like a little hamster."

"The gym makes me pay rent." I catch his eyes sparkling.

The waiter appears, brandishing a pot of fresh, pungent joe. "Coffee?"

Adam glances up politely. "Always."

The waiter sets extra napkins and cutlery on the table. "Your orders are going to be out in just a few."

Adam raises his eyebrows. "You ordered for me?"

I tug the sleeves up on my hoodie. "You were late. I was hungry."

The waiter returns with chorizo breakfast omelets piled high with guacamole, bacon, and stuffed with spinach, mushrooms, and cheese. "Apparently," Adam says.

"I'm not rude." Unlike some people, who push women off of them and toss them out of cars... But the memory of Adam's hand gently tracing the lines of my mask surfaces, and I know I'm being unfair. He did kinda come to my rescue minutes before I jumped him. I shrug. "So I ordered for you too."

Adam grins. "You should order all my meals. Save me from egg whites and sliced tomatoes."

As if.

"What's up with your shirt?" I ask between bites of chorizo.

"The hungry fairies? It's my favorite *Dr. Leto* episode."

"Why?"

Adam pauses and then thoughtfully sips his coffee. "No. No, I'm not ruining some of the greatest forty minutes of television for you."

"You're a Letovian?"

"You're not?" Another man—Daniel, for instance—would have spoken the words with irritation. Adam sounds intrigued.

"I know there's a scarf or a fez or something. I think my roommate at one point was into it." Mom loves BBC. Once, she had her book club gals over for the series premiere of the latest period drama starring hottie actors in tights. That was... memorable. A few of her friends came dressed as other notable leading BBC men (hence my knowledge of the scarf or fez), and I'm pretty sure they were all drunk and making out with each other by the end of the party.

"We can watch it together. I'm not a Letovian," Adam explains.

"I mean, I am. It's a lot of fun, especially with the right crowd. But it isn't my bread-and-butter fandom. No, we're headed to Leto Con strictly for business." He flashes a vendor badge from the breast pocket of his jacket.

"Oh, that's right. Your Nightbat escape room." I purposefully busy myself with my knife and fork. Eye contact always gets me in trouble. "You doing a demo at the convention?" Oh goldfish. Am I going to have to pretend I've never met everyone but Stace?

"No, just escape boxes. Although a full-scale demo isn't a bad idea." He leans back in his café chair. "I'm trying to find a buyer."

"What?" My fork slips and clatters on my plate.

"I franchised it. My business model is good. Especially with the tweaks my cast has made."

"They must be really talented," I say, spearing a piece of spinach.

"Yeah, I got lucky. Anyway, the setup is easy. It's mostly light and animations."

"So did you get me a vendor badge too?"

Adam tosses a badge, complete with lanyard, on the table. "It's the best way to see a convention. You have a legit cover. You can people-watch from the comfort of my booth. Work different angles."

"Like a backstage pass."

"Exactly. Should we get some cinnamon rolls for the road?"

We do, and once we make it out of Pacific Beach and are cruising south on I-5, I eat one. Or three. To be fair, I did run 12.6 miles this morning.

"So why running?" Adam asks. His wrist resting comfortably on the steering wheel is all lean and wrapped in muscle and tendons.

"Why not?" I say, focusing my gaze out at the bay. The water around Fiesta Island catches the stray rays of morning sun and sparkles.

"Why not kickboxing? Why not yoga? Why not surfing?"

I lick the last of the cream cheese frosting from my thumb. "I dunno. I guess I crave it. I have moments where I think I can't write another awful essay on Adam Smith. Moments in real life where I want to hide and never come out. I get through it because I know at the end of it, at some point in my future, it will just be me and the road, and I won't have to think. I'll be able to outrun all of my demons. All of my failures. All of my worries. Everything. I can run until there's nothing left."

"Nothing but you." He glances over with some kind of introspective look that is too brief for me to tease out.

We drive on. The alstroemeria bushes in the center divide are blooming pink and white. California is gorgeous. Even the freeways.

"Were you always a runner?" Adam asks.

"No. I picked it up during the divorce. Or before..." Talk about a conversation killer.

"I hate running. Music is essential if I have to do it. How 'bout you?"

"Sometimes. Yeah. For a while, I really enjoyed making playlists for my runs."

"Can we listen to one?"

"Because the kind of music people listen to is a direct window into their soul?"

"I'm curious. Just read off the artists on one of them."

I grab my phone and read over the artists. Cake. Movits! Fall Out Boy. Blondie. The Used. *Hamilton*. "Egmont Overture." Demi. My playlists are embarrassingly angsty—just right for pushing through the pain of those later miles, all wrong for keeping things casual with a guy as you drive down the I-5.

"Play it," Adam says, and he laughs when he catches me cringing as Aqua bubbles from the stereo. "You're a little all over the place."

"I'm a lot all over the place." I turn down the volume. "So what about you? What's your passion? Arms that toned don't just happen."

He blushes, and it is the most charming thing ever. "I'm a yoga-in-front-of-the-TV kinda guy. I mean, don't get me wrong. It's fun at a studio too. Well, hot yoga is, anyway. I've tried other stuff. Jujitsu is not my thing. Surfing is too slow. I was into capoeira for a while."

I pull off my hoodie. I'm not about to get pit stains in Adam's car. "Is that the Brazilian dance-fighting one?"

"Yeah. Most people don't know what it is, and trying to explain it usually doesn't help. They end up thinking I'm a dancer." He shrugs, and I can't help but appreciate that his shoulders, like his arms, are very toned and very not like those of a dancer. But all the dancers I've known were from my fifth-grade ballet recital. Hardly an accurate pool. "I couldn't keep up with it and grad school and my business. So I do planks and shoulder presses when I can catch the latest episode of *MBO*. Maybe when grad school ends, I'll pick it back up." He looks over and smiles. "Nice shirt."

My vintage Fem Fantastic tee is a nice shirt. "Why capoeira?"

"It was my mom's idea. I was the type of kid who would literally tear things apart if I didn't have something else to do. My mom wanted me to do dance. I wanted to do karate. Capoeira was something of a compromise."

I snort.

"What?"

"Your mom wanted you to take dance lessons. You ended up taking Brazilian martial arts that *maybe* resembles break dancing, but it's certainly not the type of dancing your mom had in mind. That's not a compromise."

Adam's lips curl into a smile, but his eyes do not leave the road. Rush-hour traffic on the five this morning is snarled up nicely. "Yeah, it is."

"No. It's a man's skewed version of a compromise. Your mom gave 95%, and because she didn't give up the last 5%, you call it a compromise. Men don't know how to compromise."

"What about this morning? I wanted to pick you up at your place, see where you live, meet your roomie, and I had to give all that up."

"Because having breakfast with me was so terrible."

"I don't know how I got through it." He smirks.

"Okay, 5% of your plan changed, but I'm still here in your car driving with you to Leto Con, where I will spend 95% of the day just as you planned."

The smirk grows into a broad smile. "Is that a promise?"

I laugh to avoid blushing and answering.

Adam changes lanes, and we inch closer to downtown. "How's work going?"

"It's good. I'm still working the bulk of my shifts in the Kids Club, but I don't mind. It's surprisingly fun."

"Surprisingly?"

"I almost didn't take the job when Tony suggested the Kids Club. I was terrified of being surrounded by infants and toddlers, but it is fascinating." I didn't realize this before, when I had my hoodie sleeves to hide behind, but my hands are a mess. Chipped nail polish reveals bits of crayon stuck under my nails. I shouldn't care about something so superficial, but I may as well have a tattoo of #hotmess across my knuckles at this point. "Did you know infants can count?"

"No way."

"There was this study with teddy bears and five-month-olds. Babies can totally count."

"Huh. I never would have guessed."

"There's this entire subset of our population that we just under-value and dismiss because they wear diapers and can't talk."

"Two subsets if you count people like my great-uncle Howard. Is your Kids Club busy?"

"Yes." I bunch my fingers into fists, trying to hide my horrible nails. "I thought it might slow down when school started, but we continue to be full with a waiting list every weekday and Saturday morning."

"Wow."

"There aren't enough preschools."

"I agree. The lack of early-childhood education in this country is a problem. I'm not going to fight you on it."

"Fight me on it?"

"You keep making fists."

Shirley Temples. "No. I'm embarrassed. I chipped off half my nail polish last night peeling the paper off broken crayons."

"Oh?"

"Coloring is a really popular activity. Or it's become one since I moved an old bulletin board from the staff room into the Kids Club." I smile in spite of myself. "The kids want to make the wall."

"Bragging rights. I get it."

"So coloring is an awesome activity. Cheap. Minimal mess. Developmentally appropriate. Nontoxic. But it's hard to hold a crayon in chubby fingers. Especially stubs of broken crayons. And no kid should have to sort through a broken mess..." Careful, or I'm not going to be talking about crayons for much longer.

I take a deep breath. "I was melting them down and remolding them. My roomie is a teacher and has a crazy collection of seemingly random things that are actually really useful if you work with kids. I took some of her silicone baking molds, melted the broken crayons in them, and now I have toddler-appropriate crayons for my Saturday morning regulars." I splay my hands out. "But really ugly nails."

"Let me see." We come to another standstill on the freeway, and Adam gestures for my hand. "I don't think it is bragging rights that are motivating the kiddies."

"What then?"

Adam peers closer, studying my hand. He rubs one of my chipped nails with his thumb. "Enthusiasm is contagious." He drops my hand. "What do the kids draw pictures of?"

Comics. I don't know why, but dividing a piece of paper into panels has been ridiculously entertaining for both the preschoolers and after-school crowd. But I can't talk about comics with Adam. #DeadGiveAway. "Kandinsky was our last artist of the week."

"You have an artist of the week?"

Cars honk behind us, and we lurch forward on the freeway once more.

"Parents can and do drop their kids off for ninety minutes every weekday. The Kids Club might be the only preschool-like experience some of these kids have." I shrug. "I might as well kill time in educational ways."

Adam gives me some major side-eye. "You're not fooling me. Go on. Let it out."

"It shouldn't matter who a kiddo's parents are. It's not the kid's fault if her parents can't afford preschool or enrichment classes. Every kid deserves to live in a society where their humanity, intelligence, and potential are validated from the start. Kids should be welcomed everywhere in the community, because they're part of our communities. Their care should not be seen as an inconvenience or an afterthought, because they aren't an inconvenience or an afterthought or... a mistake."

"Feels good, right? To not hold back. To get it all out."

"Yeah." An instinct to apologize surfaces, but the *sorry* doesn't materialize. "Thanks for listening."

He's comfortable accepting my thanks. "And school? How's that going?"

"It's good. There are too many gummy bears in the vending machines, but it's good."

"Gummy bears?"

"You'd think that buying a bag and holding it in your hand would ward off the urge for another."

"No?"

"I don't want to be made of gummy bears. I'm supposed to eat nuts and fresh produce, lean protein. Definitely not six servings of gummy bears daily."

"Hang on. I think we better stop for some gummy bears." Adam makes a big show of checking his mirrors.

"Would you drive?" I say.

He grins, and my heart is dancing Jack Black style. "As long as you tell me more about gummy bears."

"So I've taken to holing up in computer labs where food, i.e. gummy bears, are not allowed. I wish I had a laptop." I kick my feet out of my green Converse and put them on Adam's dash.

"No laptop?"

"Daniel broke mine. It's a long story. Actually, it's not. He stepped on it and then kicked it. And when I couldn't get it to work again, he said it was a crummy laptop, and we should just get a desktop. We ended up upgrading his gamer, which he kept when we split."

It was his, after all.

"You need a computer?"

"Who needs a computer when campus computer labs are everywhere?" I say, picking at the fraying knee of my jeans. I don't even give Adam a chance to respond before grabbing my soapbox. "Computer labs in theory should be helpful. Right? You pop in, log on. You do your work. Maybe you even print it out at the end. But in practice, computer labs are not helpful."

"Not even a little?"

"First of all, there is the problem of where to sit."

"How is choosing where to sit a problem?" Adam reaches for his coffee.

"You have a laptop, don't you?" I shiver, imagining what it must be like to work in the privacy of one's own space. Okay, maybe Adam's space. It's a really nice apartment. And his couch is so soft, with one of those plush, minky blankets thrown over one arm. I give myself the smallest of shakes and snap back to reality. "No, this is good. We can role-play."

Adam fumbles his cup, nearly spilling its contents across the dash. "Role-play?"

"Yeah, we do it in Kids Club all the time. It's really good for social and emotional learning to try on other people's problems."

"You have a social and emotional curriculum in addition to an artist of the week? Are parents camped out every day before your shift?"

I might be preening. Somewhere inside, I'm definitely purring. "Okay. You're me. Lecture ended twenty minutes early, which means you've got fifteen minutes to knock out an essay before you have to catch your Lyft to work—"

"Where I run a drop-in preschool on the sly for no additional fees. Do the children worship me? I mean, of course they do. Why else are they trying to make my art board?"

I want to touch him. Poke him. Give him a playful jostle, but he's driving, and I'm not fourteen. "You walk into a room with ninety-six computers. Twelve rows of eight. Where do you sit?"

"The back corner. As far away from the entrance as possible."

"Except I'm a weirdo who's going to fight you for it." I lean as far as I can into Adam's personal space while still wearing my seat belt. Maybe I am fourteen after all. "Now what are you going to do?"

Adam leans as far as he can away from me.

I strain against my seat belt to lean that much closer.

"Corners are dangerous. You run out of space quick. And this weirdo is the perfect mix of brooding and unaware to edge you out until you have no choice but to leave the lab altogether."

Adam laughs. "Okay, fine. Toward the front. Facing the door."

"Trying to keep a lookout?"

"Yeah. Avoid the weirdos."

"Distracting position to be in. You look up every time someone new walks in. How's the essay coming?"

"What essay?"

I pounce. "Exactly!" And Adam is laughing again. "You're not getting any work done. And then—"

"Then?"

"Then you make the mistake of catching the eye of someone like me. And now I'm chatting you up." I make a bro face—pursed lips, squinty eyes, slow head bob. "Hey, girl. I saw you look this way." I dramatically pause. "Do we know each other?"

"No."

"But you'd like to?"

"No."

"How dare you use me as a piece of eye candy and not swallow me whole? I'm going to sit here at this computer right next to yours, aggressively clicking my mouse and smacking the keyboard and making not-so-subtle noises of disgust until you have no choice but to pack up your stuff."

"That hasn't happened."

I raise my eyebrows and stifle a giggle. "You want to try your luck at another computer?"

"K. I'll sit with my back to the door somewhere in the middle."

"Big mistake," I say with mock sincerity. "Hey. Hey." I tap Adam on the shoulder. "Can I borrow a pen?"

"No."

"Pencil?"

"No."

"A dollar for the vending machine?"

"You're kidding."

"I had my eye on a crusty blueberry muffin. I'll pay you back. Yeah, in fact, I promise to pay you back the next time I see you." I want to reach over and grab Adam's shirt and twist it in my hands.

"Sorry, I spent all my cash on gummy bears."

I catch his eye and smile. He smiles back but does a double take when I don't look away.

I clear my throat. "Hey," I say gently.

"Hey." He's smiling. Now that the traffic is moving again, it's as if there's nothing but horizontal straight comic book hites outside our windows, blurring reality and intensifying the focus of our shared gaze. It's one of those gorgeous single-panel moments tucked into a bottom corner before the punch line on the opposite page.

"So... I'm applying for an internship, and this particular company is old-school. They double-space after periods." I crack and burst into laughter before I can finish.

"No!" Adam sounds amused but also a little disappointed.

My bro voice comes back. "Should I double-space after periods?'

"That actually happened?" Adam asks.

I chuckle. "Word for word."

We pull up in front of an enormous hotel.

"I think you're missing something," Adam says. He unbuckles and pops the trunk.

"What?" I say, unbuckling.

Adam blushes and then shrugs. "Have you tried studying someplace else on campus?"

"Like the library?" I roll my eyes. "People are after my pens and gummy bear dollars there too."

Adam is howling. He's out of the car and doubled up with laughter.

"What? It's not funny." I slam my car door shut.

"No." Adam laughs again. "It's very annoying." His lip trembles. He's struggling to maintain a frown. "The role-playing made that part very clear." Adam hands me one of his escape boxes.

"Right? Social and emotional learning can be fun."

Adam grabs another couple of boxes and slams his trunk shut. He hands his keys to the valet, and we weave our way through the hotel lobby.

"Why aren't we at the convention center?" I ask.

"Leto Con is a smaller convention. A lot more locals. Hence the Sheraton."

We show our vendor badges at the ballroom, and while we thread our way through the labyrinth of half-assembled stalls, Adam asks me if we can stop a minute by the drinking fountains. He returns with a bag of gummy bears.

We find our station. It isn't in the prime location that Adam had at Comic-Con outside the Halifax Sisters tent. But maybe this quiet back corner is strategic.

"Have you been to a convention before?" Adam asks me as we prime his escape boxes. The idea is the same as before, but the theme has been changed, of course, for the Letovians.

The lie is already forming on my lips. I'm about to deny all my comic nerdiness. "Just once."

"Really?" Adam's mouth tugs upward in amusement.

"I went to Comic-Con this year."

"And?" I swear he's holding his breath.

"It was like going to the zoo." I mean it as a compliment. The San Diego Zoo is one of my happy places. Dad would take me when I was little, and then we'd ride the train around Balboa Park and hit up the carousel.

"The cosplay is cool," Adam ventures, taking a seat on the provided card table.

"Incredible," I agree.

"Did you go to a panel?"

"Just one. We didn't want to stand in the sun for the others." Not in head-to-toe black vinyl. Adam's ears prick at the *we*. "I went with my friend. Gwen."

"You should have stopped by the vendors on the first floor."

"How do you know I didn't?"

"I would have seen you," he says.

My face feels hot.

"Here." Adam slides off the table. "Let me show you the trick to this box."

It is a nice day, and perhaps the nicest thing about it is the lack of silence. Everyone always tells me that a "comfortable silence" is the hallmark of a happy marriage/relationship/whatever. If you can be in a car with someone, spend the day with them, and not have to talk to them, everything is okay.

Daniel believed it. *Would you quit trying to find something for us to talk about?*

Silence haunted my past life. Silence was everywhere. And

honestly, I thought it was me. It was another one of my hang-ups that fed into my screw-ups.

Silence isn't comfortable. It isn't anything.

Adam wants to talk. And I want to talk to him.

Amazing the soul-searching one does while standing in line at a taco truck. Adam asked me to grab him one (one—ha!) while he finished up inside. A couple of Dr. Leto-obsessed restaurateurs were asking pointed questions about growth and return on investments. I needed dinner more than I needed to people-watch... or stare at Adam's chin. Yes, the alley. And no. I still don't know.

I'm making my way back with two boxes of tacos when Adam tugs on my hoodie. It isn't rough or anything of the kind, but with my convention track record, I jump and yelp and careen.

His arms steady me, and Shirley Temples, I like it.

"You okay?" Adam asks.

"Tacos," I mutter. I try and fail to let go of him.

"Is that a new one of your swears?" Adam asks.

Is it? Tacos, he's handsome. No. *Tacos* doesn't have the same panache as *goldfish*.

Goldfish, he's handsome.

That's much better.

"I didn't ask what kind of taco you like," I say. He's been asking me questions all day long, and I don't even know if I got him the right tacos.

"How could there be a wrong kind of taco?" Adam leads me through the considerably more crowded ballroom. The Letovians are queueing for the last event of the evening, the cosplay contest, which I am more than okay missing. Cosplay coming up in real life makes me blush, and I don't need Adam picking up on that and asking why.

"Why AJ Comics at your escape room? Why not Amaze?" I ask, but the room is way too loud to be heard. Adam leads me past his booth, where many trench-coat-wearing fans have amassed around the puzzle boxes, and out into a deserted stairwell. We camp out there on a carpeted landing. The noise of the ballroom pressing against the door from the other side makes me feel snug. Cozy, even.

Adam smiles down at his box of street tacos.

"You trying not to cry?" I say, opening up my box. I mean, tacos are beautiful.

"Yes," Adam says after a bite. "Spicy must mean something different in Pacific Beach than downtown."

"You don't like spicy?"

"I love spicy." Adam looks up. "It was the villains." He shrugs. "AJ has the better villains, and it was also orders of magnitude cheaper to license the characters."

"What came first? Your Halifax Sisters Studio internship or your escape room idea?"

"How does anyone ever answer a chicken-or-egg paradox? They both came first."

"They can't both come first," I say, taking a bite of my Korean taco. Slaw with red cabbage, carrots, cilantro, and pickled red onion was something I needed to remember to try at home.

"Sure, they can." Adam leans back against the wall. "I had the idea to angle cosplay into escape rooms. I also applied for a studio internship. Entertainment is huge business."

"And the fact that you landed on superheroes while interning at Halifax Sisters, which owns Nightbat—"

Something like a wistful expression graces his face. "I've been coming to these conventions since... since middle school. Superheroes are a safe bet."

"Safer than Dr. Leto?"

Adam grabs the grilled shrimp taco and inhales it. "There are some excellent villains in Dr. Leto."

"What is up with you and villains?" I try the shrimp taco and want to weep. They added a coconut curry sauce on top, and it is mind-blowingly delicious.

"They are more fun. A hero is only as good as his villain. The real difference between Nightbat and Magnificent Man is that Nightbat gets to fight better villains and a lot of them. Badpun, Conundrum, Mallard, Ad Hominem, the Shoemaker, Poison Hemlock, Fair Play."

Did he purposely skip Catstrike? Why? Is he embarrassed? Does he not consider her a villain but an antihero? Is he still mad at me?

"What about Catstrike?" Was the question too obvious? Should I have not said anything? Oh fudge, is he going to put it together?

His face reddens. It could have been the spicy sauce. "Everyone loves a good villain."

I hand him a Diet Hansen's soda from the pocket of my hoodie. When I pull out a second one for me, Adam laughs.

"Now the hoodie thing makes perfect sense."

"Shut up," I say.

He pops his soda open, and the hiss echoes in the stairwell. "There's a small computer lab on the fourth floor of the econ building. No one will try to pick you up there."

I recoil. "People are not—"

"Yeah, they are."

He's sitting right next to me, and I'm gripped with the need to hang on him, hold on to him, touch him, inhabit his space. We could kiss. And with the convention behind the closed door at our backs, it would be a spectacular first kiss.

Except it wouldn't be a first kiss. That happened already. Goldfish, that has happened a few times.

I stiffen. "I should get going. I've gotta get back for my shift." I stare down at my Converse and toe the swirly pattern in the grey concrete.

"Yeah, let's get you back to your second home."

"No, I'll get a Lyft. I don't want to pull you away from more interested fans and would-be franchisers."

"It's a small convention. I've already talked to everyone here."

"Yeah, but—"

"And it's over in another twenty minutes. Half the vendors left an hour ago." He rises and offers me his hand. "Let's go."

~

I call Tony, but he doesn't answer. So I send a text.

Me: I'm going to be late for my shift. We got stuck in traffic. I'll be there as soon as I can.

I call again later as we inch our way forward on I-5. Tony picks up.

I wince and lean my head against the cold car window. "I'm going to be really late."

"Hey, don't worry about it. These things happen." I hear a familiar lilting voice on the other end calling my manager's name. "Right there, Gwen," Tony calls. "I've got your shift covered, Sarah. Drive safe. I'll see you tomorrow."

"He hung up in a hurry," I say, tossing my phone down.

"Everything okay?" Adam asks.

We crawl forward a car length.

"He gave me the night off."

It's dark, but the glow of the other cars' headlights reveals that Adam is trying hard not to smile. "That's generous," he says casually.

"Gwen has that effect on people. Especially people like Tony."

"Gwen is your roomie?"

I smile. He's a dog with a bone. "Gwen's my friend. She and Tony have this on-again, off-again, cat-and-mouse... thing that I'm happy not to get in the way of."

"So if I wanted to spend next Friday night with you, I just find a way to get Gwen to the gym?"

"Your car is too clean. I need a balled-up receipt or something to throw at you."

We talk more about school. This is Adam's last semester, which makes me a little sad. We talk about my training, and Adam is shocked that I've never signed up for any official races.

"I'm not sure if you know this, a lot of people don't..." I lean in, he leans in. The traffic is at a standstill. I suppress my smile. Not as well as Adam, but effort is what counts here. "You can run for free. Whenever you want for however long you want."

Adam laughs. "For reals?"

"Why would I want to pay to run a race when I can run alone, by myself, on my own schedule?"

"Bragging rights? The smug Insta posts of before and the sweaty after? It could be fun."

"I'll pass."

"You like to be alone," Adam observes.

"No." I hate being alone. "I like to fly under the radar. You can't disappoint people if they aren't watching you."

The traffic thins, and we're driving through the gemstone streets of Pacific Beach. Opal. Tourmaline. Beryl.

"You have to tell me where you live. I can't take you back to the Green Flash."

"I'm actually going to do some weights. You can take me to my gym."

"You are not. You ran this morning. I'm going to start imagining all kinds of terrible things about your home if you don't tell me—"

"Yeah, well, they can't be much worse than living with your mom in her office/spare bedroom because you're buried under student loans and credit card debt, and there is no way you can make it in your own place until you graduate, which will take some time since you can barely scrape together tuition for a couple of classes."

My breath is shallow. And while the truth came easily enough for once, it most certainly did not set me free. I'm still in Adam's car, and we are still driving closer to my house and farther away from the gym.

"I'd like to meet your mom," Adam says. And the words are spoken with space-farmboy levels of sincerity.

"You do, and she's going to think we're dating." Also true.

"We're not dating?" Adam asks. A shy smile on his lips. I shudder, remembering a different time when I climbed on top of him and kissed those lips. But that wasn't me. I mean, it *was* me, but he didn't know it was me, and I for sure felt like someone else. "You sure?" he presses.

"I think dating looks different than meeting up for breakfast and then hitting up a convention." Yes, that was good. Because that's what friends do. I could just as easily have been one of the guys today. If Adam was a one-of-the-guys type.

"What would dating look like? Sushi, commandeering your boyfriend's favorite hoodie, and watching Netflix on a Thursday night?"

I swallow as he eases his car to a stop at Kate Sessions Park. The view of the city from this park is spectacular. And on a clear night like tonight, you can see the Coronado Islands silhouetted in the moonlight.

"Watching the city lights together?" he asks.

"San Diego is a beautiful city." I inhale.

"Absolutely stunning," he says, not turning his gaze from me. "How 'bout it?"

"Dating..." My head is foggy. "Right. I guess I'd be the worst person to ask. I haven't dated anyone... ever."

Adam turns off the car and unbuckles. "Not in high school?"

"Who dates in high school? There's no time. Did you?"

Adam shrugs. "A couple times. Sure."

My eyes narrow. "You had a girlfriend. High school sweetheart?"

"No. My first college girlfriend. My only college girlfriend. She had a high school sweetheart."

"Ouch." I stare down at my seat belt, still securely fastened.

"Yeah. It was... It was a mess. I was Allison's backup. I fell madly in love. I started pricing rings and covertly measuring her ring size. You know." He takes my hand and gently wiggles my dad's ring free. His hands feel confident, strong, and warm. "Sliding them on my fingers to see where..." Adam clears his throat and immediately takes off my ring. "My parents got married young, and it was something my dad told me he did." He hands it back. "She didn't even break up with me. She said she didn't have to because we were only ever just friends. And then when I told her that I didn't hook up with just friends, she said, 'Adam. You're not my leading man. You're the cute, funny guy in the movie with a forgettable name that makes me realize that it's always been Kevin.'"

My mouth falls open. "She did not say that."

"Allison was a film major."

"I'm sorry." *She didn't deserve you,* I want to say. *She is the world's biggest idiot. Who the fudge would ever leave a guy like Adam for a* Kevin? But I don't say any of it. #coward.

"Not as sorry as I am." Adam sighs and leans in ever so slightly, and I can faintly smell the Tide detergent on his clothes. "You busy this weekend?"

Uh-oh. That ASMR shiver is back. "I think I'm working."

Adam smiles. "Let me take you home. You already told me your roomie is your mom."

"It would be weird. My mom would want to meet you."

"Then I won't even walk you to the door. I'll just skid to a stop and kick you out."

"Fine, but only if you peel away with tires screeching. We're the little cottage on Los Altos Street." I direct him through the two turns from the park.

"Nice xeriscape," Adam says, pulling alongside the driveway.

"Mom doesn't believe in growing anything that is not edible. Unless it is to attract pollinators or something."

"What's your mom's name?" Adam asks.

"Janice."

Before I can say or do anything, Adam is out of the car and waving. "You must be Janice," he calls.

Holy fudge brownies. I grab my bag and prepare for awkwardness. I think my mom must have sprinted from the kitchen window and out the front door. "Hi, Mom. This is Adam."

"Well, hello, Adam. Nice to meet you." Mom is guarded, thank heavens.

Adam is not. "Nice to meet you." He cocks his head and stoops at a wilted plant. "Are these heirloom tomatoes?"

Oh no. Not tomato talk. But the floodgate is open. Mom launches into her hybridized verses heirloom lecture. Adam listens, and when Mom turns to pick a tomato, he winks at me.

I could kill him.

"People don't realize that our growing season goes nearly to Thanksgiving," Mom finishes at last.

Adam nods. "What's the best tomato for a burger?"

"They're all good. Right, Mom? I think Adam has to be going." I try and fail to steer Mom back inside.

"No," Adam says simply. "I'm good."

So not helpful.

Mom considers carefully. We stand in the damp night air, listening to the neighbor's eucalyptus trees shake with the breeze. "It comes down to personal preference," she says at last. "I'm partial to the lemon boys."

"The yellow ones?" Adam asks.

Mom presses her lips together in a smile. "Great on a salmon burger. Pairs wonderfully with our lemonade. But if you're wanting a red, I'd persuade you to try some of our cherries. If you put them in a grill basket just for a couple minutes, the sweetness really comes out. We throw them in with some summer squash and some basil and onions and top our burgers with the whole deal."

"That sounds incredible," Adam says.

"You should try it," Mom replies.

Adam looks at me. "I'd like to."

And before I can stop the train from derailing, Mom has invited Adam over for a Tuesday night barbecue.

"I know for a fact that Sarah will be here. She has class on Tuesday afternoon but, unlike Thursdays, no study groups."

Adam smiles. "I'll be there."

I, on the other hand, will be dead of embarrassment and composting under Mom's tomatoes.

CHAPTER TWENTY

My phone pings. The text icon angrily glares on my locked screen.

Adam: Where the hell are you?

Sabine Kennedy: I'm fired, remember?

Adam: You will be if you don't get here in the next ten minutes.

#KnewIt, and that is why my catsuit will forever and always be stuffed in the bottom of my gym bag.

CHAPTER TWENTY-ONE

"Mom, where are all my hoodies?" I ask Tuesday before class.

"Oh, honey, you've been working so hard with school and with your job, I wanted to try and help. I washed them."

I check the dryer. It's empty. I check the washing machine. It is filled with wet hoodies, yoga pants, T-shirts, and jeans—all of which are starting to smell overripe. I give a little yelp of terror.

"Oh no. Sarah, honey, I am so sorry. I must have forgotten to switch them over last night. Here, let me restart them. Better put it on the sanitize cycle." Before I can protest, my hoodies are swirling before me while the locked machine flashes that there are four hours and fifteen minutes before the cycle is complete.

"Mom. Are you stressing out about the BBQ? I can cancel it. I can tell Adam it's off."

"I'm not sure he'll believe you since I just sent him an email to confirm."

I wring out my wet hair in a puddle on the garage floor. "How do you have his email?"

"I asked for it after you went cherry red and ran inside without saying so much as good night last Friday." She tucks a loose strand of my hair back in place and straightens the collar of my bathrobe before I can swat her away. "Honey, you don't have many friends, and he seems like such a nice boy. Besides, I already invited Brent and Jen to join us."

Brent and Jen?! Goldfish, this woman. She's the one with super-powers. I give up. "Fine. But what am I going to wear?"

Mom bites her cheek. "Isn't there something hanging in your closet?"

I roll my eyes. "You almost had me believing it was an accident."

"Believing what was an accident? Those dresses are just as comfortable as your hoodies. Probably more so on a day like today. We're supposed to hit a record high."

I grab a short olive jumpsuit instead of a dress, just because I know it will bug her. And while I fully expect Mom to splash certi-fied organic cranberry juice all over my jumpsuit when I get back from class, she doesn't.

Adam arrives. With flowers. And a pink box. "Everyone likes cake, right?" he says when I open the door.

"I will murder you for this," I hiss.

"Okay. I'll know not to bring cake next time."

"You don't get it. The last boy who came to a barbecue—"

Mom appears in her cat apron. "Sarah. Don't keep poor Adam on the front step baking in the sun." I move out of the way before she bulldozes over me. "Come on in, Adam. Glass of lemonade?"

They exchange flowers for lemonade like it is no big deal. Like they are old friends.

"Brent is in the back. Poor Jen couldn't make it. She's got reverse morning sickness. Throwing up on the hour every hour after four p.m. Goodness knows she has reason to after looking into all those wide-open, disgusting little mouths of crooked teeth."

Adam swallows. His eyes flitter briefly.

"Brent and Jen are undertakers," I mumble.

Adam spills some of his lemonade. "Cool."

"Sarah! Take the cake from poor Adam and come help me with this salad."

"Can I help?" Adam asks.

"With the barbecue out back. Take this to Brent." Mom is delighted to have another person to boss around. She misses her students over the summer and on weeknights too. My mother is a complete dictator in her classroom. Somehow, her students love her. I get it, kids appreciate a woman who can run a tight ship. The principle translates even to Kids Clubs. But none of my mom's adoring students have to live with her.

"Wasn't that nice of Adam to bring a cake?" Mom is glowing as she adds the red onions, squash, and cherry tomatoes to the grill basket.

"You forgot the basil."

"I did, didn't I? Go get me some nice sprigs. The green *and* some purple too."

She planned that.

The purple basil is in the back. Near the barbecue. And because I am a chicken, I start with the green. I hear Adam and my brother talking as I pinch off the spicy sprigs.

"Orthodontists? Both of you?" Adam sounds relieved. I know ribbing is flirting under a different pretext, but I love cracking Adam's chill. It's a hill I'd die on. Daily. Hourly.

"So Jen's ill?" Adam asks.

"Morning sickness should be called morning, noon, and night sickness. I offered to stay home, but she said the smell of any cooking would make her cry. She's living off of saltine crackers and flat ginger ale."

I hear the sizzle of a burger being flipped. "Sarah was just as sick, right?" Adam asks.

Absolute silence. "You know about that?" Brent says.

"She told me."

"You're the first. She didn't even tell me. I found out by accident. The hospital called me by mistake. Serious breach of HIPAA." Brent sighs. At least I think he sighs. There are a lot of sizzling sounds coming from the barbecue. "It's just so sad. Unfair too. My sister is a shadow of who she used to be."

"Who did she used to be?" Adam asks.

Yeah. Who was I, Brent?

"She had this spark, you know? I'm not saying she was always the life of the party, but with the right crowd, she transformed. She was into... Oh, what's the word? Sorry, I've got father-to-be brain."

Don't say cosplay. Don't say cosplay.

"No worries," Adam says.

"She was into fandoms," Brent says. "You know? You did not want to get into a fight with Sarah over anything you saw on a movie screen. I told her she could make a living being a consultant for all the superhero movies and stuff."

"A producer," Adam says. "I could see that."

Brent barrels on. "She had the kind of presence that would get a crowd's attention."

"A natural leader?"

"Totally. But now. Jeez. There are days where she walks into a room, and it feels like the sun has permanently set. Jen just sobs for her. Jen didn't want to tell anyone we're expecting, but Sarah is tougher than she looks, Adam, right? Can you hand me that thermometer? The spices too."

More sounds of sizzling meat to accompany my shock. Brent was paying attention this whole time. He understood better than I gave him credit for and...cares.

"I blame her ex. She was married for almost two years."

"That long?" Adam says.

"They stayed together for a while after the miscarriage. Probably out of pride. No one wants to admit they got married for a reason as old-fashioned as an unexpected pregnancy. I thought she'd be happier now that it's all behind her."

"She said her ex is a total douche. Living in China."

"I'll punch the guy senseless if I ever see him again."

"Get in line."

Did Adam really just say that?

"So how did you two meet?"

Adam exhales. Loud and long. If he didn't seem so flustered, I'd say it sounded like a sigh. "Let's see..." More charming sounds of hesitation. "I was Sarah's TA in econ for a little bit before I switched classes. Well, before I requested to switch classes."

The zucchini vine behind the basil rustles as I catch the scaly samba movement of a lizard's tail. I yelp involuntarily.

"You stinker," Brent yells. "Have you been eavesdropping?"

Busted.

I grab a handful of purple basil. "Adam made the mistake of disparaging my hoodies."

Brent shakes his head. "She didn't tell you they were our dad's?"

"Oh, of course. But it was worse than that." Adam grins. "I said she didn't look like a runner."

"Well, she totally doesn't. Where is her enormous Apple Watch?" Brent asks.

"The tan?" Adam continues.

"The bubbly runner's high?" Brent goads.

"Fudge off." I pull up another handful of purple basil.

Dinner is good. Mom is so absorbed in eating her tomatoes that she doesn't have time to play matchmaker. She has plenty of time to play twenty questions with Adam, though.

"Adam, where are you from?" she asks.

"Here, actually. Well, Del Mar."

"Doesn't count," Brent says.

"I have a little apartment off of Beryl Street while I'm finishing my thesis."

Mom slices into her burger. She's one of the only people I know who insists on eating a burger with a knife and fork. "Kinda far from campus."

"Close to my work, though," Adam says.

"Adam is an entrepreneur," I tell Brent. Mom already knows this from meeting Adam the other day, but part of me wants to emphasize it again for her. I suppose I want her to be as impressed by Adam as I am.

"Have you heard of Superhero Escapes on Garnet?" Adam asks.

"You're the escape room guy?" Brent asks.

"I am. Can't convince Sarah to come see it."

"What? Sarah!" Mom says my name like I am the most disappointingly obtuse child in the world. What's wrong with me? Don't I understand that life is about spending time with intelligent, successful hotties like Adam?

"School, Mom. Work." They are excellent excuses—nice and succinct. Unlike the other one about Adam also being my employer/crush/TA/not TA/sometimes make-out buddy.

"And your study groups, I know. Sarah is determined to earn back her scholarship."

"You don't earn back a scholarship, Mom, if you're going to a different school."

"Who wants cake?" Brent asks.

"You should go tonight," Mom says.

I choke on my lemonade. "Excuse me?"

"You should go see Adam's escape room tonight." Mom directs her next words at Adam. "She's not telling you this, but it's the crowds that are keeping her away."

"He's not open tonight."

"True, my cast isn't there. But I could show you the rooms."

Mom has Mason jars of cake and pop-top bottles of lemonade packed for us before I can invent an excuse not to go.

"You want to come, Brent?" I ask in a burst of desperation.

Mom looks thunderously put out.

"Yeah," Brent agrees. "Why not?"

Brent makes it past the front doors, but that's about it. He pokes his head into an escape room proper then asks Adam about booking a team-building event for his office before he disappears, leaving me and Adam alone with our cake in his escape room.

A text buzzes my phone.

Brent: Know you didn't ask me to come to sniff him out, but Adam seems like a decent guy. Text if you need me.

My brother may not be a superhero fan, but he's a really good guy.

"Ever been to an escape room?" Adam asks.

"It's not my thing," I evade.

"Tough crowd. Okay. Well. I have a few different escape rooms here. I have the more traditional ones. Osric Manor Mystery. Abandum City Cyberattack. The *Daily Post* Abduction. I also have a hybrid offering, a haunted house meets escape room. Very easy puzzles."

"Let's do that one." What? No. Bad idea.

"Malum Escape it is. Just imagine my cast playing the villains in the different cells."

The door creaks and then clangs shut. "Welcome to Malum Asylum. I'm the warden. Do not under any circumstances touch the inmates. If you do, you will be escorted to an isolated cell where you will stay for a very long time. No pictures, no phones, no recording at any time.

"There is no escape from Malum. There is no justice in Malum. There is only... I can't remember the rest. 'Deputy Chief Eden' is our safe word. We make everyone practice." He pulls a lever, a bell buzzes, and the lights dim. "This way."

Another door creaks open.

Adam turns to me. "Boo!"

"I need pearls to clutch," I say flatly.

"It's terrifying when Alan does it. He's my Shoemaker, and he's usually up above." He points to the bars on the ceiling.

"How do you get out of this room?" I try the door. It's stuck.

"Well, you can always retreat. But this is a cooperative task. If the guests are really not getting it, Alan will give clues. You have to push the buttons at the same time."

I walk to the button opposite of Adam and press it. He does the same with the other button. The cell door opens.

"Who is in this room?" I ask.

"Ad Hominem. You have to get his coin and jam it into this puzzle. I mean, you don't have to. You could use chewing gum and a high heel. We've had that happen. That was a fun night."

"I remember," I say.

Adam stops. "What?"

Goldfish. "I remember working at a haunted house once... And if a particular room got backed up, it was, um, chaotic."

He seems to take that at face value.

"This next room is basically a scare," he goes on. "Cetus or Paroxysm. And the exit is through the window, which is really fun."

He vaults through and pulls me down after him. "Then Mallard. His is an actual riddle room. How fast people make it through depends on how steady our traffic is that night. I make my Mallard, Conundrum, and Shoemaker wear earpieces. Poison Hemlock, too, sometimes."

"I wondered about that."

"For Mallard's riddle, you need to borrow a page of his newspaper. It's one of those that uses the first word of every other column." He stops, looks me up and down, head to toe. "You're okay with strobes, right? We make everyone sign a waiver."

"Yeah."

"This way."

"And where are we?" I ask, stepping into the padded cell I occupy as Catstrike.

"Catstrike's cell. After everyone gets to stand and gawk, the strobes start. She disappears, usually through the same door we just walked through, as guests fumble around for this switch."

"Then we come to Fair Play's room, or Farris Cordelia Playdon, depending on what Vanessa is feeling."

"Then Badpun," I say.

"I have a manager watching Malum Escape feeds at all times. I have another two monitoring the traditional escape rooms."

"It's impressive."

Adam is obviously pleased by my praise. "You should come see it with my cast. It is something else."

"Have you gone through?"

"Oh, yeah. I've also failed to escape from my own escape rooms several times. You want to look at one?"

"Are we actually locked in?"

"No."

"Could we be?"

Adam's eyes go dark for a moment. Maybe he's living out a kinky fantasy, or maybe he's imagining the legal implications if a stunt like that were possible. "No. There's no way. Come on. Let's go to Osric Manor."

We walk into a room that is decorated to the hilt.

I gawk at the detail: gilt frames on what look like honest-to-goodness original oil paintings, Persian rugs, leather sofas and chairs with scrolled feet and those tufted buttons on the back. "How did you—" I begin before the bookshelf catches my eye. Holy fudge. I slide a book off the shelf—beautiful, leather-bound, with swirling gold etchings on the binding. All the books look equally gorgeous.

"I grew up in Del Mar. People give this stuff away every five minutes because they're redecorating. Wiring the piano was the hardest. Come on." He pulls me over to the grand piano, and I follow all too willingly. "You've seen *Nightbat Begins*?"

He plays three keys on the piano, and a closet opens. "Not an entrance to an underground cave, but cool, right?"

I examine the circuit breaker in the closet. "So you flip the switches?" I nearly jump when Adam reaches around me. He's standing so close.

"Well, you find the clues that tell you what order to flip the switches." Adam flips them. "And they unlock the safe."

"What safe?"

"The one behind the portrait." He rests an elbow against the bookshelf and leans his head against his open palm. "You dip the scarf in the fishbowl."

I've peered inside the safe to see a scarf among a pearl necklace and passports. "You do not."

"Come here. Check this out," Adam says, taking a seat on the sofa.

I poke around some more and find a box of cards in the pocket of a card table before I join him on the couch. "What? Spring-loaded?" I ask, sliding the cards out of the box. Maybe there is a clue tucked in with them.

"Nope. Just a couch. And now you're sitting on it with me. Don't we have cake?"

I pull out the glass jars from my bag and the forks and napkins from my hoodie pocket. To say this cake is yummy is too modest of a description. "What did you find?" Adam asks, licking his fork, and goldfish, I think I've found paradise in this Black Forest cake.

I give my head a little shake. A cake coma is approaching. I pick up the cards and shuffle them. It's the strangest deck I've ever seen. "Are these tarot cards?"

Adam turns crimson. "Where'd you find those?"

"They were in the pocket drawer of your card table."

Adam runs a hand through his hair.

"Not yours?" I ask.

"I didn't know there was a pocket drawer in that table," he says.

"So the cards are just random?"

"Not random, but definitely someone's idea of a joke."

I wonder how many people have sat on this couch. I wonder how many people have sat on this couch with Adam. "Allison?" Her name passes my lips without my permission, and I can't stuff it back in.

"What?" Adam says. He sounds shocked. "No, no. My sisters. Or my mom. Someone is teasing me. Tarot cards are a long-standing joke in my family. My mom's way of dishing out relationship advice. I'm warning you now; be careful."

But now I can't get Allison out of my brain. The thought of her and Adam on this couch makes me want to break things. "What do they think of all of this?"

"My mom doesn't understand why I needed to do it."

"Ah. You come from that part of Del Mar. The trust fund part?"

"Ha. No. My parents do. But they are the last people on earth who are going to invest in an escape room. I got some of their friends to nibble. Professors too."

"Of course you did. Your parents must be proud of you."

"They're wondering when I'm going to stop playing around and apply to law school."

"Are you?"

"I don't think I have the attention span to do it. Flipping businesses is more my speed. Did I tell you I found someone interested in partnering with me for the Dr. Leto-themed room? It's a couple, actually. They own a coffee shop in La Jolla, have always been fans of the show, and have space above their place right now being underutilized by storage and a cluttered office."

He sprawls out on the couch. I see where I'd fit right next to him, and I want to, but instead, I flip open my phone and hail a Lyft. I have five minutes. Nothing can happen in five minutes. I can relax now.

"Was it so bad?" Adam asks as I slide in closer. He puts an arm around my shoulders. I do not resist. "Me coming over for a barbecue? Meeting your family?"

"Having my mom basically throw me at you. Hearing about how I stayed married to save face. Put it this way." I lace my fingers into his, and it is so fantastic I nearly giggle. I realize I've been incubating caterpillars in my stomach ever since meeting Adam, because now the butterflies have hatched. "Would you like me to meet your parents?" I'm teasing him. At least it sounds that way on the surface.

He hesitates. "I would."

"Liar."

"Next to my dad, your mom would look like an indifferent ice cube. My dad would offer you a dowry to marry me."

"Is that so?" I lean into his shoulder. He smells like hickory chips and barbecue smoke. All those savory, sizzling smells stuck to his skin and even more to his hair. I want to press my nose in deep and inhale until I'm dizzy.

"It gets worse. My mom would tell you that our first son must be named Vincent, after her dad, and her first granddaughter Lily, because it's a great name. Then she'd want to do tarot cards with you, where she'd do her best to convince you that every card means a future with me." Adam blushes. "It's her favorite party trick. She'll be happy to know you've recovered one of her decks."

"Brothers?" I ask.

"Three sisters. All lawyers. They'd offer to write prenups."

"Why are they so desperate to see you married?"

"Because I'm the baby of the family. Because I was so... so stupid when things didn't work out before." He hesitates. "With Allison. It wasn't so much about her. I mean, in the moment, I thought it was... But it was more about my first serious relationship ending at a rough moment and not knowing how to cope. I failed a few classes, slept too much, ate too little. Drank a lot." I feel Adam raise a shoulder under me. "Live and learn."

I cringe. Sure. Some people get to live and learn and move on with their lives. Other people, people like me, get to live and mourn. My phone pings. "My Lyft approaches."

"Don't take a Lyft. I'll take you home."

"So you can get invited to another barbecue?" I rise and shove the empty Mason jars back into my bag. They clank against each other and my keys.

"I was aiming for Thanksgiving, actually." Adam stands slowly, until all at once he is towering over me. In my flat little green Converse, I'd have to tilt my chin way up to look him in the eye. I can't do it without a tear spilling out. "Hey. You okay?" he asks.

No. "This was fun. Thanks for showing me your escape room." I hesitate for the briefest of moments before wrapping my arms around him. I bury my face in his chest. My body tenses with a primal need. I want to sob into his shoulder while he holds me.

"Sarah." He strokes my back gently. "I know it isn't the same. I know I can never even approach what you've gone through."

There is a sob stuck somewhere in my throat. I try to take a deep breath. I try not to lose it. "Breakups are hard." My words are tight. "I get you must really miss Allison." I try to pull away, but Adam holds me tighter.

"Sure." His hand is in my hair. "At the time, I was devastated, which is absurd since Allison was never mine to love." He pulls me away and finds my eyes. "But your daughter. She's yours to love forever. And—"

My fingers slip out of my hoodie and over his lips. I need to hold on to those words for a minute. I need to wrap those words around me like a wool blanket on a cold, windy night. I need those words to stay with me forever.

Adam kisses my fingers. He takes hold of my hand and kisses the inside of my palm.

"And it must hurt like hell."

Adam has rendered my heart transparent. The shock of his understanding stops my tears. I should run away now. This is the point where I need to sprint as hard and as fast as I can. But I don't want to run. I want to stay here. I want to kiss Adam senseless, to push him back on the couch and kiss him until he can't speak or see straight. Forget his words; I want to wrap *him* around me on a cold, windy night. On all the nights.

But I can't move. I have to tell Adam the truth. I burn up with the need to bare my soul, to explain why I couldn't tell him about the cosplay, but I don't know where to begin.

I'm not who you think I am.

I'm a liar and a freak.

"Adam," I whisper.

His eyes focus on me with an intensity that approaches painful. If I could ink those eyes out into a black-and-white panel, I would. No man has ever looked at me like this. Maybe no man ever will again. My fingers trace his laugh lines, slowly, cautiously. I'm making contact with a wild creature that is both dangerous and gorgeous. One wrong step, and he'll bolt so far and fast, I'll never find him again.

My phone pings again, and I'm the one who spooks. I am out the back door and in my Lyft without even a goodbye. And as I ride away, the words I should have said to Adam come.

I can't lose you.

CHAPTER TWENTY-TWO

I check my cowl in the mirror on the staff room wall and am bracing myself for another Saturday night of strobe lights and screams at the escape room when Stacey calls me over. She's in the Redemption Ring Reboot costume, which means mere mortals are terrified into speechless submission by her gorgeousness.

"Your number has been called," she says. "Time to train you in managing Abandum City Cyberattack."

I follow Stacey and nod to Alan and Frankie in passing.

"How much do you know about Nightbat?" Stacey asks, punching in the code to the door.

"A lot." My voice ripples with sexy confidence. I follow her into a control room with multiple flat-screen TVs showing split images of the lobby and all the escape rooms.

She kicks the door closed. "Good. Then we can skip all the exposition, and you can tell me what's going on between you and Adam."

It's as if I've turned the page of a comic and been blindsided by a left-page sucker punch. Pow! My sexy confidence slips off me like mascara after an impromptu run. Not smooth, definitely not pretty.

Stacey punches a few keys into the main computer and checks

the angle of the camera's rotation. "Come on, Sarah."

I hiss at the sound of my real name.

Stacey puts her hands on her hips and stares me down. "You two are dating." She holds up an exquisite hand, complete with deflector cuff, when I try to protest. "I know about the barbecue."

My face grows hot. Had the cameras been recording when Adam and I came to the escape room last Tuesday? "Barbecue?"

Stacey flicks up the volume, and the control room is filled with quiet static. She tosses me her phone, which has been queued to a series of texts.

Stacey: Hey, any chance you could come over and help Monique out with some econ tonight?

Adam: Wish I could, but I have a date.

Stacey: Oh??? Anyone I know?

Adam: Yeah, actually.

Stacey: ???

Adam: You remember Sarah at the Student Union Starbucks?

Stacey: The runner? The one you rearranged your TA schedule for? The one who won't even consider jumping in the pool?

Adam: The very same. I've been invited to a family barbecue. Remind me to pick up a cake.

Stacey: Pick up a cake. So... what number is this? Family barbecues don't just happen on a first date.

Adam: Third date.

Adam: Ish.

Stacey: Attaboy. Can you swing by tomorrow to help out Monique?

Adam: As long as you don't grill me about the BBQ.

Stacey: We're all econ all the time over here.

I hand the phone back to Stacey. On the split screen above us, a party of four shuffles into the escape room decorated like the Abandum City Police Department. The door closes, and a set of sparks blow, making the players scream. The lights dim, and the large screen crackles to life. Smart of Adam to digitize the intro on this one.

My eyes narrow as I watch the intro through our feed. A red circle with an oversized N in the middle flickers on the big-screen TV in the escape room. My lips twitch into a smile. "Nihilism is the villain in this one," I say.

Stacey's eyes flit over to me before she clicks through to the next prompt in the program. "You're the first person I've trained who even knows who Nihilism is. This is our hardest room. It's filled with references even die-hard fans miss. And there is a manual of backstory and references"—she thumps her hand on a bulging three-ring binder—"that Adam insists every operator read before running this room."

"I bet he would." His attention to detail goes beyond immersive for his rooms.

"What is going on with you two?" Stacey asks.

I cannot have this conversation when I'm dressed as Catstrike. "Nothing." Lies. The divided flat-screen shows an image from each corner of the room. The players inside are shuffling around, looking under chairs and under papers. One finds a key.

"Key found." Stacey checks the box in the program. "You have to tell him," she says.

"Stacey, you don't get it. This..." I gesture to my ridiculous costume. "This is an act. I put on this suit, and I'm playing a part. This isn't me."

"You know I stay late, right?" Stacey checks the time, pauses, and then prompts another clue from Whalemoney, Nihilism's hacker alias. I squint and see the flat-screen in the escape room flash a message to the escapees, prompting them to reexamine the stack of letters. She swivels in her chair to look at me. "I reset, run updates on the software, close out the register." She taps the screen. "Watch that guy in the Padres hat."

"Watch for what?" The gentleman is knocking hard on all the walls around the room.

"Make sure he doesn't break something."

I'm about to ask how I do that, but Stacey continues.

"So a couple weeks ago, I'm here, counting the nickels and dimes, and Adam returns." She leans back in her chair, staring straight at me, through me. Goldfish, I might as well be naked. "Looking for all the world like he's just landed on an alien planet. His hair is completely wrecked. His eyes are all hazy, and his lips are swollen and rimmed with traces of red lipstick."

I keep my eyes focused on the screen. I stare at the little people crawling around in it, my own personal virtual ant farm.

"A berry-red lipstick," Stacey adds.

She waits for an answer.

I clear my throat. No trace of my sexy femme fatale voice now. "Adam is on drugs and experimenting with makeup?"

Stacey prompts another clue. "I know a post-make-out look when I see one. Adam is my friend. He's Monique's friend too. So you're going to tell me what 'the fudge' is going on."

I stare at the screen. The guy in the Padres hat appears to be knocking on all the surfaces, his date wandering around aimlessly behind him. "With the escape room people?"

"With you and Adam!"

I know. Goldfish, can I just go to my padded cell now?

Stacey prompts another clue and mumbles something about spoon-feeding not being in her job description. She glares up at me—and Shirley Temples, I'm scared.

"I don't know," I mutter. "He was upset. He said I was fired. I may have kissed him."

Stacey folds her arms across her chest. "And meanwhile, you're dating in real life but playing hard to get?"

"Stacey, you don't get it. I've got a past. I can't rush things. And I can't let anyone know that this is how I'm paying for classes. If anyone finds out..." Goldfish, it would be worse than the first time. My costume is a thinly veiled dominatrix caricature. The fact that I enjoy wearing it is proof that I am a depraved lunatic with sexually repressed and sexually anxious fantasies. No one would want to have anything to do with me if they knew.

But Gwen knows. And Stacey knows. They haven't bailed on me.

Yet. And if I left through the front door of the gym like a normal person while in costume, Tony would probably know, too, and he wouldn't care. But if Tony knew about my cosplay gig, then he'd also know that I've been lying about my schedule. I groan. That, he'd definitely care about.

"What?" Stacey demands.

"I'd lose my job at the gym." If lying about my schedule didn't get me fired, vaulting the wall every Thursday and Saturday night would. And while it may not be breaking and entering, I'm pretty sure it's a serious OSHA violation. My employee membership would be revoked. I'd never see the inside of the Kids Club again. Once again, I'd be fodder for Brent and Jen's front desk.

Stacey's eyes narrow. "So you think you can make out with Adam all you want when you're in cosplay because no one will find out?"

"No. It was one time." I grab my cat ears. My cowl feels way too tight tonight. "Maybe two, although that could have been someone else."

"You're making out with other people too?"

"No!"

Stacey spreads her hands wide on the table. I've never seen her upset, and it is frankly terrifying. "Look. I get the fear. It's scary to tell the truth, especially when it means you finally have to start being authentic with everyone. It means things will change in big ways. But, Sarah—"

The sound of my real name has me instantly riveted.

Stacey's voice softens. "Do it sooner rather than later. Not just for Adam. But for you."

My phone pings. My real number, not the Sabine Kennedy one. It's Adam.

Adam: What are you up to tonight?

Me: Working.

Adam: Can I come say hi?

My heart skips.

Me: Yes.

Yes. Come. There's nothing I'd like better than to prance around in my skintight vinyl while Adam looks—oh fudge. He means the gym.

Me: No.

Me: No!

Adam: Too late. Already on my way.

Oh, Shirley Temples. Blind panic starts pumping and forging new, unthinkable thoughts and sensations. Adam can't find out. Not like this, not tonight.

"Stacey, I need a favor."

Her eyes are fixed on the screen. "No."

I can't lose him, and the moment he walks into the gym and finds out I've been lying, he's gone. He told me that it was the deception that hurt most about Allison, and then if I turn out to be just like her —it will be over.

I close my eyes, already loathing what I'm about to do. "You're right. I have to tell Adam the truth. Tonight." My back is to Stacey, and she can't see my face twist at the lie.

I hear her huff and some angry clacking of computer keys. Probably toggling through camera feeds.

My phone pings again.

Adam: Can't wait to see you.

"It's Adam," I say, turning to Stacey. "He wants to see me. Please, let me go just this once. I need to talk to him in person." I close my eyes and wince. "I need to tell him the truth."

Stacey softens. Her eyebrows knit together in the most beautiful picture of concern. "Go. I'll break you. Go."

I run out the back door, and when I get to the alley, I grab my phone and dial the gym. "It's a great day at Fit Gym 24 Pacific Beach. This is Kate. How may I help you?"

"Kate, this is Sarah. If a guy named Adam comes in looking for me, will you tell him that I picked up a shift in La Jolla?"

"Will do," Kate replies in her chirpy voice.

"Thank you."

"But next time you pick up a shift, could you ask me first?" Kate groans. "I'd die to have a Saturday off."

"Absolutely."

I run and skid to a halt in the alley behind the gym. Stu is out back with his phone and cigar.

"Hey, Stu," I call.

"Hey, crazy lady."

I run past the doughnut shop and weave to the small parking lot on the side street. If I had a car, I'd have happily parked it here every night and changed in it rather than vault the wall outside the gym. I look and light up with relief when I see Adam's Mustang. He hasn't left for La Jolla. Now it's just a question of stopping him from going.

I take gulps of fresh air, trying to catch my breath. I can't tell the truth. I can't take off my mask. I'd lose him before I'd have a chance to say, *Surprise, it's me. I'm crazy. Just ask Stu.* Adam would be gone and out of my life for good. And my life without Adam in it... would be like a backyard without a Meyer lemon tree.

If I take off my mask, Adam would have a complete, detailed picture of what a crazy loser I really am. He'd never let me kiss him again. And I need to kiss him again. I need to give vent to my feelings. Because even though I'm not sure what is at the top of the feelings escalator I'm riding, I do know that feelings have developed. Big ones. Ones that have me up at night. Ones that have me out for runs in the early a.m. again.

Ones that have me desperate to buy more time.

Adam, keys in hand, appears. His phone is out. No doubt he's googling the location of the La Jolla gym.

"Well, well, well," I say, leaning against the driver's door of his car. The lighting is better on this side street than it is in the alley. Pink and blue neon signs add a soft glow to the brighter streetlamps. My vinyl suit shines under them.

Adam jolts to awareness. "Sabine? You're working tonight?"

"It's my break," I purr.

"Well..." Adam takes a lingering glance at my vinyl before

returning to his phone. "I'd love to stop and figure out what you're doing here, but I have plans."

"Mmm, so do I." I grab his face and kiss him. I catapult myself onto him. I kiss him with the intensity of everything I felt Tuesday night and then some. I kiss him until he melts and kisses back. I kiss him until a dialogue develops between our kisses.

I really didn't want to do this, his kisses say. *I'd like to pretend that this isn't one of my fantasies, but damn, Sabine.*

My kisses taunt and tease. *Tell me about your plans now?* they say. *Am I a part of them?*

I slither his hands down to my waist and hips. I push him against his car and climb on top of him, straddling him until he has to hold me back.

He pulls away. "We can't do this."

"Why not?" I say in a voice so rough I hardly recognize it as my own. "We both want to."

Adam is out of breath. "I can't kiss you and pretend that you're someone else under the mask. It's not fair to anyone."

I pull him back to my lips. He's found the hinge of my jaw and kisses it until I shudder. "And I can't kiss you and pretend that I'm someone else too?" I ask. Although it sounds more like begging.

Adam squeezes me tighter. He has a hand on my back and one on my thigh. "I'm seeing someone. A real person."

I move my hand from his heart to low on his hip. My tongue is thrusting against his. Goldfish, I've never kissed anyone like this. I've never wanted to kiss anyone like this. "Everyone wears masks, Adam." I whisper the words. "Some are just easier to see."

He groans against my lips. So I focus on his neck. I am at a clear advantage, as his is not buried under vinyl. I nip at it gently with my teeth. In an alternate universe, the one where I am not a liar, liar, pants on fire, I find the courage to take off my mask and tell Adam the truth. *Hey. It's me, Sarah. I'm really into you. I have all kinds of feelings for you, but because I screwed up so badly at my first rodeo, it's easier to just hide behind this mask and make out with you.*

"Sabine?"

I must have frozen. I lean in for more kisses, but he pushes me gently back. "Why are you here?"

"I missed you." Fudge brownies. Is that even true? My face flashes red. I don't need forty-five minutes of rowing followed by some intervals to get to the bottom of that one. It's a lie. I'm here because I don't want Adam to find out my secret. I'm here because I'm scared of what would happen if he did.

Adam's eyes narrow to slits. His lips—swollen and rimmed in berry-red lipstick—tug into a frown I don't like.

I slide my feet back to the ground. "I don't see you much at work anymore. When I do, you hardly look at me. One kiss in your car hardly seems worth that level of avoidance."

I'm back beside him, making out gently with his neck. "But I could be wrong. Why don't you ask this real person of yours what she thinks? I'm sure she'll be wondering why you're covered in hickeys and lipstick."

"No, Sabine. Just... no."

Adam insists on driving me back to the escape room before he disappears.

Stacey is waiting for me, arms folded across her chest. "You didn't tell him."

"I tried, but... You're not going to rat me out?"

"No. But I'm done covering for you. By the way, you better figure out something to say to Mike when he gets back from starring in his play."

I freeze. "What?"

"Mike and your double left together the night she filled in for you."

My phone pings. A text on my real-person number.

Adam: Okay. You win. But I can't stop thinking about you. Brunch tomorrow?

CHAPTER TWENTY-THREE

Gwen isn't returning my calls.

So I text.

Me: Every time I go into work, I have to do the walk of shame for a make-out session I never had.

Gwen: Honey, you were doing some sorta walk of shame without my help.

Me: Just. Why? You made out with a dude in clown makeup. Scary, psycho, Badpun clown makeup, but still.

Gwen: He had nice arms.

Me: What about Tony?

Gwen: What about him?

Me: Is everything okay? Did something else happen after the escape room?

Gwen: Dunno. It's been so long, and I was promised a debriefing over breakfast that never materialized.

Shirley Temples. I totally forgot. I've been so busy. None of these excuses matter.

Me: I'm really sorry.

Gwen: I know.

Me: I'll make it up to you.

Gwen: Tomorrow?

Me: Can't. Brunch with Adam.

Gwen sends me a very smug-looking emoji. I wish I felt smug. Is there an emoji for frantic?

Gwen: Don't worry about Mike. Meant nothing. And he was switching jobs anyway. That was his last night. He left to star in some play.

I explain the temporary nature of Mike's play. And Gwen sends back a plethora of egg-faced emojis.

Gwen: I'll take care of it.

CHAPTER TWENTY-FOUR

"I didn't know there were tide pools in La Jolla," I say.

"Sure, you did," Adam replies. "Tide pools and stinky sea lions. It's La Jolla's thing."

Brunch was awkward as fudge. And because it was so awkward, we are now at the tide pools, extending the awkward misery.

Adam is surprisingly chill, having come off of an epic make-out session with Catstrike last night. I, on the other hand, keep staring at his neck, wondering if the polo he wears is strategic.

"So I've been thinking about you," Adam says.

"Want to hold a sea slug?" I pick a purple blob up and offer it to him.

"Um..." It has the exact effect I was going for. Total mood killer.

"I think there are anemones over here."

He plops the slug back in a pool and follows. "I missed you last night. You were all I could think about."

"Sounds like you need to start cross-training." I poke a sea anemone studded with hundreds of bits of shell into a tight circle. I jump when Adam crouches next to me.

"Easy," he says. "You don't want to fall into a tide pool."

"I think there is a crab in this one."

"You've got some sand on your face. Hold still."

"I do not."

He leans in. Oh, no. He's going to kiss me. And if he kisses me, he'll know. And if he doesn't know... If he can't tell my kisses from hers. I mean, mine...

This is too fudged up.

"What are you doing?" I say.

"I want to kiss you."

"You didn't ask."

Adam is still chill. "Please, may I kiss you?"

"No."

He smiles, his eyes crinkling in that gorgeous array of wrinkles I like so well. Until they don't. "You're serious?"

"We're not dating. And even if we were, I'm not..." I'm not giving myself away. I'm not taking the risk that he'll remember how I taste. I'm not giving Adam an opportunity to connect the cosplay dots. And I'm certainly not going to be here when he realizes I'm not the sexy, tongue-thrusting, kiss-first-ask-later, full package. That's an act. That's not me. Sorry to disappoint you, Adam, but I'm not going to show up for this. I'm not giving you the chance to run away from me in real life. "I'm just not," I finish.

Adam swears. He's angry.

I want to run. It is all kinds of messed up. If you care about someone and fantasize about someone and have snogged that someone on more than one occasion, you should want to kiss them. And I did, but how do I explain, *Oh yeah, by the way, I've been lying to you this whole time. I work for you. I'm your Catstrike. I dress up every weekend, and I've done things to you that I'm not proud of.*

Even in my head, it sounds wrong.

"You want to tell me why?" Adam asks.

"I just can't."

"You just can't? Sarah. 'I just can't' isn't a good reason."

"Do I need a good reason? I don't want to kiss you, Adam."

He stumbles backward, like he's just fallen off a treadmill. He slips a little on the wet rocks and is now standing knee-deep in a tide pool. He sloshes out but manages to get even wetter.

I reach in for his wet loafer that didn't make it out. "Can we just be friends?" It kills me to ask. I don't want to be his friend. I want to be his last thought before drifting off to sleep and his reason for getting out of bed in the morning. I want to be the author of his favorite meal, his *Mississippi Bake-Off* buddy, and the keeper of his inside jokes. A good man, but a better one for me. And yes, I want to bite his bottom lip and run my hand across his stubbled cheek while I purr in his ear... But that isn't me. I mean, it is me. Me dressed up like a caricature of a woman, a superhero who is more about sexy one-liners and black boots than anything else. Goldfish, if he knew, he'd run away screaming.

"Sure," Adam says with little to no enthusiasm or sincerity. A *sure* spoken to save face. My face. His face. Goldfish, his face is gorgeous. Even now, when he's looking for all the world like he needs a run and a good ten rounds with a punching bag. "I'll see you around."

CHAPTER TWENTY-FIVE

I miss Adam. He isn't at the escape room. He isn't on campus. I'm worried, and I'm angry at myself. I sucked him into my crazy. He doesn't deserve to be in my crazy. He deserves the truth. And if telling him the truth is what it takes to see him again and to extract him from my den of crazy, I'll do it.

He's not responding to my texts, so I send them from my Sabine Kennedy number.

Sabine Kennedy: Still there?

Nothing. Nothing for hours.

I try again.

Sabine Kennedy: Haven't seen you in ages.

More nothing for hours. If this is what life is like without Adam, I don't want it. I can't take it. Staring at my phone every five seconds, trying to will it to ping. Swiping back and forth between my texts and email to see if anything has changed in the half second since I last refreshed my screen. Feeling an empty, sinking weight pressing against me until all my breaths are uselessly shallow.

I grip my phone, and my heart hammers. Adam is the real deal. Not a speed bump. He's the one I want sitting beside me on the epic cross-country road trip. I want him in the front seat with me, keeping me focused and awake on mile two hundred.

This car analogy thing is getting weird. The point is, I know as I hold my cracked phone, which is still inert, that this awful I'm feeling isn't going anywhere and will only get worse with time. I let a man, an understanding, kind, sweet, and gorgeous man, go. Unless I do something about it, the awful will grow into a devastating regret. And as scary as doing something about it is, it's worth the risk. Adam is worth all the risk.

Sabine Kennedy: Maybe we should meet.

My phone pings. A text from Adam. My heart beats so fast it hurts.

Adam: Lost my appetite for costumes. Thanks just the same.

Sabine Kennedy: Meet in real life.

My phone radiates energy. I can feel Adam on the other end catch his breath. I can feel him trying to think up the right reply.

I throw him a bone.

Sabine Kennedy: Where will you be tomorrow?

Adam: SDSU.

I have to shake out my hands and vent some nervous giggles before I type the next text. Holy wow, Nightbat. I'm really doing this.

Sabine Kennedy: Let's grab coffee.

Four miles of interval sprints this a.m., and I can barely stand for my shift at the gym. Not a big deal since my clientele usually insists I join them on the floor. But yes, it took sprinting for my life for half of every minute for four miles to achieve my current state of calm.

"So you're going to do it?" Gwen asks. I texted her on my break about my rendezvous with Adam later today, and now she's at the coloring table with me. Her perfectly-sculpted eyebrows are arched as she awaits my answer.

"I am. No more lies. No more excuses. I'm going to tell him it was me all along." I've hurt Adam. I've taken the nicest guy in the world, run him through my grinder of crazy, and dropped him cold. Adam doesn't deserve that kind of torture. He deserves the truth.

"And are you going to tell him anything else? Talk about your feelings, maybe? How you 'greatly esteem' him?"

"K. Watching *Sense and Sensibility* with you was a mistake."

"Would you pass me the green?" Gwen asks.

I take a deep breath. "Don't you think he'll piece it together on his own?" I hand over the green crayon.

Gwen rolls her eyes as she adds swirls of green leaves to her still life. It's not a bad picture, but it's not making my art board. The competition these days is way too fierce.

"Hey, what happened with you and Mike that night you filled in for me?" I ask.

"Mike?"

"Badpun?" I whisper. We may have a comic corner in the Kids Club, but I'm not about to introduce any of these kids to a psychotic clown.

A wistful smile appears on Gwen's face. "Oh, yeah. We shared a kiss or two after the escape room thingy. I invited him out for a drink, but he's a teetotaler. Nothing happened."

"Is he going to come sniffing back?"

"I doubt it. There wasn't much chemistry. It was more about the costumes, really. Ever notice how sexy those make you feel?" I shoot her a playful stink eye. "Oh, right. Sorry."

I bend down to retrieve a fallen dinosaur. "Who dropped a stegosaurus?" I ask my remaining kiddos, but I know whose it is.

Laura runs over, pigtails bobbing. "Can we make a picture for Steggy?"

"Sure," I say. "What do you think Steggy would like a picture of?"

Laura considers. "A birthday party!"

"Again?" The number of times I draw Steggy eating cake has gotten out of control.

"He wants to wear a tutu and tiara this time!"

"Okay, but you color it. Deal?" I grab a new sheet of paper and reach for a pencil.

Gwen's giving me a look.

"What?"

She pauses. "You know, not everyone is as tough as you, Saire. You're about to throw Adam a big curve ball. I'm all for it, but... Just, be patient with him."

"I'm not tough." I hand over the doodle to Laura, who squeals and immediately starts coloring the cake blue and the tutu purple.

Gwen puts up a hand. "Just promise to try, okay?"

"Okay," I say. "I promise."

Gwen drops me off at Mom's so I can properly shower and get ready. As tempting as it is to hide behind a hoodie, I reach for a pretty yellow shift dress.

I've changed shoes too many times, waffling between wedge and gladiator sandals. I pick neither and grab my green Converse. My Lyft approaches. I need to get to the driveway before it drives away without me. I grab my keys and my backpack and bolt out the front door.

I nearly collide with the UPS guy.

"Sorry!" I say.

"Sarah Miller Jonson?"

I go cold at the mention of my married name.

The UPS guy holds a large, battered envelope in his hand.

My stomach sinks. The memory of that stupid phone call on that stupid night blunders to the forefront of my pathetic existence.

I fumble for my key and struggle to lock up. "Yeah. That's me. Or it was..." I mumble. Trust Daniel to get my name wrong.

"I need you to sign."

My Lyft pulls into the driveway.

I hesitate. I don't want to sign. Not the UPS guy's little black tablet thingy. Not the legal papers inside the yellow envelope. I don't trust Daniel with my past, but... I really don't want to relive it. I don't want Daniel telling my story, erasing me and my love for my daughter with his hurtful words. If there was a way to outrun any of this, I would have done it by now.

My Lyft driver honks his horn.

"You have to sign," the UPS guy says.

I'm not strong enough for the cascade of nasty, hurtful, terrible things that would come at me if I refused at this point. I want Daniel gone. Forever. "Yeah." I press a hand to my forehead and wince. "Yeah, I'll sign."

My Lyft driver taps his horn again.

The UPS guy hands me the envelope. "Good thing I parked on the street."

Like a shadow, I slip into my Lyft. Daniel's name in his bold, careless scrawl stares up at me from the corner of the envelope. Laughs at me. Tells me what an idiot I am to imagine I could ever be more or do more than pretend I'm not a sad little failure.

Adam is waiting for me in the Student Union Starbucks, and maybe, for a moment, I think big silly thoughts about how my life has been building to this point, and all will have been worth it, because here is my Prince Charming and happily ever after.

I have the weight of Daniel and Daddy Ray's stupid papers in my backpack, reassuring me that I am no fairy-tale princess.

I screwed up my life before it even got started, and for the rest of my life, I get to live with that failure—except for the hours on Thursdays and Saturdays when I pretend to be Catstrike at Adam's escape room. Then I get to escape. Then I get to be sexy and confident. But that's over now too. I'm here to tell Adam the truth, and he'll see that I'm a sad, pathetic, little failure, and he'll be gone. Like my dad, like my daughter. Like the future I tried to claw back for myself.

I thought coming here would be proof that I'm brave. But it just proves that Daniel is right about me. I am such an idiot.

"Hey, Adam," I say, my mouth flicking into the briefest of smiles. He looks up.

And I wait for the ball to drop. For the recognition. For a coy smile and the light of understanding to shine bright in his eyes. For him to fold me into his arms and for everything to be okay.

Instead, he drops his head to look back down at his book. "Hey."

"Mind if I sit here?" My heart is hammering.

"Yeah, actually, I'm meeting someone." The words are so pointed, they make me flinch.

"Cool." I sit down. In hindsight, it is a mistake. "Who?" I take a sip of my tea, a bitter chamomile and lavender. The barista must have forgotten to add the honey.

Adam looks up at me, and unbridled rage floods his features. "What do I have to say for this to end?"

I smile. I laugh. And then a pit forms in my stomach. People see what they want to see. And even though it is clear as mud that I am Adam's Catstrike, his Sabine Kennedy rendezvous, Adam won't see it because he doesn't want to. He wants someone else. He hopes, and has always hoped, that there is some other woman behind that cat mask. And honestly, right now, I wish I were someone else too. Because I'm not the sexy, strong, confident girl I was pretending to be this entire time. I'm a nobody who doesn't even deserve to explain her past. I'm a loser who's still too scared to do anything about it.

Fudge. Fudge it all.

I'm here. I might as well find out who Adam wishes is behind the black vinyl. "Tell me about who you're meeting. It must be someone special for you to iron your shirt." I finger his sleeve. He swats my hand away.

"So what's her name?" I ask.

He huffs.

"Did you meet her in Econ 101 too?"

"No."

"Are those new Vans? Wow. She must be special."

Adam snaps his book shut. "I know what you're doing. I went through it with Allison. Remember?"

Allison. His ex-girlfriend. I am now in her boat.

Adam leans forward. "I'm your backup plan," he snarls. "I'm an insurance policy. But I'm not doing that again. I'm not going to be the friend you confide in and hang out with. I'm not letting myself fall in love with someone who is just using me because she needs to break a heart to prove something to her ex-husband or herself."

"What the hell, Adam? Daniel was and remains a douchebag." I've got the papers in my backpack to prove it.

His eyes narrow. "You made it completely clear that you aren't into me." He pulls out a notebook and slams it open.

"You misunderstood," I said. But he doesn't give me a chance to tell him more.

"Not wanting to kiss the guy you've been dating sends a pretty clear message." Adam slowly underlines something in his notebook.

"You're such an idiot," I say. Of course I wanted to kiss him. I just didn't want my entire life to unravel afterward. And look at me, I'm at last telling the truth.

"I'm smart enough to know to stay away. And now that I have... You're jealous that I've moved on."

I laugh. I'm jealous of another woman who happens to be me? How in the world did it ever come to this? "Maybe I should just stay until she gets here. Who are we looking for? Come on. Give me some details." Knowing I don't live up to the fantasy in real life hurts. So do my hamstrings from all the sprints I ran this morning. My Prince Charming hates me, and my rose-gold thoughts of future happiness are going up in flames. As a result, I might not be fighting fair or even thinking rationally.

Adam swallows. He tries not to flush, but he reddens all the same. "You are the most stubborn woman I've ever met. Let it go, Sarah."

"How am I the stubborn one?" Adam's the one who refuses to see what is right in front of him. "You're the one refusing to share."

Adam digs his fingers into his hair and lets out a tortured groan. His phone buzzes, and his desperation when he grabs it is almost heartbreaking. He slams it back down on the table.

"Did she cancel?"

The exasperation on his face is palpable. "If I say yes, will you leave?"

"Why not text her? Call her? Maybe she's stuck in traffic. Maybe she woke up with food poisoning." Maybe she's sitting right across from you, and it took everything she has to show up today, and now there's nothing left. I kick my backpack under my chair with my heel. Not that it matters.

Adam pushes away from the table. His chair makes an awful screeching sound, and heads turn toward us for a moment. "You know I liked you, Sarah. I did. Drama and all. I liked you. But you are crazy. I get it. It's hard to move on—"

I am about to object, but he plows on, and what he says next breaks me.

"I was hoping I'd be the one who made you want to. Now"—he shrugs—"I'm just lucky I got out alive. Go live your life. But leave me alone. Okay?"

I'm trying to blink back tears. "You're right. Have a nice life, Adam."

CHAPTER TWENTY-SIX

Adam: I was really looking forward to meeting IRL and dropping the act.

Adam: You stood me up.

Sabine Kennedy: You double-booked.

I'm not about to invent some sad little story about traffic for the sake of his ego.

Sabine Kennedy: I came. I found you chatting up a pretty little blonde.

Adam: I don't think we're even friends anymore.

Sabine Kennedy: Really. You looked friendly.

Adam: Wait.

I see ellipses on my screen. Then, all at once, my phone pings with a bombardment of texts.

Adam: Wait. You think I was playing you?

Adam: Oh no.

Adam: Nonono

My phone lights up with frantic texts.

Adam: I swear I'm not that guy.

Adam: Let me explain.

Adam: Give me another chance?

Sabine Kennedy: I'll think about it.

CHAPTER TWENTY-SEVEN

The fountain in the little waiting room of the student wellness center aggressively fountains. No gentle trickle here. No babbling-brook associations. If anything, this fountain is a faucet that was turned on to full and left running.

A fake ficus tree in the corner collects dust, and the carpet tiles near my chair are no longer meeting at right angles. I'm pretty sure this waiting room is a metaphor for my life.

The door to the office swings open. "Sarah?"

Why is it that all dudes in the mental health arena have beards? Did they sign something that said they must honor the legacy of Freud by growing facial hair?

"Hey," I say.

"I'm Brad," the bearded one says. "Come on in."

The university therapist's office is much cheerier than the windowless waiting room. Filmed windows filter in some natural light. A large, overstuffed couch faces an armchair, and a box of tissues is positioned conveniently and prominently on the table between them.

"Janet called and said you needed to come talk." Yes, I told Janet, the counselor who got me set up this semester, that I'd hit a speed bump, and she set this up. "So what's going on?" Brad asks, and I swear he smooths his beard.

"I'm crazy," I say.

He laughs in the affable I'm-a-professional-and-we-will-see-about-that way. "Why do you say that?"

"I'm twenty-two. I'm divorced. The only reason why I'm not still married is because I have an incompetent cervix. I literally run away from all my problems. Today alone, I've gone out for two four-milers. I swore off all relationships, and despite that, I'm now in two relationships with the same guy."

The therapist furiously writes notes. "When you say you are in two relationships, are you saying you *feel* like you are in two relationships? Or—"

"No. I am in two relationships. He thinks I'm two different people."

Brad clicks his pen into action but seems stumped as to what to actually write. He frowns at his notes.

"You want me to start at the beginning?" I ask.

"N-no. If you had the choice, would you still like to be married?"

"No. Daniel is an idiot. He's writing his memoir about fatherhood and marriage and living in China. He called me, for the first time ever, and was upset when I didn't want to give him carte blanche to all the personal details of our relationship. Is that wrong?"

"No." Brad is still writing. "Why did he call?"

"His dad made him do it." I pull the sleeves of my hoodie over my hands.

"What about your parents?" Brad asks.

"My dad died when I was ten. Stupid car accident."

More furious scribbles. "And your mom?"

"My roomie. When my marriage ended, I moved back home. She's very... routine-oriented."

"What was her reaction to your marriage and divorce?"

"She was disappointed. She kept saying things like, 'If only your father were here, none of this would've happened.' 'If he could see you now,' etc."

Brad, who has filled several pages of notes, flips through them. "I want to come back to this idea that you are in two separate relationships with the same man. Why do you feel this way?"

"Because I first met him while cosplaying—"

"Meaning?"

"I was dressed up as..." I close my eyes and wince. "As a superhero."

More furious notes on Brad's end. "Why were you dressed up as a superhero?"

"Oh, for the love. Have you been to Comic-Con? People dress up. I was dressed up as Catstrike, full-blown '90s freak fantasy. My own mother wouldn't have recognized me. Adam saw me and offered me a job cosplaying at his escape room."

"Why did you say yes?"

"Why not? I needed the money."

"And it was fun to be someone else?"

"I wasn't someone else. I was just a different version of me. I don't get to be sexy and confident. I'm the loser who screwed up so bad she had no other choice but to marry the village douchebag. And then I miscarried, my own fault, just a colossal screw-up screwing up colossally. I lost my baby and was supposed to be relieved because, 'Hey, Sarah, Daniel and you can make a clean break. Isn't that great? You have nothing to be sad about, Sarah. It could be so much worse. Don't be sad. Smile, move on.'"

"Did you move on?"

"Do I look like I moved on? Am I sitting here with bags under my eyes and talking to a therapist because I moved on? My life at twenty-two was over before it even started."

Brad stares at his notes. "Tell me about the cosplaying. You say it's another version of you?"

"When I put on the cat costume, no one knows anything about me. No one knows how bad I've fudged up. No one knows they should look at me or my body and feel pity. No one knows I was once a mommy. No one knows I was once some idiot's wife."

Brad puts the point of his pen to his lips and sits in thought. "And you were content to just make believe, but then something happened?"

"I was going to keep it separated, all of it. But then the guy who hired me to cosplay..." I roll my eyes because Therapist Brad is scribbling notes again. "Not in a pervy way. I mean, staff his escape room in costume. I met him in real life as myself. He was my TA for a while."

The therapist looks at me, nodding. Goldfish, I am crazy.

"Adam and I started not-dating. Before that, he had to stop being my TA because people thought we were actually dating, and that is a clear conflict of interest."

"And you told him you were also cosplaying at his club?" Brad asks.

"No!"

"Why not?"

"Because that would have been like stripping in front of him."

Brad takes a not-so-subtle deep breath and reexamines his notes.

"It would have been mortifying," I clarify.

Brad pockets the pen and sets aside his notes. "I think you didn't tell him because you were trying to play it safe. You were trying to see if Adam would have the same connection to your authentic self—how you present in the real world—as he did to your cosplay. Did he?"

Holy fudge brownies. He did. "Yeah."

"How do you know?" Brad asks.

I twist my dad's ring around my thumb. "He saw me at my worst, and he didn't run away."

"So what's wrong with that?"

I pick up a stray fidget spinner on the arm of the sofa and flick it. "I didn't want him to find out about the other part."

"What other part? The cosplay part?"

It's my turn to take a not-so-subtle deep breath. "That I have to pretend I'm someone else and wear a costume to feel strong and sexy."

"Why?"

"Because it is still humiliating."

"Why is it humiliating to be strong and sexy?"

"Because I am not strong and sexy. It's all fake. It's an act. It's part of my costume. And I lied to him. Right? I didn't tell him the truth."

The therapist shrugs.

"Don't shrug! You're supposed to have the answers. You're supposed to tell me that what I did was cowardly and wrong and that I have to quit lying to this poor man—"

Brad folds his hands in his lap. "Have you ever tried to tell him the truth?"

"I tried. After we stopped not-dating, I sent him a text and said we should meet for coffee in real life. And when I showed up... he didn't see it."

"How did that make you feel?" Brad asks.

Now it is my turn to shrug.

The therapist takes out his pen and makes some more notes. "So you showed up and said, 'Surprise. It was me in the mask'?"

"I didn't get that far," I mutter. "He told me he was meeting someone important and wanted me to leave."

"Did you?"

"He was meeting me. You get that, right? He was meeting me? I was the someone he wanted to meet."

"But you didn't tell him the truth."

"I tried. The fact is... he didn't want me. People see what they want to see. If he had wanted me to be me, he would have connected the dots."

"Maybe. Maybe he was feeling too scared or too vulnerable to process all the information. After all, you were inhabiting two very different parts of his life."

I check the time on the clock behind me. "So are you going to tell me why I'm so messed up? Are you going to tell me that no grown woman would ever parade around in a catsuit?"

"No. Were you hoping I would?"

"I'm crazy. Adam said as much."

"Did he?"

"Yeah, scribble that in your notes. He said I was crazy. He said to leave him alone. And he's right. Only crazy people sit on couches like these."

"The really crazy ones don't sit. They lie down."

Funny. My therapist is funny. Fantastic.

"Listen, Sarah," Brad says. "I don't think you're crazy. I think you're creative. How do you handle the trauma and grief of losing not only your first child but your marriage? You started distance running. Not drinking, not abusing food or other substances. You enjoy running?"

"I love it."

"You found something constructive, and yeah, maybe you need to think about ways of scaling back—eight miles sounds excessive. You found a similar outlet that let you explore your sexuality. You dress up and help people escape on Saturday nights. You get to play a role and be confident. What is wrong with that?"

"The deception. The shame," I stammer.

"Ah. Those. Why do you need to hide your second job?"

"It's embarrassing."

"If you were dressing up as a fairy princess, would it be equally embarrassing? What if you were acting in a play? What if you were going to Comic-Con again?" Brad tucks his pen into his shirt pocket. "You want to know what I think?"

"It's why I'm here."

"I think you should tell someone what you've been up to. In fact, I'm going to give you a homework assignment. Pick one person you trust and tell them all about it. See what happens. When you're ready, come tell me about it."

CHAPTER TWENTY-EIGHT

Creative. My running and my cosplaying are proof that I am creative. I'm a badass, working her way through a lot of Shirley Temples in creative and constructive ways.

That's what I tell myself when I ask Stacey if we can talk after my shift at the gym Friday night.

She's kind enough to agree to meet me in front of Superhero Escapes. The thought of bumping into Adam inside is more than I can handle right now. I want to get there. I'm going to get there. I just need to take care of a few things to prove to myself that I can.

I walk the couple of blocks down to the escape room, and I am shocked to see the people lined up to get in. My cosplay shifts have always been busy, but I didn't realize that there was this much demand.

The door opens and out steps Stacey in her cosplay. Cheers erupt from the people in the queue. Stacey registers none of it. "I got to make this fast. We have back-to-back bachelorette parties arriving in five. What's up, Sabine?"

"It's Sarah, remember? Sarah Miller, actually. I wanted to make a donation to the escape room's communal cosplay closet." I pull the paper bag stuffed with my *Nightbat Returns*-inspired catsuit out of my gym bag and hand it to Stacey.

She peeks inside before crumpling the bag flat to her chest in shock. "You serious? You're not quitting, are you?"

"No. Nothing like that. I've outgrown it is all." I toe my Asics into the sand-dusted concrete. "And I was thinking of trying something new anyway. I've been working on a third costume that I'm excited to try. See you Saturday?"

"I'll leave the back door open as always."

I shift my gym bag onto my shoulder. It's lighter without the costume and boots. "Keep it locked. I can handle the front door." My Lyft pulls up. "Good luck with the bachelorette parties."

Catstrike was just a place to start. I don't need to hide behind a costume anymore. That's what I tell myself throughout my Saturday morning run. And I believe it, too, right up to the point where I walk into the kitchen and see Mom juicing a pile of lemons, oranges, ginger, and carrots. Turns out the fresh juice is here to stay and not just a summer pastime.

"Hey, Mom. Can we talk?" I ask.

"What's up, honey?" She feeds a handful of carrots into her juicer, and they are buzzed, pulverized, and sifted until only the juice remains.

"I'm sorry," I blurt out.

"What?" Mom can't hear me over the juicer.

"I'm sorry!" I yell.

She turns off the machine. Her lips press into a tight frown, and her worry lines are all over her forehead.

"If I could go back and have a do-over, I would never have gone to that stupid party. I'd never have even spoken to Daniel. I'd definitely never have had sex with him." I involuntarily shudder. " I—"

"Oh, baby," Mom says, swatting her hand through the air. "Water under the bridge."

"No, let me finish. I know I disappointed you. I lost my scholarship. I was an embarrassment—"

"Sarah, you were never an embarrassment," Mom says firmly.

I reach for the ginger and begin peeling the fragrant root. Mom is meticulous about her kitchen knives. Annoying, until you realize that a super-sharp knife makes nearly every kitchen chore go five times faster. "You kept saying, 'If Dad were here—'"

"If your father were here, I thought he might have been able to help you through it all better than I could. If he were here, he could convince you right now that none of it matters. That Daniel wasn't worth two cents of your time." Mom pushes a pile of lemon peels out of the way.

Mom sighs. "I thought you loved him, sweetheart. I thought it was what you wanted. All of it."

"Mom, I was pregnant. And I didn't love Daniel ever, but I loved my baby."

Mom's pale as almond milk. We've never talked about my pregnancy. She's never asked. I've never shared. I assumed Brent told her, but he certainly never told her how much I loved my daughter.

"I was excited. I wasn't scared." My knife makes precise and pleasant *chop, chop* sounds against the bamboo cutting board. Having something for my hands to do makes the words come more easily. "I mean, I was scared of other people. But not scared of being a single mom. That's what you've been all these years, and it's worked out." I close my eyes. The memories are still painful, but not in a raw way. "The day I found out, I went out and bought this yellow dress with a snail on it, because, you know, maybe she'd be a slowpoke like me."

"Your father gave you that nickname, just because you were five years younger than Brent, and I never liked it. You are not slow. You've never been slow in any way." Mom huffs but drops the hands from her hips. "Sorry, honey. Keep going. I'm listening."

"I married Daniel for her, and yeah, there was pressure." I scoot the chopped ginger over to Mom. "But I thought maybe she'd need a dad for a little while. Or whatever."

I reach for a couple of oranges to peel, but Mom places her hand on mine to stop me. She looks me in the eyes, and I can see worry there, but also love.

"I had a miscarriage."

"How far along?"

"Twenty-four weeks."

My mom cries out as if she's been stung by a honey bee. A bright burst of sunlight reflected from a passing car outside temporarily blinds me. Next thing I know, Mom wraps her arms around me in a viciously tight hug. "Oh, Sarah." She's struggling for composure. "I wondered if you were pregnant. I should have asked. I told myself you'd tell me in time if you were. A few friends asked me if you were, and I wasn't going to lie outright. So I made a point of not asking."

"It's okay, Mom."

She wipes her eyes with the back of her hand. "It was stupid and selfish. And now I have lemon juice in my eyes."

I hand her a clean tea towel.

She smooths the towel in her hands. "Did you have a name picked out?"

I lean against the white porcelain of the farmhouse kitchen sink, which uncharacteristically is brimming with dirty dishes. "No. I had a few I wanted to ask her about when I met her." I inhale low and long and catch a whiff of fresh bread mingled with all the citrus and ginger. "Elinor was my favorite."

My mom blows her nose, loudly, into the blue dishtowel. "Oh, honey, it isn't fair." She tosses the towel in the sink. "It isn't fair that you had to walk through any of it, and it especially isn't fair that you don't even have your daughter with you now. I'm the one who's sorry." She folds me up into a tight hug again. I have to stoop, because Mom is four inches shorter than me. "You've been through so much. And I... I didn't know what to do. Even when I knew what was going on, like with the divorce, I didn't know what to do about it." She releases me from the hug only to rest her hands on my cheeks. She's still crying.

"The lemon juice still stinging your eyes, Mom?" I ask gently.

"I worried I was losing you. I worried you'd given up on everything. I should have been there for you. I could have put my foot down or reached out. But I convinced myself that you were tough. And you are." Mom sniffs and reaches for a new dishtowel. This one's a bright yellow. "My girl, my strong girl, running goldfish knows how many miles, working her tail off at that gym, paying down her student loans, and still finding time for all her study groups."

I groan and rest my head on the kitchen counter. "Mom. I have something to tell you."

"Oh goldfish, honey." Mom sounds absolutely panicked. I hear her furiously cutting into her pile of oranges. "I don't know if I have enough citrus to get through this. I've failed you before—"

"You've never failed me, Mom." I slide over and give her a hand. "I have a second job. A side hustle."

"Tell me you're not selling drugs on the corner of Grand and Balboa."

Seriously? "You know the escape room on Garnet Ave?"

"Baby, I need a drink." The juicer is on again, and the ginger is reduced to a pale, milky dribble, followed quickly by the pile of peeled and quartered oranges. "The what now?"

"The escape room," I yell. "Adam's escape room. You solve puzzles and stuff to unlock doors?"

"Okay," Mom says, flicking off the juicer and pouring two glasses of carrot, ginger, lemon, orange juice.

"I work there. And it's themed."

Mom mutters a prayer under her breath. I'm pretty sure she is promising her pension to the church in exchange for my deliverance.

"Superheroes," I say.

"Superheroes?" She swigs her juice fast, like a shot. She's added so much ginger, it may as well be. "You mean like Magnificent Man?"

"Nightbat, actually."

She adds a pinch of salt to the juice remaining in the large glass pitcher. "Who do you dress up as?"

I take a deep breath. "Catstrike."

Mom considers, swirls the pitcher, and pours out another two glasses of juice. "1960s camp?"

I shake my head.

"Not the one with ripped leather pants?" She hands me a glass.

"No! The '90s Catstrike from *Nightbat Returns*."

"For reals?" Mom laughs and clinks my glass. "That's the best one."

"For reals." Now I down my juice like it's a shot. Ooh! Not doing that again. "Since when do you know superhero movies?"

"Since book club."

I give her some major side-eye. "Book club?"

"Just because we like to talk about books doesn't mean we only talk about books. Did you make your costume?"

I nod. "I made a suit from the animated series, too, and another I haven't worn yet. I was paranoid someone would recognize me, so I went for costumes that have a lot of coverage."

"Why didn't you want anyone to recognize you?"

I stop cold, realizing that I'd had it wrong this whole time. I wasn't worried Mom or Brent would find out. "Because I wanted an escape. I wasn't proud of my life or myself. It was nice to leave that all behind on the nights I cosplayed."

Mom smooths a lock of hair behind my ear. "And what about now?"

"There's still stuff I'm working through, but...I'm pretty proud of me." I laugh through a stray tear. "Costumes and all."

Mom presses her lips together and pats my cheek dry. "That's my girl." She folds me up in a tight hug. "I love you, Saire Bear."

And she starts to cry. Hard. "It's okay, Mom."

Mom blows her nose, reaches for the cooking wine, and pours a glass. "Does it pay well—your costumed escape gig?"

"My cosplay escape?" That has a nice ring to it. "It's why I've been able to take classes while still paying down my student loans."

"I knew you weren't studying every Saturday night. I thought it was some boy. Hoping it was that nice Adam who tried so hard to butter me up over my tomatoes."

"You saw through that?"

Mom looks at me over her glass of juice. "Have I or have I not taught school for twenty-five years?"

I suck in. "So you're not mad?"

"Should I be? My baby is hustling her way through school. I'm proud." Mom squeezes my hand. "Just do camp sometimes. Sampling the whole spectrum is not strange. But, Sarah, leather harnesses don't count."

"No worries, Mom. She wasn't even canon."

"Ripped leather pants. What were they thinking?" she mumbles and sips her wine. "How come I've never seen you leave the house all dressed up?"

"I change at the gym. You're seriously not scandalized by the overtly sexy costumes?"

"Oh, honey. I quit worrying about all that years ago. If Jesus doesn't care, why should I?" She hiccups and then laughs. "So Tony knows about your cosplay hustle?"

I shake my head. "I slip out the back door."

"Discreet."

"And maybe climb over a wall."

Mom laughs. "Everyone has a past, honey." She heads out of the kitchen, through the living room, and into the backyard, wineglass in hand.

I follow and am met with the beautiful breeze of a near-perfect San Diego Saturday morning. "You don't," I say, collapsing into a patio chair.

Mom is sprawled out on her chaise. "I do. But it is my business. I get to curate what parts of it I share."

"But everyone knows my past."

"Oh, honey, you give people more credit than they deserve. What do they know? You got married young, like your mama. You divorced young. You're going to school at SDSU now and working at the gym." Mom laughs again, and the breeze knocks out a quiet melody on her wind chimes to match. "In this day and age, people don't know anything. They hardly have time to keep even their own lives straight."

I pull out my phone and search #Catstrike #superheroescapes on my IG.

"All lives are curated," she goes on. "And not just the past. You get to decide who gets to be a part of your present and who stays around for your future." Mom curls her toes in the sunshine like a cat. "You sticking around for lunch? I've got bread baking and fresh lemon curd in the fridge."

I was planning on heading out early to lift weights. If I hustle, I might be able to get some core work done too.

The wind rustles the leaves of the little Meyer lemon tree. "Actually, yeah. A quiet lunch sounds nice." I join Mom on the chaise and show her my search results.

She laughs. "That's my girl. When are you working? I want to come escape. I'll bring Brent and Jen. No, I'll bring my book club ladies!"

"You sure you aren't mortified? Mine isn't the only skintight costume."

"I'm just glad to know you wear something else besides a hoodie."

It turns out that being honest is habit-forming. I take great delight in calling Daniel overseas before my walk to the gym. It's three a.m. his time. He's either sleeping or clubbing, and either way, I don't care.

K-pop blasts in the background when he answers. "Did you sign the papers?" he says by way of greeting.

"No, Daniel. No. Turns out I'm not cool with everything. No. I'm not going to sign some stupid contract from your daddy or your editor. But thanks for asking."

The music becomes more muffled on the other end. I can hear my ex working up a whine, but I don't give him the chance to let it out.

"You either own that every word of your lame-ass book is fiction, or I email your daddy right now and tell him about Tiffany and Charlotte and all of your other camping buddies."

"Forgiveness..." I can hear his teeth clenching even on the crackly international call. "Forgiveness is a higher road. I chose to forgive and forget. I thought you did too."

I crack open the burgundy leather-bound book I dug out of Daniel's boxes. "Molly Brightmore, is it? Your editor? She came to our wedding. I'm staring at her name in our guest book now."

"I can't believe you kept all that junk," Daniel says in his nastiest voice.

"Oh look, here's Tiffany too. And goodness, Charlotte and Dixie came alone. Didn't remember that, but there they are, with cutie hearts and x's and o's all over the page." I sit up in Mom's office chair. "Listen, why don't I send Molly Brightmore an email and let her know that if she publishes your book and it has me in it, she can expect to get sued for invasion of privacy, defamation, and anything else a good lawyer can come up with."

"People can write what they want to," Daniel whines.

"Sure. Write whatever you want about yourself, but not about me. And I have a feeling that your daddy, the lawyer, is going to have the last word on this one. Like he always does. Enjoy Africa, Daniel. If you ever contact me about something this stupid again, I'm going to call your dad's office and ask how restraining orders work. I've got his website pulled up now." I recite his dad's office number. "Should we give Daddy Ray a ring and make this a conference call?"

Daniel quickly hangs up, and I'm about to close the Web browser on my phone but decide to screenshot a picture of Daddy Ray's contact info. His mailing address could come in handy.

~

Life feels less frantic. Maybe that's what happens when you stop vaulting a wall and using back doors on your commute. Or break up some of your runs with a slower walk on the beach. Or take time for some stretching while the surf plays tag with your toes. I must say, I don't mind this pace. It's easy to see how this is an upgrade, and I'm ready for more upgrades.

I'm back in the waiting room of the student wellness center, the one with the aggressively gurgling fountain.

"How did it go?" Brad asks, ushering me into his office.

"It was no big. I'm ready for more homework."

"Great."

"What's next?" I ask.

"You decide what the next step is."

"But—"

"You're not crazy, Sarah. You never have been. You've got this." Brad assures me that his door is always open, but the message is clear. I'm a big girl now, and I know what I have to do. And while I'm not ready to tell Adam just yet, I am ready to take baby steps and make a plan.

I start small. I have no choice but to start small. Adam's been a no-show since Sabine "stood him up." I can't say I blame him. I find Vanessa as she's streaking her pigtails blue and red before our next night of cosplay begins.

"Vanessa?" I say.

She turns around.

"Hey." I pull off my mask. "I'm Sarah. You wanna walk up to Mr. Frostie with me on our break tonight? They brought back the pistachio soft serve."

"Sarah? I'd love that!" Vanessa smiles. "It's really nice to officially meet you."

She's right. And I feel silly for not embracing a possible friendship sooner. "Yeah. Sorry it took so long. I'm working up the courage to meet everyone officially."

Stacey's at the door. "Take your time. No one is going to out you here." She's beaming. "Villains, let's get to work," she shouts.

Old Sarah would have panicked about stepping through the front doors in her cosplay. But I don't panic when Vanessa and I grab ice cream, and I don't panic when the night is over, and I head back to the gym. In fact, I'm proud. I can do this. My smooth night of cosplaying is proof. My mom knows. Vanessa knows. Stacey knows. Soon, everyone including Adam will know. And I'm perfectly okay with that.

It's after midnight, and the gym front doors are locked, requiring my gym card. I slide it through and am nearly to the women's locker room when I hear a man's voice.

"I was wondering when I'd see you here again. Back for more proof that no one kisses you like I do?"

Tony grabs me and pulls me close. He would have kissed me had I not screamed bloody murder.

"Jeez, Gwen!"

"Not Gwen," I say, pushing Tony back.

Tony looks terrified. "Sarah! What are you doing in Gwen's catsuit?"

Oh no. I pull off my mask. Wearing it when Tony knows it's me underneath feels ridiculous. Worse than ridiculous. Mortifying. Maybe I'm not as okay with all the world knowing about my cosplay escape as I thought. "It's mine actually. Or it was. I forgot to pack my other suit tonight..." I awkwardly shuffle in my boots. The story of my forgotten costume is probably not important right now. "I asked Gwen to fill in for me one night when I was... when I wasn't up to it. I work Thursday and Saturday night at Superhero Escapes."

"You've been lying about the study groups?" Tony groans and slowly drags his fingers down his face.

"It's how I've been able to pay for classes this semester. I love working here at the gym, but it all goes to my student loans. I needed a side hustle. I should have told you the truth, but I was embarrassed. It's a pretty ridiculous gig." I pull off my gloves and try to hide them behind my back. "You mad?"

"Yeah. I'm mad. You've been needlessly lying to me and everyone else on the team."

"You going to fire me?"

"No. Are you kidding? You work like a dog. You know most of our members and their kids by name. If it weren't for what I thought were study groups, I'd have asked you about co-managing. It comes with benefits."

"Are you serious?"

Tony looks offended. "Yeah. I'm your friend, Sarah."

Tony's my friend? "You're my boss? And you're my friend?"

"Yeah," Tony says impatiently.

Okay, then. "What the fudge is up with you and Gwen and your on-again, off-again—"

"That's Gwen's choice. You should ask her."

"Yeah. Yeah, I will." I pull out my phone, about to text her, but remember something. "Hey, Tony? Can I have some time at the next all-staff meeting?"

"Sure," he says.

I text Gwen.

Me: Can I take you out for that omelet? We need to catch up.

I wake up the next morning to a text from Gwen.

Gwen: Finally.

I meet Gwen for breakfast the next day at a little bistro that specializes in French omelets and pain au chocolat. We sit outside in the October sunshine. "So you and Tony were always a thing? From the beginning?"

"Not from the beginning," Gwen swirls her coffee and smiles. "Since Comic-Con."

"That was pretty much the beginning. So you two were never off, always on?"

"I didn't want to be a distraction, and he had some certification thingy he was working toward. He wanted to be exclusive. I didn't want him to feel that kind of pressure. Not that I dated anyone else."

"But you did end up kissing Mike, the Badpun?"

"Yeah, I blame it on the costume."

Our waiter comes out with our steaming omelets and an assortment of pastries.

"What happened that night?"

Gwen giggles. "First off, your suit barely fit me. Couldn't even get it zipped up all the way. So I was hanging out everywhere. Your Fem Fantastic was, like, rolling on the floor, laughing. Wouldn't let me take any photos with the clientele. Which was more than okay with me. Except I got bored really fast, so I started flirting with Mike. I mean, he was in a crazy costume. I was in a crazy costume. Catstrike and Badpun are like a thing, so why not get into character, right?"

I choke on my omelet. "They're really not." Seriously, Gwen's lack of comic savvy is astonishing.

"It was his last night." Gwen rolls her eyes. "Or it was his last night for a while. I was getting into my character. But... it wasn't any fun. Like, it was awful. I ran to the gym in the catsuit, told Tony that no one kisses me like he does, fell apart, and went home with him, where we spent the night mapping out our two kids, dog, and minivan future." She rests her left hand on our bistro table. A gorgeous diamond surrounded by emeralds dazzles in the morning sunshine.

I blink. "Are you serious?"

"I wanted to tell you in person."

"Holy fudge Shirley Temples, Gwen! Can I be the flower girl?"

"If you want to meet us at the courthouse the Friday before Thanksgiving. So how are things going with you and Adam? Have you told him yet?"

"Not yet, but I've got a plan."

≈

I make time to stop by Stu's doughnut shop before the all-staff meeting at the gym. "I'd like four dozen doughnuts, please."

Stu is behind the counter this afternoon. "Any particular kind?"

"An assortment, please."

He looks up. His eyes narrow. "I know you..."

"Crazy lady." I smile.

"Yeah!" Stu says with the realization. "How you doing?"

"I'm good. My name's Sarah."

"Nice to meet you, Sarah. I'm Stu. You going to a party?"

"I'm going to apologize."

"Oh..." He continues to shove doughnuts into a box. "Well. I think you look nice without the mask. Not crazy at all."

"Thanks, Stu."

"Don't mention it." He smiles and rings me up.

I carry the pink boxes of calorie bombs back to the gym. "I brought doughnuts," I say at the meeting.

"That's a good start," Tony says. "In fact, Sarah, you asked for some time. What is it you want to talk to all of us about?"

"I just want to thank everyone for covering for me and my shifts. Um, and I want to apologize. I have been going back to school, but it wasn't study groups that had me off on Thursdays and Saturdays. I've been working at Superhero Escapes." I catch myself from looking down at the floor and instead look out at my colleagues. "I'm their Catstrike."

"No way!" Kate says.

"Yeah. And I should have told everyone, but I was embarrassed. I mean, dressing up as a supervillain every weekend is kinda embarrassing for me." I wince. "I should have told everyone the truth from the beginning. And to say sorry and to say thank you for understanding and for all the support, I bought passes for everyone to Superhero Escapes." I reach into my pocket for the stack of gift cards.

Thank goldfish for employee discounts. "Good for two rooms. Please come. I'm often in Malum Asylum."

"Sarah, this is so nice," Alice says.

"You didn't have to do this," Nathan says.

"I really did," I say.

"Wait," Kate says around a mouthful of cherry-filled doughnut. "If you were working at the escape room on Saturday, why did you call to ask me to tell that hottie that you were working in La Jolla?"

I feel my face go bright red. "That was my other boss. And I need to take doughnuts over there next."

Kate looks confused until Henry whispers something in her ear. "Oh!" She giggles.

"Right," Tony says, reaching for his clipboard. "Next order of business. As you know, I'm stepping down next month as club manager because"—he smiles at his clipboard—"I will be a certified chiropractor."

There are cheers. Chiropractor? I look around the room. Literally everyone knew this but me.

"Thank you," Tony says. "And while I'll still be around as a personal trainer, Nathan will be your new manager, which means we have a spot open for an assistant club manager. I was wondering if any of you could recommend someone for the job."

"Sarah," Alice says. "You should do it."

I bray involuntarily.

"What? You don't want to?"

"I—"

"Who better to sell more memberships than the girl who practically lives here?"

"She can run circles around most of us."

"All of us."

"True. Speaks volumes that she was the one who got a job parading around in a jumpsuit," Kate says.

"Hey, now! Be nice." I blush.

"She's got the right temperament for the Kids Club and all the new parents, and that's our fastest-growing demographic, right?" Nathan adds.

I straighten. "Hey, Tony..."

He looks up from his clipboard, an amused smile on his face.

"I'd like an application, please."

Tony hands me an application. "When can you interview?"

I'm back at Stu's. "Four dozen doughnuts, please."

"Crazy lady is now my best customer."

"Well, I have a lot of explaining to do." Doughnuts definitely help apologies go down smoother. Not that I owe everyone at Superhero Escapes an apology. Just Adam. Still, introducing myself to my coworkers is a good first step. And doughnuts can't hurt.

After I introduce myself to everyone at the escape room, dough-nuts and all, Mike wanders forward. "But you're not..." He looks desperately confused. I think he is trying to put together that I am not the woman he smooched, but that he most definitely did smooch someone in a Catstrike suit. "How many Catstrikes does Adam have?"

"Doughnut?" I ask.

"Who says no to a doughnut?" Mike grabs a chocolate twist.

Stacey pulls me aside. "So does Adam know?"

"Not yet. I'm working up to it. Is he going to be here tonight?" I ask hopefully.

Stacey shakes her head.

"Is he okay?" I ask.

"Yeah, he's thrown himself into the Dr. Leto Room in La Jolla. If you wanted to head over there, I could cover for you—"

"No more covering for me. I'll find a way to tell him soon."

I send Daniel's boxes of junk back to Michigan by way of his father's law office. I snap photos of the pages of our guest book beforehand, just in case I need the evidence later. The closet door in my mom's office shuts all the way now. It's almost as satisfying as imagining the phone call Daddy Ray will make when he unpacks the box of camping equipment.

As I walk out of the campus post office, I bump into Adam. Literally. I was digging in my bag for my phone, and Adam must have been on his. He dropped it when we collided. Maybe my smile should be shy, but I can't help but grin. I haven't seen Adam in days. He looks so... real. Reach-out-and-hold real. And I'm on the verge of doing just that when I remember what I have to say, what I swore I would say the next time I saw him.

His phone landed by my feet. I grab it and try to hand it back. "Hey," I say.

He swallows. "Hey." He's not moving.

Oh goldfish, he's terrified. I reach for his hand and, as gently as I can, place his phone in it, wrapping his fingers around the screen.

"Look, I'm really sorry about the other day. I shouldn't have teased you." I pause as a group of freshmen pass by us. "I'm having a nice life. It's just... I wish you could be in it."

He stares at me, still holding his phone awkwardly.

I'm worse than a dog with a bone. "How's it going with..."

"It's not," he says.

"That's a shame." I catch his eye for a minute before he looks away.

Adam is clearly struggling. "She thought that you and I were..."

"Not dating?" I smile. "Hand me your phone. I'll text her now and clear that right up." I make a grab for his phone, but Adam pulls it out of my reach, and suddenly I'm standing inches away. Another step is all it would take to close the distance between us.

"Somehow I think that would do more harm than good," Adam says quietly.

"This is none of my business—"

"I have a feeling that's not going to stop you." There are notes of exasperation but also amusement in his voice.

A breeze finds us, and my white skirt dances, and I have to pull strands of hair out of my face. "Why her? Is it just the mystery? Is it the mask? Are you going to meet her in real life and realize she has a nasty, hairy mole the size of a quarter on her neck, and that's going to be the end of it?"

A dry sort of smile tugs at Adam's lips. He folds his arms across his chest and stares at me. "She doesn't have a mole."

"What if she has a disfiguring scar, or worse? What if she has the ugliest tattoo ever? Creepy, chubby dolphins with fluffy eyebrows diving into her nether regions."

Adam stares at me. I wish he'd laugh. "I don't want to be a cliché, but she has the wryest sense of humor. She's confident. Clever. Sexy as hell."

I clench my fists. "Are you twelve-years-old?"

"Probably. I get excited when I'm standing next to her. Why wouldn't I want to be with her in real life?" He looks at me cautiously, and it's like he can read my thoughts. "What's up?"

"Ask her to homecoming," I say.

"What?"

"A swoony dress. No girl can resist the chance to wear a swoony dress."

"I can't ask her to homecoming."

"Why not?"

"I'm working that night. Which reminds me, I have to tell my cast. We got booked by the school."

"What?"

"For homecoming. We're setting up the escape room in the student center. They gave us twice the space, so I'll be able to run two escape rooms at once. Well, with modifications." Adam checks his phone before returning it to his pocket. "You know what? I will ask. She won't be able to say no. She'll be there working. Thanks, Hoodie." He tugs on the strings of my sweatshirt. "Hey, are you coming to homecoming?"

"I... Yeah. Absolutely. Wouldn't miss it," I say.

Adam brushes a hand through his hair. "Lucky guy. I'll see you there."

Later, when I'm home after my shift at the gym and reading my econ chapters while my mom is catching up on her BBC before dinner, my phone pings.

"I think I should get a cat," my mom says.

I swipe through an email from Adam detailing the homecoming schedule for the escape room. "For reals?"

Mom takes a sip of her beet juice. "Want to come with me to the shelter on Saturday and pick one out?"

"My Saturday is really busy. The escape room is working homecoming." My phone pings again with a text.

Adam: Come with me to the dance Saturday?

Sabine Kennedy: I'm working.

Mom looks crestfallen. "Maybe it was a bad idea anyway."

"I don't think so. What if we went now? Grabbed fish tacos on the way home?"

Mom brightens, looking simultaneously scandalized and delighted. "I'll get my keys."

Another text buzzes on my phone.

Adam: So you can't say no. Meet you there?

"Ready?" Mom asks.

I tap out a text and press send before tossing my phone down and following Mom out the door.

Sabine Kennedy: I'll be waiting.

CHAPTER TWENTY-NINE

"Let me get this straight," Gwen says. We're in the gym on an unusually quiet Saturday afternoon. "You're going to homecoming as yourself, as Catstrike, and as Adam's real-life Sabine Kennedy?"

"And my mom got a cat. Try to keep up." I pull up my mom's feed of Sir Bartholomew Fluffy Pants while Gwen squeals. She has every right too. The black furball is just as adorable as my mom's smitten smile.

"So why do you have to go to homecoming as three different women?"

"Because what I have to work out is, does Adam like me for me? Or me for Catstrike?"

Gwen grabs the sides of her treadmill and groans. "Oh, you are such an idiot. You're the same woman!"

"Okay, you're right. I am the same woman, and he clearly likes both of me. But what if..." I can't quite find the words to tell her exactly what scares the Shirley Temples out of me. What if once I tell Adam the truth, he walks away and never looks back? How would I recover from that? I'm not even sure I could. I've fallen hard for him, and the thought of losing him...

"What if what?" Gwen prompts.

I can't put it out there, not yet. It's too dear. "I was thinking if I get the right dress, I could wear my suit under—"

Gwen slams her treadmill down to a slower speed. "You march your sorry butt right over to that escape room and tell him the truth."

"I've played this out in my head a dozen times. The only way this works is if I am in literally the best dress in the world—has to be floor length to hide my Catstrike boots. There's loud music, the crowd parts, and all that atmosphere finally descends on him, and he realizes it has been me all along."

Gwen looks at me with eyes that say, *Get real, girl, please.* "What movie did you see this in? Because you did see this in a movie. This is not a real-life thing that can happen."

"Just come dress shopping with me. There has to be some way to pull this off. I could maybe—"

Gwen is glowing with sweat and panting. "Tell that poor boy tonight. Do the right thing. Give him a chance to save face." She jams the speed button down on her treadmill. "And I have the perfect dress for you."

I slow down the speed of my treadmill. "What are you talking about?"

"An LBD. Too small for me. Perfect for you," Gwen huffs and puffs.

"No. The save-face thing."

"It's not always the big fairy-tale ending in real life," Gwen says. "Sometimes you have to work up to it."

Panic burns inside me. "You mean what if he doesn't want me once he knows?"

Gwen groans. "I mean what if he needs a chance to cycle through a lot of emotions before he lands on the fact that he's always hoped, always wanted, etc., etc., etc."

I should have this conversation with Gwen when she isn't out of breath and hurting from forty minutes of cardio. Even without hashing out the etc., etc., etc. territory, I know Gwen is right. I know I have to tell Adam tonight at the escape room.

I text him when I get back home.

Sabine Kennedy: Can you come early tonight? We need to talk.

Adam: I'll try. Have a meeting with some investors. Going to be tight.

Adam: You found a dress for homecoming?

Sabine Kennedy: A little black one. See you tonight.

"Is Adam here?" I ask upon arriving at the escape room.

"Not yet," Stacey says. "Nice costume."

An evolution in my Catstrike cosplay seemed appropriate for tonight, and while never represented on the big screen, Daphne Cooke's Catstrike is still iconic and easily recognizable—athletic-cut leather catsuit, boots without the fudge-me heels, circular zipper pull reminiscent of a cat collar, and, most notably, goggles. She was a reimagining of the character from a caricature to a real woman back in the early 2000s. She is just as sexy, just as dangerous, as the other incarnations, but more joyful and real. Needless to say, this cosplay is way more comfortable than my other costumes, and much more... me.

"Felt like I needed a little more authenticity tonight," I say, adjusting my mirrored goggles on top of my cowl.

"Right. And still very comic bookish. So have you told him?" Stacey asks.

"He was supposed to come early." I scan the guest list. "Half my gym is coming tonight. I need to tell him before they tell him for me."

"Don't worry," Stacey says.

"Easy for you to say," I mutter.

Stacey narrows her eyes. "You're actually doing this? You're telling him tonight?"

"I have to." No more games, no more subterfuge, no more hiding. Tonight, I come clean, and if I'm lucky, Adam will love me anyway. Or, goldfish, he'll at least still *like* me enough to give me a chance to be my authentic self with him going forward.

"I'll juggle the list. I'll make sure you get to tell him. Okay. I've got your back."

"Thank you, Stacey!"

She flips her brunette waves behind her shoulder. "But you're going to invite me and Monique to the next Tuesday night barbecue. Adam has been raving about the tomatoes and lemonade nonstop. Deal?"

My voice catches in my throat. Stacey wants to stay friends. "Yeah. I'd like that."

"Go on to Malum. I'll sub you out as soon as he gets here."

It is an epic night at Malum Asylum with all of my gym coming through the escape room. Kate and Henry scream when they see me. Gwen and Tony cheer.

But where is Adam?

"It's packed tonight," I say to Vanessa. "Have you seen Adam?"

She hasn't. No one has.

My mom arrives with her book club ladies. They need extra help posting their celebratory pictures on Instagram after the photo op. A slightly nauseated Jen, accompanied by Brent, comes through. Nathan and his husband circle through twice, and Alice with her grandkids give me high fives.

It's eleven p.m. before Stacey finds me. "Adam's not coming," she says.

My stomach plummets. "Did he say why?"

Stacey shakes her head. "Just that he was headed back to his place and that he'd call me in the morning to talk details about the homecoming operation."

I stick it out for my last round of escapes and then leave. This time through the front door. I grab an electric scooter and weave my way through the PB nightlife (and a smattering of raucous shouts of recognition) to Beryl Street and a block of apartments with well-worn steps.

If ever there was proof that I am crazy creative, knocking on

Adam's door at midnight dressed as Catstrike would be it. "Adam!" I shout when he doesn't answer.

"It's open," he calls.

I step into his apartment and feel like a cat burglar must feel. Adrenaline, fear, desperation—it's all there. My cosplay is too conspicuous for white T-shirt normal life.

Adam is on his couch, watching the spice-week episode of the latest season of *Mississippi Bake-Off* on his enormous screen.

"We need to talk," I say, in a voice that is desperately, painfully my own.

I expect Adam to jump or swear. But he turns off his TV and remains where he is, sitting calmly on his couch, eyes focused most definitely not on me. "Those are never comforting words."

"I need to quit. I can't work for you anymore."

"What?" Adam says, rising. He takes in my costume and the spectacle of me dressed in resplendent cosplay in the everyday confines of his apartment.

My eyes are hidden behind my mirrored goggles. "I'm giving you my two weeks' notice. Although when I'm done talking, you'll probably want me gone sooner."

"You want to tell me why? Without the mask?" He looks at me. "Sarah?"

He knows. I'm still in cosplay and he knows. I don't know whether to shout for joy or panic. I feel as if ice water and hot oil were dumped on me at once. So I say nothing.

Adam cracks. He's on his feet and standing in front of me. "Tell me it's you under there. Because if it's not, I need to run up to Los Altos Street and wake you up for a long-overdue apology."

I suck in hard. I peel off my goggles and hood and rough up my blond hair. It's me. I'm right here. I'm sorry. I think I love you. Tell me more about this overdue apology. "Hi," is all I manage to say.

Adam's shoulders sag. I want to attribute it to relief, but it could easily be exasperation. Or despair. "Hi," he says. He takes a step closer.

My eyes dart from the pile of textbooks on his kitchen table to the jade throw over the arm of his couch. "I don't think I should keep working for someone... I have feelings for." I press my lips together. "And I'm sorry for lying to you."

"That's it?" Adam asks. He's closer still.

He's close enough to either strangle me or kiss me. I can't even look at him, but I note the clean grout of his tile floor. "I'm *really* sorry for lying to you."

"Why?" His words are almost a whisper.

Why? It's my favorite question. Why did I marry my ex? Why did I have to lose my baby? Why would anyone love me? Why would anyone want me? "I was a loser. A nobody with a sad little life. But you offered me a chance to escape. When I was your Catstrike, I got to be sexy and confident. That's why." I close my eyes. "And because you asked me." I press a gloved hand to my forehead. "I'm a nerd who loves cosplay," I say, peeling off my gloves. "And when I wear the costume, you don't look at me like I'm a sad, pathetic, little failure."

"I've never looked at you that way."

I can feel his breath on my neck. I can almost hear his heart beating. "Um... No, you haven't. What I should have said was... When I'm cosplaying, *I* don't feel like a sad, pathetic, little failure. I borrow my character's confidence and tell myself that the heart eyes and flirting are all part of the cosplay and don't count. But I got carried away. I let myself get more carried away the more I got to know you."

Adam opens his mouth like he's about to say something that can't be unsaid. I can't chance that.

"It would have made sense to tell you it was me, right? But I couldn't lose you. What if you were disappointed? What if I couldn't live up to..." My eyes find his. "To your fantasy?"

"My fantasy?" Adam looks almost amused, or he is just very practiced at enabling crazy-pants like me.

The campus therapist was wrong, completely full-of-Shirley-Temples wrong. I'm certifiable, and I know it. It's the only explanation for what happens next. "Why'd it take you so long to find a

Catstrike?" I ask, and I know my confidence exists outside of cosplay because I'm doing Mom's power stance in Adam's kitchen, demanding answers. "Why the obsessive search?"

Adam swallows. "I wanted someone who could do justice to my favorite character."

"Catstrike is your favorite character."

Adam sighs. From a lesser man, the exasperated gust of frustration would be accompanied by an eye roll. "Obviously."

"And waiting for me in the alley after Customer Cosplay Night?"

Adam's eyes narrow. "You knew it was me?"

"No." I tilt my chin up. I want him to feel what I say next. "But I hoped it was you."

Adam sets his jaw. "Why are you telling me this now?"

"I wanted to tell you at homecoming when I was in a pretty dress and irresistible, but that wouldn't be fair. Or even possible. Do you know how complicated getting in and out of my cosplay is? And finding a dress that is floor-length, long-sleeved and turtle-necked to cover it—" I'm rambling. I take a centering breath. "I couldn't bear thinking I am in the same boat as Allison for another night." I lean against his kitchen counter. "I didn't kiss you at the tide pools because I didn't want to lose you. I knew you'd either kiss me and find out I was your Catstrike all along—which clearly you didn't want to be true, because you could have put it together. I mean, hello, I'm the same person—or you'd kiss me and not realize that you'd kissed me before. And... maybe that would be worse because it would mean one of our kisses was forgettable." The adrenaline has left my body, and I feel weak. And scared. "I know your last big relationship was untenable because..." I close my eyes and say it. "Because someone was a liar, liar, pants on fire. And you're too great a guy to have to repeat that history." Oh no. Tears burn in my eyes. I swore I wasn't going to cry and make this weirder than it already is. "It's been me the whole time. Just me. I'm not your superhero fantasy. I'm a dork who lives with her mom, has a loser past plus sob story, and was too scared to kiss her crush in real life."

Adam leans against the counter next to me, his arms folded across his chest. "I knew it was you."

I breathe out, and I swear my heart is rattling inside me. I feel all empty and deflated. "You knew it was me?"

"There are only so many women who swear by taking a goldfish's name in vain."

"Fudge brownies," I mutter.

Adam chuckles. "And the baked goods. What's the other one?"

"Shirley Temples."

"Shirley." Adam laughs. "Shirley Temples."

I open my mouth. My head is spinning. I don't know if I feel elated or completely defeated. "How long have you known?"

"I've known since the first day of Econ 101. You wear a mask, not a paper bag over your head. Don't you remember? I sat right next to you and tried desperately to play it cool. Which wasn't easy, because I'd barely slept since I'd seen you last, and, um... I was trying hard not to blush or get caught staring at you." He rubs the back of his neck. "Between class Wednesday and Friday lab, I wavered. I mean, I could have just been manifesting fantasies into existence. I showed up early—not just on time, but early—to lab hours because I needed to know. And yeah, there was no walking anything back after that."

A timer starts beeping. "Is something burning?" I ask.

Adam reaches for an oven mitt and retrieves a couple of tins from the oven. "I thought you knew that I knew."

"Why would I keep going with the alter-ego thing if I thought you knew?"

"Lots of reasons. Method acting. It was fun—"

"I think they need to go back in." I gesture at his cake pans.

"They're burning."

"No, the stuff that spilled over and is now on the bottom of your oven is burning." I grab a clean fork from his drying rack and prick the cake. "These are still gooey." I set the timer for five more minutes as Adam pops the cakes back in the oven. "Meeting up at the Student Union Starbucks wasn't fun."

"Ah." Adam tosses the oven mitts down. "I was over the game we were playing, and I was worried that it was only a game. I mean, you kissed me"—he pauses and catches my eyes—"passionately the night before, but you wouldn't let me come near you the morning after."

I wince. "And then I asked to be just friends."

Adam exhales, and his breath comes out shaky and fast. "Yeah. But then you texted me and wanted to meet in real life. And yeah, I ironed my shirt and was a complete ass. I'm sorry. I thought we were done with games and going to just talk, but you kept on playing. But of course you did. You thought I didn't know you were you and also you in cosplay. How could you ever want to be with a guy who dated two women at the same time?"

"We weren't dating," I say. Adam tries to object, but I hold up a hand. "I think it's why I never thought of you as a player. Did you make frosting too?"

Adam pulls out a bowl of white fluffy frosting from the fridge. "What were we then if we weren't dating?"

"We were two friends spending time together. I knew it wasn't your fault that some crazy kept jumping you at every opportunity." I dip my finger in the bowl of frosting, taste it, and immediately grab a paper towel and spit it out into it.

"Now you're just being mean. It's not that bad." Adam dips a spoon into the frosting and has a bite but then gags.

"What did you put in it?"

"Butter, powdered sugar, and vanilla."

I hold up the bottle of fish sauce on the counter. "This vanilla?"

"Yeah. That's... not vanilla." Adam slides down to the floor of his kitchen, defeated.

I join him, and in the friendliest way possible, as far removed from I-want-to-grab-you-and-kiss-you-senseless as I can manage (because I still want that), I nudge his shoulder with my own. "I did go see a campus counselor. You had me convinced I was crazy."

"Oh, this is definitely... something."

"And... now that you know?"

"I have questions." He considers. "The most pressing being, are you still going to be working for me homecoming weekend, or do I need to find someone else?"

CHAPTER THIRTY

Gwen wraps my hair around the barrel of her curling iron.

"I don't know why you're doing this," I say, picking at the hem of my dress. Well, Gwen's dress that she's letting me borrow on the condition that I took the hem up by four inches. "It doesn't matter."

"It does too matter. You're going to homecoming with Adam."

"As an employee." I sigh. "We parted, after I bared my soul and gave voice to my feelings for him, with a scheduling question."

Gwen pulls a curl loose before spraying it. "Meaning?"

"He wanted to know if I was working this weekend. That's friend-zone territory at best."

Gwen chuckles. "Did I not tell you happily ever afters take a little more time in real life?"

I pout. "You sure this dress is a good idea?"

"Bare legs, and a lot of them, after all the catsuits?" Gwen laughs. "Yes, I'm sure."

I brush a speck of glitter off my black skirt. "He didn't ask me if I was still going with him. He asked me if I was working."

"Honey, the man was shell-shocked."

"You mean terrified. You mean run-now-if-you-hope-to-live panicked."

"Look. He's still your boss. You told him after work. He had a lot to unpack. He was preoccupied with the fear that you thought he was a douche for dating two girls at once." Gwen rolls another section of my hair. "And you shouldn't have worn a new suit. He's probably still trying to do mental gymnastics with that one."

"I had to wear a new suit. I'm never going near my old one after Tony mistook me for you in it." I shudder. Gwen laughs. "Why would a new suit matter? It's still me."

"Oh, I know. And, believe me, he knows. He can't sleep at night, he knows so bad."

"Or make vanilla frosting."

"No, he may just be crap in the kitchen."

I laugh as Gwen twists a few of my curls back and swipes pink lip gloss on my lips. The very same lip gloss Brent and Jen give their team to wear to work. Turns out it's the most amazing lip gloss ever— gluten-free, vegan, fair trade, with SPF 30. "Adam has your every angle memorized. Which is why you are in a flirty cocktail dress that shows a lot of leg and shoulder. Show me your mask."

I hold up the glittery black cat-eye mask.

Gwen adds a slim gold headband with cat ears to my soft, shoulder-length blond curls.

"Classy," I deadpan.

Gwen tries hard not to laugh. "I mean, you are working tonight."

The Student Union is outfitted with red and black streamers and many disco balls. Nothing but the finest for homecoming.

"I thought you were joking about the little black dress," Adam says when I show up for my shift. His gaze falls to my bare legs, and he looks for a moment like he's in pain.

"Hi," I say.

"Hi." Adam takes my hand, and my heart beats faster.

"I forgot my mask."

"Okay." He's in a pair of dark jeans with a blue plaid shirt and skinny tie. "Dance with me?"

Butterflies take flight inside me. He pulls me close, and I smile into his shoulder. My fingers lace with his, and I rest my other hand on his strong shoulder. "I'm sorry I was too chicken to tell you the truth sooner."

"The timing had to be yours. But I always hoped you'd tell me. When you were ready."

"Hoped?"

Adam speaks quietly into my ear. "Who doesn't hope that the smart, witty, gorgeous girl in the hoodie is also the clever, confident, sexy badass in the catsuit?"

"I don't believe you."

"Well, like I said, there were clues. Your cosplay schedule shifting with your new class schedule. The times I heard you swearing under your breath at work. The same cracked phone. Our chemistry. And you may have run by my escape room every morning after Comic-Con for two weeks. I caught you on my Nest."

I blush.

"That was a fun discovery." Adam smirks before he pulls me closer. "Why didn't you tell me that first day of Econ 101?"

I scoff. "If I had said, 'Hi, I'm Sarah. I actually work for you, and by the way, I think I licked your face the other night...'" I pause. "Who were the other people with you that night? Badpun and Fair Play?"

"I was walking through the escape room with my contacts from Halifax Sisters. *Undercover Boss* meets thinly-veiled fantasy."

"You didn't count it as a kiss later at the Student Union Starbucks."

"It doesn't count if you don't get a chance to kiss back."

I purr softly and slowly. "If I'd told you the truth in econ, what would you have done?"

"I would have grabbed your hand and run to the nearest empty office, where I'd ask you to give me a legitimate chance at forever before I knelt and kissed every inch of you."

"Every inch?"

Adam presses a kiss to my bare shoulder. "Every last one."

I'm surprised I'm still standing. "You would not. You would have blinked and then transferred not just TA assignments, but departments."

"You underestimate how cute you look in a hoodie. I would have asked you out, switched class assignments, and promptly fallen hard. So really not at all different from reality."

"Why did you never cosplay as Nightbat again?"

"I met you in real life."

"And when I kissed you in cosplay?"

"I closed my eyes and pretended you weren't wearing a mask."

"Really?"

"You said I was obsessive in my search for a Catstrike cosplayer. I wasn't. I hire quality, talented people. And while one of my cast members could have played Catstrike, they couldn't have done it the way you did. You think you were playing a role, escaping into some character, but it was all you shining through." His hands urge me close. "You wanna get out of here? Maybe go walk the tide pools?"

I smile. "Or head back to your place for Korean tacos and more *Mississippi Bake-Off*?" I lean in close and enjoy how I fit against Adam's chest. "Wait. Aren't you working?" I pull away. "And don't I need to start my shift?"

"I took us off the schedule tonight. One of the perks of being the boss."

I wrap my arms around Adam once more. His hands press against my back and waist. Each touch deserving of its own panel—one frozen, essential moment of a story.

"I have to fire you. You're right. Flirtations are one thing, but shared feelings are a clear conflict of interest. Completely unprofessional." His words, hand-inked and slanted, fill the space around us, pressing us closer together.

My words join his until there is no blank space left between us. "And we wouldn't want to repeat history."

"I would," Adam says. "If it gets me here with you." It's another moment to capture in pencil, ink, and color.

I press my lips to his. "Me too."

The white margins between the panels expand and grow, until I realize it would take an entire lifetime to imagine what goes on in between them. For once, I'm happy to explore what happens off-panel, especially since I have Adam to do it with me.

NOTE TO MY READERS

Thank you, dear reader, for taking a chance on Sarah and Adam. Sharing their story with you means the world to me. I am beyond honored that you gave us a slice of your time. I hope you had fun and enjoyed this, the first book in my Escape to Love series. Yes, series. Escapist happily-ever-afters (of both the contemporary rom-com and fantasy fairy tale persuasion) are all I want to write and read these days. I'm very happy to share that I've got more books in the works. Pop over to my website, amytrent.com, for more details or to say hi. I love to hear from my readers!

If you'd like to stay current with my new releases, discounts, and writerly life, I publish a newsletter when I have something to say, maybe four times a year. I promise I will never sell, swap, or give away your personal info, and it's easy to unsubscribe. More details about the newsletter at amytrent.com.

I'm also on Instagram and TikTok @authoramytrent. However you like to keep in touch, know that I will always be wishing you,

Happy Reading!
Amy Trent

ACKNOWLEDGMENTS

I would not be a writer without the support, love, and mentorship of my aunt, the amazingly talented Grace Burrowes (graceburrowes.com). Love you forever, Aunt Grace. Thanks for helping me get this story off the ground. Thanks for believing I was a writer when even I wasn't so sure.

I've been so lucky to work with talented editors on this journey. A big, heartfelt thank you to Deborah Halverson (deborahhalverson.com). Thank you, Deborah, for being a champion of New Adult, and thank you for being a champion of this story. I've never had more fun with an edit letter! Thank you to Joyce Lamb (joycelambediting.com). You are a copy-editing superhero, and I am so grateful for your help!

Everlasting thanks to my talented cover artist, Bailey McGinn (baileydesignsbooks.com). Thank you for your patience, your compassion, and for figuring out how to work in my love of comics and Ben-Day dots into the perfect rom-com cover. You are amazing! It was so much fun to work with you!

Sincere thanks to my talented and wonderful proofreaders: Sarah Rosenbarker and Arianne Costner. Y'all are geniuses!

Cookies to my sisters who spent untold hours talking with me and teaching me about Puccini and pop songs, gym life, running, and mom life. Mirror cakes to my brother whose enthusiasm for this project and knowledge of superheroes is unmatched. I'd be nothing without my sibs, and I am so gosh darn proud to be your sister.

Big thanks to my loving and supportive parents. Thanks to my father, who blazed the author trail with his debut novel. Thanks to my mom, who has always been my cheerleader and hero.

Eternal gratitude to my kiddos—I am so proud to be your mommy. Lucky too. You both are amazing and wonderful, and I love you always. This book would not exist without you. Thank you! Let's celebrate with a goldfish, fudge, and Shirley Temple party!

And finally, biggest and brightest thanks to my husband. This book would have stayed in my computer forever were it not for Mr. Trent, who said on our wedding anniversary, "Hon, I know we don't go in for big, dramatic gifts and stuff. But I was thinking... Let's celebrate us by publishing one of your books. Do you think that's a good idea?" Baby, it was a fantastic idea. Thanks for being one of my proofreaders. Thanks for telling me why this book made you laugh and smile. I love you forever. Now, please stop teasing me about the kissy-smoochy scenes. It's not fair.

Made in the USA
Las Vegas, NV
05 February 2022

43171986R00154